REVERENT

AN ANTHOLOGY OF DIVINITY

ALICE SCOTT
SHEPARD DISTASIO
KATE DUARTE
SOLAR HOÀNG
ANDROMEDA RUINS
JEANEA BLAIR
MIRANDA JENSEN
OLIVE J. KELLEY
CASPER E. FALLS
IVY L. JAMES
DC GUEVARA
ENGEL WILLIAMS
BUCKY A. WOLFE
HARVEY OLIVER BAXTER
RILEY DAEMON
ARES MACABRE
PERLA ZUL
C.J. ELLISON
VIKTOR E. GRACE LANG
K.T. ANGELO
HELEN Z. DONG
TEA CAMPBELL
ENOLI LEE
TIEN LEE
AIDAN SPARKS
ELISE GEORGESON
A.R ZEITLER
ALEX HARVEY-RIVAS
H.S. WOLFE

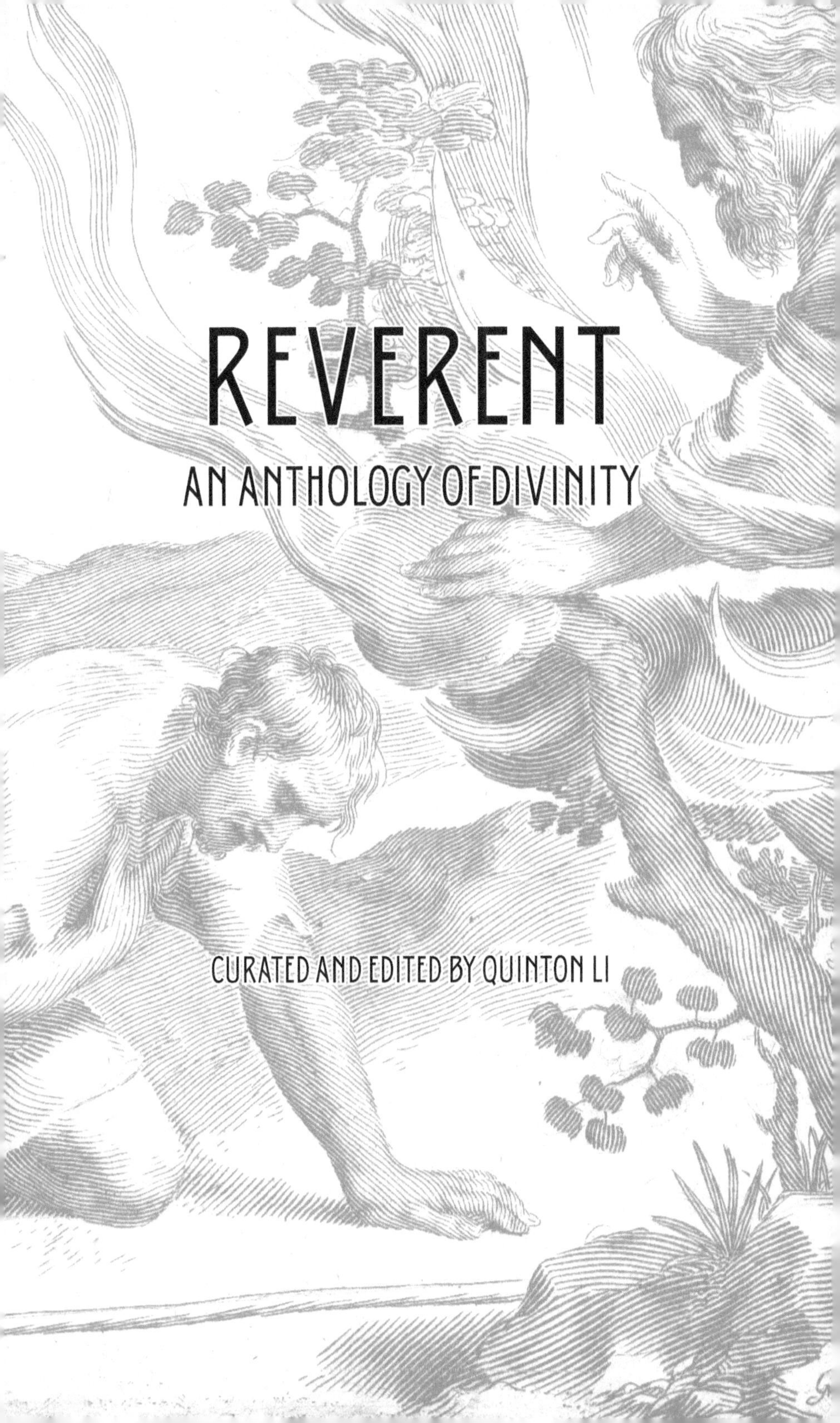

REVERENT

AN ANTHOLOGY OF DIVINITY

CURATED AND EDITED BY QUINTON LI

REVERENT: AN ANTHOLOGY OF DIVINITY
First Edition

Contact: Quinton Li (www.quintonli.com)
          More information: https://quintonli.com/reverent-anthology

Cover: Harvey Oliver Baxter (@topazsunzart on Instagram)
Typesetting and Interior Design: Jun T.N. (https://ko-fi.com/advalentinus)

Set in 10pt EB Garamond and 20pt Donau Uppercase.

ISBN: 978-0-9756222-0-9
Ebook ISBN: 978-0-9756222-1-6

EDITOR'S LETTER

To release my second curated anthology with twice as many contributors and a beautiful, vast theme feels divine in itself.

From the moment I published the predecessor of this anthology, another one was brewing at the back of my mind. It took a while to pinpoint the exact theme I wanted to capture. I wanted to make it something *more* than angels — and angels are already hard to contain, if they can be contained at all.

Divinity is special to me. Not only for my connection to angels, but the history of my faith led by family tradition, and my current devotional practice. I also find divinity in my queerness, transness, and disability. That is to say, this anthology and its writers are special to me, too.

If we haven't met before, I'm Quinton Li, the curator and editor of this anthology. I'm ever pleased to present this collection by a group of writers, familiar or not, who engage with the theme of divinity as deeply as I do.

Alice, Shepard, Kate, Solar, Andromeda, Jeanea, Miranda, Olive, Casper, Ivy, DC, Engel, Bucky, Harvey, Riley, Ares, Perla, C.J., Viktor, K.T., Helen, Tea, Enoli, Tien, Aidan, Elise, A.R, Alex, and H.S., it was a pleasure to work with you and it's an honour to share your work.

Harvey, your incredible and thoughtful artwork inspired by our shared vision is a blessing to this collection. Thank you for your dedication and enthusiasm.

Jun, your formatting talent carried an unbelievable weight in bringing each piece and the entire collection of works to life. I will always be thankful for your patience and time.

To every ARC reader who expressed interest in REVERENT, thank you! Your passion for independent publications, the authors in this anthology, and the theme of divinity means so much.

And, I can't forget every angel, divine being, or lover of the divine reading this anthology. This is for you and I only wish that something resonates in these pages, or perhaps you learn something new.

Enjoy the REVERENT ANTHOLOGY!

TABLE OF CONTENTS

CONTENT WARNINGS

THE FAR TOO HOLY AND THE ANGELS FALLING SHORT: Child abuse from a parent (physical, emotional, and psychological); Transphobia such as deadnaming; Ableism; Violence, including murder, talked about but off page

GENESIS 19:1-11: Religious trauma; External and internal transphobia; Body dysphoria; Traumatic birth; Suicidal ideation/imagery; Parental neglect

RELICÁRIO: Menstruation; Murder; Sexism; Vomit (mention at the start of the story); Childbirth

CONDEMN ME: Religious bigotry; Transphobia (on page in the first section & some internalized throughout); Gore; Body horror; Desecration of religion

I AM A GOD AND SO IS EVERYBODY ELSE BUT THIS IS ABOUT ME!: Death and suicide (mainly off page but one scene where the moments leading up to the attempt is described)

PSAPPHA'S PROGENY: Catholic themes of prejudice; Exorcism; Blood sacrifice (cut on palm)

POSTS FROM GOD: Ableism; Societal neglect; Transphobia; Relationship betrayal; Chronic illness; Covid pandemic; Unemployment; Threat of homelessness; Neglectful parents; Retching/vomiting; Reference to stalking and murder

A SONG FOR THE ROOSTERS: Parental neglect; Verbally abusive parents; Brief mentions of blood, periods and pregnancy; Mild sexual content

THE BREATH OF LIFE: Animal death; Mentions of death; Depictions of blood; Violence

THE GIRL I WAS BORN IS THE BOY I'VE BECOME'S KNIGHT IN SHINING ARMOR: Mild gender dysphoria

SEVERIN AND THE DARK: Gender dysphoria; Implied eating disorder; Transphobia; Hallucinations (one with sexual implications); Mentions of hate crimes and murder; Implied death/transcendence

A KISS FOR MY BELOVED: Suicide

THE PATRON SAINT OF ONE-WAY TRIPS: Death

HEAVEN IS NEAR: Sexual content; Dubious consent; Blood; Death; Vomit

MOONTIDE: Blood; Gender dysphoria; Body invasion; Body horror; Genitals mentioned

LIFE, DEATH AND DAISY CHAINS: Death (specifically of family members and a child)

THE AUTOPSY OF ICARUS: Autopsy/corpse; Mild graphic descriptions; Death

THE COMFORTS OF HOME: Ableism; Vomit

BLUE SCREEN ORACLE: Major character death; Implied mild cannibalism; Mention and discussion of severe chronic illness; Corpse

THE FAR TOO HOLY AND THE ANGELS FALLING SHORT

Alice Scott

The creature standing in her bedroom doorway wept golden.

Sitting in the dark, Monday Deora couldn't make out much else beyond a hulking blur of wings obscuring the true shape of its body—but when it stepped forward just a fraction and the light spilling in from the hallway caught its face, multiple pure-white eyes blinked back metallic tears. She pulled the blanket back over her head with a yelp like she was still a little girl.

Monday, go to your room. Close your eyes, cover your ears, her brother had told her about half an hour prior, an d to Monday's credit she'd half listened. She'd sat under the comforter with her eyes squeezed shut, wings folded over her face in case she tried to look, but she couldn't bring herself to cover her ears, not this time. So when she'd heard her brother's footsteps in the hall, after all the screaming stopped, she'd dared a peek, and—

"Fuck—Monday, it's okay, it's alright."

Looking now, the only thing she saw was her brother kneeling by her bedside. He was shirtless, pale scars crossing his already pale chest that hadn't been there before, shaped so much like the wings that bracketed their faces. He'd chopped off his ponytail as well, though she hadn't noticed in the kitchen what felt like hours ago. It was still him though; silver-haired and golden-eyed, looking at her with so much concern, same as always.

No, that wasn't quite correct. Monday couldn't say she'd ever seen her brother cry.

He scrubbed a hand over his face, wiping away clear, ordinary tears as he tugged her hands from where they strangled the quilt.

He said, "They can't hurt you anymore."

Perhaps it should've been clear that the house of Deora wanted status symbols more than they wanted *actual* children, seeing as no one bothered to think of baby names beyond the days on which said children were born.

The child who would eventually call himself Severin was their perfect daughter for too short a time. With how many generations back in the Deora family tree sat that angel blood, it hadn't been enough to manifest anything impressive in ages. The delicate, birdlike wings beside their heads cut quite a figure, but wings and nothing else from an old-money, old-magic family wasn't much when compared to the nouveau riche magicians of their social circles. But Severin was supposed to change that. The Deoras had the money to spend on obscure folk remedies and commissioned rituals, anything to guarantee that *this* child would be the one to bring renown and magic to their name once more—and on one Saturday evening they thought their hard work had finally come to fruition. They doted, as much as people like them could dote, and all was well.

It didn't last. It couldn't. Not when it became abundantly clear that Severin hadn't the slightest magical ability. "The first pancake always comes out a touch unfortunate," the family said, as though they weren't wealthy enough to pay someone to make their pancakes for them perfectly. "This time we know."

That "first pancake" was promptly shunted off to an au pair with as much dismissal as returning a pair of shoes that didn't fit . Severin was three years old.

Had he been old enough to remember it, he would see that the little sister—born about a year later—-didn't receive the same doting. Their parents were something close to gun shy, insisting that this daughter would be the "right" one while secretly preparing for her to be another dud.

This baby they named Monday, and when the au pair asked little Severin if he wanted to see his new little sister, h e asked if they could return her and get a baby giraffe instead.

When the two were old enough to realize just how messed up the situation was, his sister would sit on the edge of Severin's bed and they'd speculate together how, if things had been different, would their parents have kept going until they had a whole clutch of faintly angel-blooded children, one for every day of the week?

But at that small age, he did not hate her. Hate was too strong an emotion for his tiny body, and hating her would've required more understanding of the situation than he possessed, but the urge to return her didn't dissipate. He knew enough to know that things were different and in some unfathomable way he was wrong. Monday was their perfect little angel, and he was *not*.

And then Monday got teeth.

"Monday, go to your room. Close your eyes, cover your ears. I'll come get you in a minute." The words barely escaped through gritted teeth and for a moment he feared she'd assume the anger was meant for her. "I need to have a talk with our parents."

Monday didn't need to be told twice, clutching her bleeding arm to her chest as she scampered out of the kitchen.

"I'm not asking again." How long had he been out in the garden that it came to *this* right away? They jumped his sister like a pair of goons the minute she got home from the mall? How much of her had they taken before he walked in? "What are you doing to my sister?"

His father set the tweezers down on the pristine kitchen table that never saw use for family dinners, rolling his eyes like he was the slighted party. "Satur—"

"No! None of that!" *It's not like you put a lot of thought into naming me so you shouldn't be that mad when I discard it.* He pointed in the direction Monday had run. "I want to hear you say it."

"Your sister's...condition has gotten worse lately," his mother interjected. If his father spoke like he was the victim, she talked down to him like he was still three years old. "Harder to hide."

"Shouldn't you be happy about that? The visual proof of the perfect magical child you wanted?" He ignored her grimace at the word *perfect*.

"Not when—"

"Not when she's too holy that her body can't contain it?" Severin asked, knowing he wasn't enough and she's too much. "You wanted magic, but weren't prepared for divinity to be feral? That seems like an oversight on your part!"

Spineless, his father only bothered to speak up now. "Do not talk to your mother like that."

"Then don't rip parts off my sister!" Something coiled in his gut, the anger he thought he'd starved out long ago now perking up like a snake inside of him. He'd never cared how they tossed him aside, always told himself he couldn't miss what he'd never had, but—

But Monday was *good*. She was everything they wanted and she still wasn't enough. They could hurt him to their hearts' content, with the distance they held him at and the casual cruelty only deigning to acknowledge him with criticism, backhanded barbs, and pretending they *still* didn't know his name.

But not Monday.

As soon as he'd been old enough to realize that she wasn't enough for them either, he'd wanted to protect her. Until now, he hadn't known how, and he had let it get this bad.

"Do you really think that's the best way to handle this?" To leave her bleeding and scared at the hands of her own parents just because she doesn't fit their aesthetic? "Can you answer me that?"

"It's...complicated," his father said, refusing to meet Severin's eyes.

Fine. He'd *make* them look at him.

Severin shut his eyes and took a steadying breath. They'd be happy to know they got their wish. Two powerful, magically inclined children here to make sure everyone knows the family name, just like they always wanted.

"Can I let you in on a secret? Our angelic ancestors, they look more like her than they do any of us. Did you ever consider that?"

Only now did his mother's perfect porcelain composure start to crack. "How do you—"

Severin ignored her. "I can honestly say I didn't want it to come to this," he said, so softly it was more to himself than them. "But to say I'm sorry would be a lie."

When he opened his eyes again to see the horror on their faces, his tears were running gold.

At least by the time she turned eighteen, their parents had long given up on trying to file Monday's teeth down. It quickly became clear that her little fangs would keep growing back, like a rat or a rabbit, but never longer than her face could hold.

Despite her other so-called *imperfections*, Monday was the magically gifted child they'd so desperately wanted, and that meant pretending everything was fine. Long sleeves and longer skirts so out of place on a girl her age, tucking her wings over her face in what their mother called an "air of mystery" but instead caused her to bump into things, and a debutante ball that made everyone miserable.

The fight to get Severin in dresses had ended in childhood, despite the fact that he'd never been able to put a finger on why. When Monday stole his frilly skirts a size too big and hissed like something unholy when asked to give them back, he was grateful in a way he couldn't put into words. Unfortunately, this was "a high society affair," which meant both of their daughters had to wear nice dresses and pretend to enjoy it. He found his sister on the patio that night, long after the guests had gone home, staring out into the perfectly manicured gardens and scratching at the lacy sleeves of her dress until they tore.

"It catches on the shards. It hurts," Monday said.

"Let me help," Severin said and she did, allowing him to fumble with the zipper that went all the way up her neck with a collar like a Victorian schoolmarm.

"It hurts," she repeated, a note of disdain in her voice not solely meant for the sleeves. "The fabric. The texture feels so bad it makes me want to rip my skin off."

"I know." He didn't, not personally, because his own discomfort in this attire was rooted in something else, but she'd told him enough. The clothes their mother picked out, the ones she chose to hide everything "unusual" about Monday, were a special form of hell on her senses. He stepped out of sensible flats.

"Trade with me; your feet look like they hurt." Because heaven forbid either of them walked back in barefoot and tracked dirt across the floor.

"I looked for you," she said. "I had to smile and shake hands with everyone our parents know and I wanted my sister there. I was miserable, Saturday, and you left me alone."

He winced. "Not...completely alone," Severin said. "I told you what to expect. This was your party, Mother didn't want to detract attention, I had my own a few years back..."

It wasn't what she meant and he knew it. Their mother had planned this whole party to make Monday seem perfect, no expense spared, everyone she wanted to impress invited; she'd even gone so far as to commission magicians for the décor, for twinkling lights that bobbed and instruments that played themselves, all to make everyone in attendance forget they didn't have enough magic to do such tricks themselves.

Monday was to be the star of the show, *not* her unfortunately ordinary older sibling, and he'd stepped back and let her be, even when she didn't want the attention. She *had* looked for him in the crowd and he'd slunk away, lest he end up in the spotlight too and incur their mother's wrath. At least that's what he told himself.

"I'm still shocked they presented you to society when they like to pretend you don't exist," Monday said. His fingers stilled on the buckles of her strappy heels and she seemed to realize she'd said the wrong thing. "...Sorry." It was a mumbled apology, but more than he deserved.

"Don't be," he said softly. "You're correct. And truth be told, I wish they hadn't."

"At least they didn't make you cover your face," said Monday. "Do you know how hard it is to dance trying to peek out from between your wings? Angels are supposed to be graceful." She rolled her neck, flapping her wings slightly like she was trying to work feeling back into them. "Mother's gonna be mad I kept stepping on their toes."

"She's the one who thought that was the best way to cover your 'little skin problem,' so she has no room to judge," said Severin.

"And if I told her that she'd slap me for *disrespect* or whatever. *You* might be able to, though."

But he couldn't. Wouldn't. Same thing, right?

"I didn't notice any horrific missteps," he said instead.

"And thank our angelic ancestors for that," Monday groaned. "I felt hopeless out there. Boys *can't* dance!"

When he laughed she went quiet again, looking out at the lawn and not at him. When she spoke, her voice was almost a whisper.

"Saturday," she said, "I don't think I like boys. Not like that. I like girls."

It wasn't the confession he'd expected from her, and when she looked to him again to gauge a reaction, her tears were already starting to form. He knew then that he'd been quiet for too long, that she feared he was about to judge her like their parents did, that this was something else like her appearances and her "little idiosyncrasies" to make her even less perfect than their parents pretended she was.

He rushed to wrap her in a hug before the tears could fall.

"It's okay," he said. "I don't care. I mean, it's you, I care about you being happy, but I don't care like they would." He ran a hand through her silvery hair as she sniffed into his shoulder. "I love you, it's you."

"You're not upset?"

"Why would I be upset? And if we're making confessions..." He paused. He'd already let her down tonight, leaving her to fend the crowds without her big sister. This would either make it worse, or ... "You don't like boys, and I think I am one."

She pulled back to look at him, and in her heels he finally had more than an inch over her.

"Truth be told, I'm not surprised," Monday said, and a bark of laughter scrambled out before he could stop it. Of course she wasn't, had it been obvious to everyone except him? "What do I call my brother then?"

He'd thought about it, passively, knowing if anyone would care enough to ask this it would be here, but hadn't expected it so *soon*.

"...Severin, I think," he said finally.

"Severin," Monday repeated, no trace of the hurt in her voice that had been present when she called his old name. "In that case: Sev, I don't think I like boys."

He hadn't expected how much it would mean to hear *his* name from the one family member who cared enough to ask.

Severin hid in the downstairs powder room, trying to work up the nerve to do *something*. Much the way he'd been trying for the last forty-five minutes. He'd had the good sense not to grab the kitchen shears, instead swiping the scissors his sister used to cut her bangs out of her bathroom cabinet. If all went well, they'd be back in her medicine cabinet before she got home from the mall, none the wiser.

All had *not* gone well for the aforementioned forty-five minutes. He stood before the mirror with the scissors held to his ponytail hesitating every time until his parents' voices floated in from the kitchen.

"—s getting worse."

"I really thought after puberty we'd be done with the worst of it."

"I did too, but layering isn't going to hide it anymore; the scales are tearing her clothes, she's got bruises from bumping into things. It's getting to be too much."

Too much? Too fucking much?

He wanted to burst out of the bathroom and remind them that Monday was everything they wanted, the magical child, the angel of their ancestors. Yes, she's not a cherub but she's nothing short of divine. If they weren't prepared to have a child that was *too much* then they shouldn't have tried at all.

It would be deliciously ironic if it wasn't so damn sad: her far too holy, him the angel who fell short.

He was so caught up in the indignity of it he almost missed his mother's next words.

"—going to have to start plucking. She's got enough magical prowess to fix any cosmetic scarring."

"She's used to wearing layers anyway."

"And fixing that up will be easier than mending her torn sleeves."

"We'll talk to her when she gets home, then. I'll find the tweezers."

Plucking. Tweezers. Cosmetic scarring. Monday was his *sister*, and they were talking about her like she was a decorative bonsai to be pruned.

He stormed out of the bathroom, Monday's hair shears still in hand, and out the back door. He barely heard his parents calling the name that was no longer his, demanding to know how long he'd been "lurking" in there.

He didn't know where he was going, or what he intended to do, but Severin knew this: he would tear his parents apart if he could.

At least, that was the conclusion he came to when he finally stopped walking, slumped in some corner of the family's sprawling gardens. If his parents followed him, they wouldn't find him here; they paid other people to tend their gardens rather than learn their own way around.

It made sense that the self-centered and image obsessed house of Deora would have fountains topped with statues of angels, though the one Sev found himself looking up at had seen better days.

"She gets it from you all, right? Everything they say is 'wrong' with her?" Even he didn't know if *you* meant their family in general, or the angelic ancestors that gave Monday all her holiness and left the rest with only wings. "Did you all look more like her than...this?"

He gestured up at the weathered stone pouring water from a jug, into a basin he and Monday had tossed coins into as children before they were scolded to stop being wasteful.

Did he look ridiculous, hollering at a statue like it was actually responsible for his sister's pain? Probably. But was it also a touch cathartic? Yes.

"If she gets it from you, do something to help her! Before they hurt her again!" Or help him protect her, he realized as his anger solidified. "I'm her brother, I'm supposed to keep her safe, and I've fucked it up until now! I let it get this bad and I can't let it get worse!"

A tiny voice in the back of his head, one kinder to him than his usual self-admonishments, pointed out that *he wasn't responsible for their parents' abuses, he didn't* let *anything happen.*

"It doesn't make me *feel* any less responsible," Severin said. "They can hate me all they want, that's fine, whatever, I'd rather they treat *me* like that than her."

What must've been his conscience continued: *What all are you willing to do for her? You think of yourself a coward, unwilling to risk their ire until now, what changed?*

"Their vehemence," he answered aloud. "Maybe if I distract them. Make them madder at me for something I can control than something she can't."

It wasn't what he wanted, not really, but it was the only thing he could think of in the moment, the only thing he *could* control.

That would be an awfully bold assertation

It would, but he didn't care. With the hair scissors gripped in one hand, he draped his ponytail over his shoulder and chopped. His hair had been almost as long as Monday's until now, and hers reached her waist. Their mother had never let him cut his hair, as it was easier to pretend he hadn't told them he was a man that way. She wouldn't do something as dramatic as kick him out of the house, that would stir up too much gossip, so maybe she'd just slap him, maybe she'd reinstitute the feminine dress code of his childhood to keep up appearances, but no matter what she would be *angry*. Perhaps, *hopefully*, angry enough that she'd forget—

The second his discarded hair hit the water of the fountain, his vision swam in gold.

You have my attention, son of mine. What are you planning to do with it?

Ah. No wonder the voice in his head was too nice to him; it wasn't his at all. The use of *son*, though...

Oh, how his parents would fume to find their angelic ancestor, the being they so longed to emulate, saw him as he is.

Looking at them directly was near impossible because they were pure iridescence; near consumed by feathers that looked more like shards of rainbow glass and a halo to match, too many eyes like chunks of pink quartz, all sharp edges and radiance. In this ancestor of his, divinity was feral...

And they looked like Monday.

Or rather, the extinct megafauna version of Monday. The pieces of her that their family hated, all exaggerated and glorious and if only she could see it.

"Our parents always resented me for not being special, not being magical," Severin continued, trying to sound more confident than he felt with his newly hacked off hair and lack of a plan. "So let me be everything they thought they wanted."

How so?

"If Monday is too much, I want the power to be *more*." It made so much sense now that he finally said it aloud. "To make them afraid to ever hurt her again, so afraid that they won't overlook me anymore now that they know *this* is what's protecting her."

And what will you offer in exchange?

"Shit, flesh and blood good enough?" Severin asked, putting his hands on the swell of his chest. "They don't quite fit the whole *I'm a man* thing."

The entity that was his ancestor hummed a bit in consideration.

Blood is a powerful bargaining tool, yes

"Hell, take my womb as well. We're a dynasty of misery and I think our genes are cursed. I'm not gonna want children, and if I can get *more* from that...?" He tried to play it off like a joke to mask the fact that he was terrified. What if whatever he became, it hurt too much to bear? The little mermaid walking knives with every step? What if he couldn't turn back? That dramatic, declarative haircut wouldn't mean much if he was a mass of eyes and feathers forever—

You're a very caring brother, Severin

He hadn't been, but he would be, and that would make whatever he was about to endure worth it.

"At this point, I'll take whatever you can give me."

In that case, this will only hurt for a moment, my son

The creature wept golden.

When he first snapped back to himself in the garden, he thought he'd dreamed it, and that left an ache in his chest: once again, he'd failed his sister. When he realized that ache *was* his now flat chest, and when he'd gone inside and let his anger wash over him and remake him, it was euphoric. A creature decked in shimmer and feathers; no one could look at that and immediately, incorrectly assume womanhood when they were too busy counting eyes.

And besides, the people who mistook it so insistently never would again.

He scrubbed a bloody hand across his eyes and the feathers came away streaked in gold. That was new. A part of Severin hated himself for crying, for mourning them. Neither him nor Monday had been truly wanted enough to feel properly *loved*, and yet he wept nonetheless. Perhaps he mourned the family the four of them could've had if things had been different, or maybe the pain came from the fact that it ever got this bad in the first place.

Whatever the case, they were gone, and it was time to go find Monday.

As drooping wings dragged behind him, he wondered, *could* he turn off this new face of his? He could feel the feathers falling away, the wings starting to retract, the extra eyes closing and resealing so hopefully...

When he reached Monday's door, she must've heard the floor creak because she looked up and saw him like *this* and flinched, ducking immediately back under her quilt with a yelp.

The last thing he'd wanted was to scare her. That was the trigger, it seemed, for this visage to slough off in a shed of bloody feathers as he collapsed at his sister's side.

"Fuck—Monday, it's okay, it's alright." He tugged her hands from the blanket as she took him in, hair shorn and flat chested, blood in places that hadn't been covered by the feathers. "They can't hurt you anymore."

He hadn't realized he was still crying until Monday brushed a tear from his face, back to its normal clear. She was crying too, and it was a relief that he wasn't alone in his misguided mourning.

"Are they dead?" she asked.

Severin nodded. "We're on our own now."

The impossibility of it stretched ahead of them like a chasm. He hadn't been thinking through a plan for the future as he'd ripped their parents apart, and now reality hung heavy in the room. What were they supposed to do with that?

"I want to go," Monday said, the wings beside her face fluttering like a nervous pigeon as she shook her head to clear it. "I wanna grab all the shit we can carry and leave this stupid miserable place behind. Go somewhere that I can pick out clothes without worrying about people seeing my shards and can kiss all the cute girls I want. Where you kiss all the cute boys, and nobody knows you as anything but Sev. Fuck the Deora name, can we do that?"

Severin kissed his sister's forehead like he'd done when she was very small. "Yeah, Monday. We can go wherever you want."

GENESIS 19:1–11

Shepard DiStasio

if my mother had treated me kinder
perhaps I would have been

better

she tucked me in with a kiss to my forehead
and told me not to fear the

Devil

i should have been grateful
and maybe then i could've been a better

daughter

she tells me i'm an angel
and that i can do anything because i'm

special

because i'm her daughter
and her daughters are good

girls
very good girls
girls

girls   *girls*   *gi**rls***   ***girls***   ***g i r l s***

a shooting star, she tells me,
make a wish!

                    a wish?

when the doctors told my parents ***not to have me***

                        and when i came out screaming with blue lips and
                        bulging eyes

my umbilical cord fashioned as a noose

   i   *wish I had been born a son of God and not my mother's*

                                    daughter

RELICÁRIO

Kate Duarte

Relicário

Maria's vomit splashes onto the tips of the priest's shoes, ruining a shoeshine boy's work.

It's the incense that has always made her nauseous, or perhaps angel Miguel's gaze fixed on her, or maybe something has upset her stomach. These are the excuses Mama gives Father Inácio, repeatedly, a regretful sinner's tone dripping over every word. Maria blinks, trying to relieve the itchiness—it's the incense that has always made me nauseous, Maria lies.

Papa doesn't ever blame Maria for any of her flaws, but Mama's eyes are pointed at her in accusation. You see, Maria is a reliquary-girl, one of those born to be put on display. One day, she shall fulfill her destiny. The same way a reliquary's only function is to keep the saints' secrets safe, Maria's is to carry on her husband's name, a pompous secret made to fit inside a womb and belong to someone else.

Maria clutches her ivory skirts, stained with ruby, but it's impossible to hide: her nausea isn't incense-induced, after all. Mama drags her away from the chapel, as demure as she can in such cases, to hide away Maria's shame. A myriad of maids awaits her when she returns home. Maria is a woman! Mama announces. Maria is a woman... the maids echo, staring at Maria as if mourning a corpse dug out of its white coffin and planted in the ground to provide for the worms.

O anjo

She barely had any time at all to be a girl. At fifteen, Maria was tossed into etiquette classes (too late) and, on a sunny Sunday, Papa took her to the house. He chose the man himself, bargained Maria like his prized racehorse.

It was a short engagement. They had a few encounters at the manor's gardens, chaperoned by a watchful aunt. The man was always polite but never warm.

Please, call me Madalena, she requested on her boldest days. Maria, he corrected every time.

On her last engagement night, Maria dreamed of the angel Miguel. He was cloaked in sky-blue, traced in delicate watercolor brushstrokes, eyes almost faded. On the fabric of his clothing, the angel prompted flowers to bloom into golden hues, beautiful, dainty things. It was a promise of good news—but what of the strain of her stomach, the smell, the itch! Maria Madalena drowned in her silk sheets, a red sea flowing down her legs, sweat washing her fair skin. And Miguel lost his wings, as the dream grew dim. He had her father's eyes, or perhaps her fiancé's... but was every man not the very same one? And every woman, mirrored on her mother's childbirth's scar.

A casa

Her husband's house was erected during a glorious architectural period, entirely white, entirely cold. Tiles adorn the corridor walls, the furniture is the most expensive in town, and the maids braid Maria's hair with the care of a dear sister. Vacant eyes and frosty hands, they share the appearance of the religious maidens perched on Father Inácio's altar. If they fall, will they break? If they break, will Maria's husband care? Each of them is as young as Maria, and she wonders how they can exist not to be a reliquary, too, but merely the attentive hands that take care of one.

Yet the moon rises, and the maids dissolve into the shadows. Maria is alone in her husband's room, and all is gloom. In her mouth, her tongue is glued to the roof like sacramental bread. Why does it roll back, then, to choke her? Isn't her mouth holy, aren't her kisses supposed to be sacred?

Every night, she prays for the candle to be snuffed out later, and every night he blows out the candle with ruthless punctuality, then lies over her body with that same scent of incense ingrained into his limbs. His kisses aren't divine, they're asphyxiating.

Eventually, Maria is fulfilled. Her belly rounds from day to day, until it blows up like a balloon, all the maids surrounding her, so many cloths, so much encouragement. Push, push, push, until they hear a strained cry. It's a girl, one of the maids says, and she doesn't sound glad.

It's a girl, therefore, it's mine, Maria decides.

Chuva

A maid opens the day with the promise that it's going to rain, whispered into Maria's ear. Through the window, the sun shines with the will of a thousand. Still, Maria nods in agreement.

Her husband drags her into the manor's chapel, in hopes that prayer might cure her. Melancholy, the doctor concluded, common enough illness. Despite clinging to the child in her arms, she refuses to take a single bite of food.

Madalena follows the private mass with arduous, fixed eyes—dark as if they have swallowed the shadows in the corners of her bedroom. She claims every ugly thing as her own: the maid's tattered skirts, the hunting boots her husband forgot about but could still endure a ride, the ceremonial dagger the careless priest sets down on the altar.

She waits for night to fall, so she may slide out of bed unnoticed. She believes she sees every angel carved into the wooden ceiling of her bedroom, a choir whose symphony inspires no divinity, only fear. Her husband is fast asleep, the plains of his chest exposed. Madalena does not fear as she sinks in the dagger into his heart. It's a girl, so it's hers. She shall not be like Maria. She won't be a pretty girl as her grandmother was, and her great-grandmother before her, and the group of women who let their dreams die inside this manor's attic.

There are no angels, it seems. Instead, it is every maid in the house scattered around the room to aid Madalena. One holds a cloth to the hot drop that stains Madalena's bosom, another pins his arms, a third one closes her fingers over Madalena's to help her plummet the dagger further into her husband's flesh. Each of them dons the same dress they donned when they first entered the manor. Maria Madalena is different, since she bore the blessed fruit and did not die on the delivery bed like they did. Maria Madalena is the only one who could make it past the manor's gates.

She wraps her daughter against her chest, against her heart, and leaves behind her silver rosary. She allows herself a single glance over the shoulder, to watch the red rain cascade from her husband's bed—look how it rains!—and the women who came before her.

LANGUAGE OF THE GODS: THE USE OF MUSIC IN VIETNAMESE SHAMANIC RITUALS

Solar Hoàng

When the ritual began, it needed no introduction. A hush swept through the crowd and we settled down without being told to. I shifted to fold my legs into a more comfortable position as the lights washed the room in red. In the darkness, the features of the priestess kneeling on the stage morphed from human to statue. Her lips were redder and cheeks pinker with rogue. The chosen attire resembled one of a rich landlady in the feudal days - deep navy blue to match the crown on her hair, highlighted by gold embroideries of the dragon dancing with the phoenix. The temple was so quiet, I could hear the pearls on her ears and the clink of bangles on her wrists from where I sat. Wordlessly, I marvelled at the way she could sit so still, all while a straw mattress imprinted onto the skin of my legs. But the stillness dissipated when the music began. The high notes of a đàn nguyệt, the moon lute, and the metallic sound of a cymbal drew the priestess to her knees. With each addition of a new instrument, she rose a little higher. By the time she was on her feet, the ritual became a celebration of music. The votive dance, namely 'lên đồng,' means "to mount the medium" or "going into trance." But its more formal name 'hầu đồng' offers a clearer understanding of its purpose - to serve.

'Chầu văn,' the music genre used in these shamanic rituals, has its roots in the rural areas of the Red River delta. Its golden age lasted from the end of the 19th century to early 20th century until 1954, when the tradition of lên đồng was criticised for its association with superstition and consequently banned. After 1990, chầu văn was restored as a shade of the Northern Vietnamese cultural tapestry[1]. Its name, chầu văn, literally means the "text" or "the literature of

---

[1] Dân Trí (2007)

a ritual." As I sat among the audience, listening to a song in my mother-tongue, I lost my grasp on its meanings until Vietnamese became foreign to my ears. Then again, perhaps it was not mere Vietnamese. It was a new language that combines the text with the ebb and flow of music, allowing the medium to assume new identities and engage with spirits beyond this realm[2].

As the music became the only thing I could hear, the ritual felt similar to attending an orchestra. A 'cung văn' is a musical group consisting of three to five musicians, commanding a variety of traditional instruments, mainly the moon lute, trống ban (small drums), clappers, and cymbals. In different hearings, the group could also include trống cái (big drums), đàn tranh (zither), đàn nhị (two-stringed instrument), flute, đàn bầu (single-stringed instrument), and in some, but not all cases, singers. With music dominating the ritual, chầu văn is an organic combination of a musical genre and the folk belief[3]. Except for the shaman mounting the medium at the centre of the stage, the musicians all wore impassive features, losing themselves completely to the song. The man that held the moon lute stood out to me the most. Draped in black traditional dress, he held the wooden instrument close to his belly. His eyes dimmed as he nurtured it, feeling each vibration of the plucks echoing in his body until he, too, was a vessel of the music.

The shaman held long candles between the grips of her fingers. With four in each hand, she splayed them out like a fan dance. After the first verse, one of the candles was lit on fire. I gasped in amazement of the whole production. Someone sitting in front of me dropped her head and started to murmur something, her sniffling drowned by the sound of music. One by one, the candles were lit until the shaman was wielding fire in her hands. I didn't understand the implication until the next part of the dance began. On both sides of the stage, offerings piled up on plastic trays. Each tray was prepared by one family in the audience. The rituals involved pooling a selection

---

[2] Norton, B. (2000)
[3] Norton, B. (2009)

of goods, food, special delicacies, and other trinkets together-items
that the spirits of the loved ones once adored-with the money prepared
by the temple and the shaman. I lifted my eyes when the woman swayed
in the air. Money rained down. In East Asian custom, the act of burning underworld money was not a strange activity. During New Year's
Eve or death anniversaries, we invited the dead back to celebrate the
day with us, and at the end of the celebration, we burned money to say
goodbye to them. Watching the money raining down, it felt the exact
opposite. We, the audience, were invited to the world of the medium.
And the shaman, she who led the rituals, ripped the border between two
realities. Did she invite the ghosts to come to us, or us to them, of
that I can't be sure when there was no division.

Rouget and Biebuyck (1985) in their book "Music and Trance: A
Theory of the Relations Between Music and Possession" coined a key
distinction: the shaman functions as the "musicant" (where they ac-
tively sing or play an instrument), while the possessed individual is
"musicated" (with music performed for them by musicians). As a "musicant," the shaman projects her own imaginary world onto the audience,
whereas the possessed individual is "musicated" by the imaginary
world. They argued that music induced the adept to identify oneself
with their deity and allowed them to express this identification
through dance[4]. However, in the specific case of lên đồng, the shaman
acted like a medium for the spirit to pass through and communicate
with the audience. To me, the line between the two terms the author
proposed blurred until the musicant became the musicated, until the
possessed became the possessor, until reality blended into the spirit
world in stitchless perfection. In shamanism, Rouget views music's
primary function as "incantatory," bringing the unseen imaginary
world to life and being "infused with magical power."

As we approached the climax of this orchestra, I closed my eyes
and soaked in the entirety of the experience. Sitting here, among
other people in the audience, I thought about the erasure chầu văn
suffered for more than thirty years and how it returned as an intan-

---

[4] Rouget, G. and Biebuyck, B. (1985)

gible heritage. I wondered what drove the restoration: was it because it had become so significant in the cultural custom of Vietnam or was it because the music was so tightly linked to our ethnic identity? Buchanan and Stokes (1995) highlighted how music embodies and enacts political and moral order, sustains communal values, and aligns individuals in bounded groups[5]. Peeling away the religious setting, the shamanic dance often centres around a certain activity, such as to heal a sick person, to cast away ghosts, to read a prophecy, or to pray for prosperity. The kind of mundanity in such activities that is so easily understood by every person in every class.

And so, hầu đồng is a reflection of the people. It expresses the people's wishes and aspirations, for their family, and for national peace and prosperity. It praises the Saints who have contributed to building and defending the country. Though indirectly, it contributed to patriotism and the act of remembering the roots of our nation. Each hầu đồng ritual is a story about a hero, talented and virtuous in their lifetime, who has contributed to the people and the country. Serving the shadow of those Saints is an honour for each artist, and through that I understand more deeply the history and culture of the nation. Hầu đồng is a form of theatre, art, a living museum preserving folk cultural forms through music and dances.

The music peeled back like the spirits departing. One by one, each musical instrument dwindled to a stop. First the drums ceased, bringing the tempo of the dance down to a soft flow, much like a leaf floating in the air. The fire was extinguished from the candles between the shaman's fingers, leaving only the warm light of the altar behind her to coax us back in the darkness. The person in front had stopped sniffling. Soon, there was only the moon lute and the shaman who was still on her feet. The shaman didn't look as graceful as she was at the beginning. Her forehead beaded with sweat and I could see the tiredness lining her eyes. Suggested by her movements, she was still in communication with the ghost, wrestling and grappling for one last thing. I have heard spirits do that sometimes. They dueted

---

[5] Buchanan, D.A. and Stokes, M. (1995)

for another verse before the shaman knelt down on her knees. I waited. I didn't know how it would look to see a spirit departing, so I waited. The moon lute slowed and ended with the last note hung like a question. I continued waiting.

Then the shaman opened her eyes and smiled.

REFERENCES

Buchanan, D. A., & Stokes, M. (1995). Ethnicity, identity and music: The Musical Construction of Place. *Notes, 52*(2), 427. https://doi.org/10.2307/899032

Dantri.com.vn. (2017). *Hầu đồng - Hành Trình đi Tới di Sản Văn Hóa được UNESCO Vinh Danh.* Báo điện tử Dân Trí. https://dantri.com.vn/van-hoa/hau-dong-hanh-trinh-di-toi-di-san-van-hoa-duoc-unesco-vinh-danh-20170113105036834.htm

Norton, B. (2000). Vietnamese Mediumship Rituals: The Musical Construction of the Spirits. The World of Music, 42(2), 75-97. http://www.jstor.org/stable/41699334

Norton, B. (2008). *Songs for the spirits: Music and mediums in modern Vietnam.* University of Illinois Press.

Rouget, G., & Biebuyck, B. (1985). Music and trance: A theory of the relations between music and possession. University of Chicago Press

CONDEMN ME

Andromeda Ruins

"Forgive me, Father, for I have sinned." My voice trembles at the confession. I don't know why I am here; I do not believe that what I am doing is wrong. "It has been six months since my last confession."

I am simply fulfilling God's will for me, fulfilling my parents' prayers for a son.

"These are my sins: I have been doubting who I am meant to be." There is no doubt, I know who I am meant to be, but I can't tell the Father that if my parents' reactions are anything to go by. "My clothes have become uncomfortable on my body and I wish to wear the clothes of my brothers. I wish to change my flesh to make myself more comfortable in it."

I've done the research on it—the surgeries that will make me feel more like *me*. I look forward to the day I can use them to make my body truly mine.

"My friends tell me that I can change my name and they will accept me, but when I spoke to my parents they told me to come here and confess my wrongs."

The words stumble from my mouth, unapologetic in their tone. I'm having a hard time trying to convey the depth of the feelings I have, but if I'm being honest, I do not care what the priest says about my confession.

I know who I am. I know what I wish to be.

This is not a bad desire, just as my parents' decades worth of desire for a son is not bad.

"For these are my sins, I am truly sorry." God, I pray that the priest cannot hear the insincerity in my voice. I wish for the priest to comfort me, but I do not expect him to. This is a trial I must see myself through and I know he will not see it as such.

"That is concerning, my child." I am not his child, I have not been His child for months now. But he cannot know that. "It seems you have fallen to the age-old temptation to make yourself God."

That's an option? I could create myself in an image that I see fit and call myself God? The corner of my mouth ticks up as I imagine what it might be like to be God. Would I be as merciful as He is said to be? Would my believers accept those like me with open arms?

"You are damning your soul to Hell. If you repent now, I may be able to save your eternal soul. But you must repent and never stray from His will again."

The Father continues speaking, but I do not listen. Even just a year ago, I would have hung onto every word he said. But his teachings have been filled with hate in a way that I can no longer believe. He has spoken of miracles and acts of God Himself, calling them abominations and failures.

As the Father's speech comes to a close, I prepare my rehearsed recitations.

"My God, I am sorry for my sins with all my heart."

I am not. I could never be sorry for simply fulfilling the prayer of my parents, for living my life in a way that honors both God's creation and my own desires.

"In choosing to do wrong and failing to do good, I have sinned against you whom I should love above all things." The prayer falls from my mouth, despite my heart not being with the words.

It is enough, though. The Father ends the confession, removing us from the confessional and telling me, "The Lord has freed you from your sins. Go in peace."

For the first time in a year, I believe him. I believe that He freed me, but not in the way the Father believes to be true. The black sludge of sin will eternally run through my veins, but I shall embrace it and mold it into something beautiful.

"Thanks be to God," I mumble. The words taste like ash on my tongue as I turn to leave. My training tells me that I should enter a pew and fall to my knees in supplication to God, but I can't. Not anymore.

I continue down the hall instead, past the basket asking for offerings and out the front doors. As I leave the building, I let one final prayer leave my lips:

Lord, please forgive me for abandoning you. I simply refuse to believe in a God that would condemn me for struggles that He put me through.

The large wooden door slams shut behind me, sealing what remained of my faith in the coffin of its inception.

"I would like to thank each and every one of you in this room for joining us today! We always love seeing your beautiful faces," the president of the club says, their voice a comfortable rumble that commands the room.

"I would like to extend a special thank you to our newest member," they say, turning to point at me. They smile, a true smile like one I've only started seeing since leaving the church, and a healthy levity fills the air.

It had been an adjustment period, allowing myself to be around people who so clearly defy the word of the Lord. But I have found that these people, the ones who welcomed me into their ranks with nothing more than a simple "hello, welcome!", are full of light in a way that I refuse to believe is sinful.

"Would you care to introduce yourself?" the president asks me.

"Sure," I respond, shifting in my seat as I think of what I wish to say.

"My name is ███████. I, uh..." I stumble over the words. I don't know how to describe myself; I don't think I've ever purposefully brought attention to myself like this. I can feel the gaze of each person in the small classroom on me, staring at me with a weight I am unfamiliar with. The Father would say this is an act of sin, one I should absolve myself of.

I embrace it.

"I am questioning my identity and I hope our discussions here will shed more light onto how I view myself."

"I'm glad you've joined us today, ███████. I know Mack has been speaking highly of you for the past few weeks. If you need anything," the president leans further over the table to catch my gaze, looking deep into my soul as they speak, "anything at all, please let me know."

I nod in response. Having their eyes on me is becoming overwhelming. I wish for them to look upon someone, anyone, else.

The president smiles before leaning back, starting their spiel on gender identity—the topic of the meeting this week. This was what made me cave to Mack's request, what made me attend the club meeting with her. I am hoping to learn about that which the Father told me was sinful. Maybe I will find an answer for who I am.

The insight I seek evades me until we start talking about transmasculinity. The wish to be perceived as a man, or something close to it.

I don't know if I will ever see myself as a man, but there is a part of me that rejoices at the idea of people mistakenly assuming I am one.

I need to think about that. I wish to pray to God and see if He would love me still if I were to make myself a man, but I know He will not answer me. Not after I cast myself out of His light without a second thought.

Instead, I will pray to myself.

"Do you think there is a God out there who would accept us for our sins, instead of despite them?" Mack asks me one day. We are sitting outside of the church after Mass. Both of us are silent on the concrete steps as we process the vitriolic hate that the priest spewed at us.

I don't know why we went, really. I think we wanted to try reclaiming the faith that meant so much to us for so many years, but it wasn't meant to be.

I never realized just how targeted and painful the teachings are, how they enforce that we must all be the same. That anyone who is slightly outside of what God would consider "normal" is to be shunned, pushed out of His love and His light. And it hurts.

It shouldn't, but it hurts to have my fears confirmed. It hurts to know that I will never be loved by Him again because I will never hide myself again. I know now who I am, what I am, and I never wish to revert to the miserable person I was before.

I can see by the look in Mack's eyes that she feels the same. Even her new gods cannot dull the pain of betrayal from the one she was raised with. But we will not hide any longer, we know who we are to become and if God does not wish to have us, then so be it. We will move forward without Him.

"I believe that if there is not, we will create one ourselves."

I'm not sure what's changed, but in the past week I've noticed that people are more... attentive to me and the words I say.

I noticed it at first when my peers started turning to me for answers in class. I have never been a particularly active participant in any courses I take. My parents have already reprimanded me for my choice to pursue a degree. I did not want to bring them any further shame by making a spectacle of myself.

And yet, the number of times I have seen a room full of students turn in their seats to listen to what I can contribute... It's starting to freak me out.

I thought, at first, it was just that particular class. That I had somehow convinced those peers I am more knowledgeable about calculus than I actually am. But Mack thinks it extends further than that, that I should try paying more attention and seeing if it happens elsewhere.

Of course she was right, she always is.

I've found myself talking to more people, including myself in conversations that I never would have been included in before this week. People have been nicer to me. My opinions have been heard and considered in a way that I've never experienced before!

But this new consideration came with something more. People have started bringing me things, even if I never asked for them. Sure, I may have mentioned off-hand that I was thirsty, but I never asked for the professor to stop my presentation to fetch me a bottle of water.

This is becoming too much. I am not sure how to make people stop.

When I ask them to kindly leave me alone, they get this look in their eye like I just damned their soul to Hell. I do not have that power, nor would I wish that upon them.

I just want to be left alone.

It's freeing to see clumps of hair fall to the floor around me.

I'm sat on a stool in the bathroom of my apartment with Mack behind me. This was her idea, now that I'm not living under my parents' thumb. She said that they can't talk me out of doing what I want with my body anymore, that I do not have to worry about seeing their disappointed gazes or listen to their lectures on sin.

And so here we are. With Mack holding a pair of shears in one hand, cutting the long blonde locks from my head.

"Look at that handsome face," she coos, cupping my chin in one hand and forcing my eyes up to my reflection. There are tears in my eyes; I can't believe that is me.

The new haircut is short, something much more masculine than my long hair had been. There is no more hiding behind the barrier my hair provided. Now, the cut frames my face and brings out the warm honey brown of my eyes. I can see the man I am becoming in this reflection, even if I don't quite feel like him yet.

I watch a smile creep onto my face. *That's me.*

"You did an amazing job, Mack," I say as I cast my eyes upon her. "Thank you, you are the best."

Something flashes in her eyes, but I don't look long enough to figure out what it is as I turn back to the mirror. She really did an amazing job, I cannot wait to show off—*God, forgive me for this brazen display of want, even if you won't forgive me for my desires*—the new look on campus tomorrow.

There's a burning desire in my gut, one that's steadily grown warmer since the first day that I introduced myself as ███████. I wish to stoke it further, even if I end up drawing more attention upon myself to do so.

For the first time, I find that I do not mind the looks that I am receiving. People are staring at me as I walk to class. They are watching my every move.

I like it.

I like the way they look at me as if I am something to behold, the way they say my name as if it is something to worship. The way they gaze upon me is downright heretical, and I cannot get enough of it.

I am holy.

I return to my apartment after class and find Mack in my kitchen.

I gave her a key when I got the place and told her that she was always welcome in my home. I'm glad to see her using it, even if the look of concern on her face brings me to worry.

"The priest caught me on my way out of class today," she says. "The one from your church."

I haven't even taken off my shoes, set down my bag after being gone all day. "Oh?"

"He asked me if I had seen you recently. He wanted to talk to someone who is familiar with your quote-unquote 'fall into temptation' and could talk some sense into you, ██████."

Her voice is cold and the way she leans back against the counter tells me that she is trying to remain calm. I wonder what the old man told her to get such a reaction.

"He said that the church is suffering in a way that he's never seen before, that the only people still attending mass on the regular are your parents. He believes that everyone else has abandoned their beliefs and that you have something to do with it."

I have something to do with it? Now that is odd. I've never told anyone to change their beliefs, nor would I want to. *But I do like when they dote on my every need—is that my Sin?*

"How strange," I reply, shrugging my backpack off and setting it on the floor next to the shoe rack. Mack watches my movement with a palpable exasperation, like she thinks I'm not taking this seriously enough.

I could not care less.

"Who am I to tell someone what their beliefs should be? I never once spoke ill of the church. It is my own personal issues that I have. If people are now seeing that their God is flawed, that He can't both be merciful and all good if He discriminates against His own creation, then who am I to say otherwise?"

I walk into the kitchen, stepping up in front of Mack and separating her hands. She had been wringing them as we spoke, and I don't wish her to hurt herself with her concern.

Her voice is small as she responds, "Do you remember when we sat in front of the church and I asked you about the possibility of a merciful God existing? Do you remember what you said to me then?"

She refuses to meet my eyes. I don't know what she is asking of me.

"You said that we'd create one. What if we have? What if people started worshiping you as a God?"

I can't help but laugh.

"I am nothing special," I whisper to her, "nor am I worthy of being a God. It is preposterous to think that I could ascend into Godhood when I am just a silly little man standing in front of you after a long day of math lectures."

Mack sighs, adjusting her hands in mine to intertwine our fingers. "You're right." Her voice drops to match mine. "It's not possible. I'm just worried about what the priest will try to do to you if he sees you as a threat to his authority."

"And I appreciate that concern," I say, bringing our entwined fingers up to my mouth and pressing a kiss to our knuckles.

Then I step back, raising my voice and forcing a wide smile onto my face as I ask, "Now what do you think about spaghetti for dinner?"

I have not been able to stop thinking about our conversation the other week.

Do these people really believe me more important than their faith? Do they worship me as their God? Do I *want* them to worship me as their God?

The more I look, the more evidence I find that they do.

They dote on me. I knew this, of course. I even nurtured it at one point. But now I see it in a different light.

While I thought at first that they were just being kind, that they were treating me as just another man in this world, I now see that they are treating me as something more important. They bring me what I need and make sure that I am as comfortable as I can be at all times. One professor even brought in a container of soup the week that I had started to feel under the weather!

Not only that, but they follow me around. This is a recent change, but I've found that whenever possible they travel with me. They follow me from class to class. They wait out in the halls for a chance to see me as Mack and I leave the dining hall. They trail behind me as we walk to the local theater to watch a show. It's weird.

Then, there's the whispers. They whisper about me when they think that I cannot hear them. I have made an effort to keep an ear out for what they say. They call me merciful when I forgive them for bumping into me when we cross paths. They call me generous when I share the fruit from my lunch with someone who couldn't afford lunch that day. They call me humble when I apologize to the professor for answering a question incorrectly.

And finally, there's the way they gaze upon me. They look at me the way that I look at Mack, as if I am their entire world. As if I hung the stars in the night sky. They look at me with the same reverence that an art student might look upon the works of Bernatelli or Michaelangelo.

I have done nothing to deserve this attention and I fear that they may think me something I am not. I am as human as they are, not divine.

Something is wrong.

I startle awake, launching myself off the side of our bed. Something is wrong. I am nauseous.

The steps I take to get to the bathroom are shaky. My focus is on keeping the contents of my stomach where they are. I don't pause to turn on the light, instead falling to my knees in front of the toilet mere seconds before heaving a thick, dark liquid into the bowl.

I hear footsteps behind me before familiar fingers card through my shorn hair. It is a vain effort to comfort me, as it is quickly followed by a shrill scream.

My stomach roils, but I reach up to wipe at my mouth with the back of my hand. It's a poor attempt to make myself presentable before turning to face Mack, one I didn't need to make as I see her stumbling away from my hunched figure.

Her hand fumbles on the wall, searching for the light switch. She finds it a moment later, the light flickering on as she screams again. There is a clump of my hair in her hands.

"What the fuck," I whisper, just as another wave of nausea causes me to turn back to the toilet and heave. Only this time, I can see the contents of the bowl.

What I see makes me gag once more, adding more chunks of meat and viscera to the mix before me. Blood covers the white porcelain and coats my tainted fingers. I try to wipe my hand on my thigh, only to find my skin loose under my fingers.

"What the fuck," I say, louder this time. I dig my fingers into the flesh of my thigh, pulling it off with no effort.

Mack is sobbing behind me.

I turn towards her once again, unsure of what to do. What is happening to me? Why is my body falling apart?

Mack's sobs begin to form words, a desperate prayer to her gods as she begs for answers about me. I wish for a response.

It is only then that I remember our conversation from months ago. From the night when Mack told me about her conversation with the Father.

Then, I remember his words in the confessional booth well over a year ago. Is this what it means to remake myself? Am I creating my body in my own image?

"Did I ever tell you what the priest said to me that day?" I ask Mack. I know I haven't, I haven't spoken of the day my faith fractured to anyone. But now, as I hold clumps of my own skin in my hands, I know that I have to.

"He told me that I was sinful, of course," I laugh. The sound is rough, raw as I reach up and claw at my throat. "But there was something else he said. That I was falling to the age-old temptation to make myself God."

I watch her eyes widen as I speak. I watch the concern in them bleed into fear as the skin of my shoulder sloughs off, plopping obscenely onto the tile floor. She gags as viscera splatters next to her foot, droplets landing on the bottom hem of her flannel sleep pants.

I feel as if I am stepping out of an ill-fitting suit. Each piece of my body that falls away lifts an insurmountable weight from my soul.

"Does this feel like becoming God to you?" she asks, her voice trembling beneath the weight of her fear. Her eyes refuse to leave mine, even as I feel my skin melting between my fingers.

She must see the answer in my eyes, as she looks to the heavens and takes a deep breath. I verbally answer her anyway.

"This feels like an answer to my prayers, like a chance for me to be who I was always meant to be."

I am being given a chance to rectify the hate that the Father has spread, that is why my peers have been worshiping me. I will create my image the way I see fit. I imagine an ancient sculptor using his tools to create a new vessel for me, my skin chipping away to reveal the divine creation of God underneath.

"This is our chance to create a God that will accept us for our sins, just as we've been looking for."

I AM A GOD AND SO IS EVERYBODY ELSE BUT THIS IS ABOUT ME!

Jeanea Blair

THE INTELLIGENCE SOCIETY RELEASES THE PSILO PAPERS: A REPORT ON THE POSSIBLE SCIENTIFIC DISCOVERY OF GOD

By Shannon Laront

December 19, 2071

In the days preceding and following the Meeting of the Minds, it was all anyone could talk about in boardrooms, at coffee shops, on internet forums. Ever since the dismantling of the United Nations in 2064, there had not been seen a congregation of international leaders on such a scale. Retired presidents, leading scientists, Olympians, celebrities: gone are the days of ill-intentioned representatives as we bare forth a time where creators of culture are recognized in the way that old money and older power have been. The Meeting of the Minds Conference was a place where someone like Apryl Langette-three-time Olympian and author of seven best-selling novels, four of which have been made into movies-can appear on the same stage as Lola Sturgeon, who you've likely never heard of but has piloted the most successful zero-waste hospital on the planet.

Unfortunately, in the wake of such synergistic performances, other talks went unnoticed and even unattended. Dr. Lionel Frank, the president of the Intelligence Society, had a curious crowd of only eleven people for his talk titled, "I Am a God and So Is Everybody Else." Before the podium, with no sense of irony, he reported as follows:

"Ladies and gentlemen, you don't know it now but you're about to be harbingers of great change. If you were brought into this room today to receive this message, it was not by coincidence and that's not to say it was by design, either.

Twenty years ago, my team of scientists sought out the discovery of god. What really is god? Who is god? Not unlike questions you've probably asked yourselves, what intelligent folks you all are. I must say, I've attended a few of your workshops so far and I'm affirmed to be stood here among such greatness today. But yes, the questions we've all asked, so there must be some truth there, no? In a sample size of ten billion cognitively functioning adults, 99% of them will have raised a question of god.

So, we mined for this truth-in sunsets, in birth and death, in awe, in despair, in nuclear science-in any and every moment that someone has felt the presence or question of god. Which has been felt-you guessed it-in every moment. If something as mundane as a smile or a juicy peach can bring someone to godliness, then there must be the potential for godliness in all of us.

At the Intelligence Society, we've discovered that god is not out there; god is every single one of us. Living or dead. Conscious or previously conscious. Animal or plant. All of it. Anything with a life force is god and everything without one is god too, but in a way we haven't quite yet discovered. The point is we are all god, and I mean that in a literal sense. We all have immense power brewing in our chests."

Dr. Frank, like others were optioned to do, selected for the entirety of his transcript to be available publicly, which can be found at the Meeting of the Minds Conference webpage here. As you can read, he then goes on to describe the "God Frequency" that radiates subliminally through all living and previously-living things. It is, according to Dr. Frank, an underlapping frequency that cannot be attributed to heart rate, electric charge, movement, magnetism, or any other known catalysts for frequency.

Apparently, some of his attendees believed him, reportedly crying or stunned into silence when they returned to the main hall. Five of the attendees so far—Elias Grady, founder of Tidal Amnesty; Abby Destroyer; pop icon and queer activist[1]; Monica Diaz, former first daughter; Dr. Davis Chatterley, quantum physicist and nuclear mechanic; and Mother Larae Koving, the Vatican's head nun—all have made public statements in support of the Intelligence Society's claims in the week following the transcript publication. We got the chance to speak with Dr. Chatterley, one of the lead scientists who discovered the threads of consciousness.

"I've always respected the Intelligence Society," he says with his ankle crossed over his knee, sunken in the brown leather couch across from me. "We wouldn't have found the threads of consciousness if it weren't for their research on meta-thought a few years prior. Everything we know about ETILFs comes from the Intelligent Society, and Dr. Frank specifically. He understands better than anyone that all physics was once meta-physics, so the answers lie in the meta."

Not long after the Intelligence Society befell new leadership under Dr. Lionel Frank in 2049, they released the Everglade Files, a federally-funded report on the interactions with Extraterrestrial Intelligent Lifeforms (ETILFs) aboard the Magpie Station that circumvents Venus. On the eve of the Conference, the Society released the Psilo Papers, which sat mostly unnoticed until weeks later.

"Read the Everglade Files and then read the Psilo Papers," Dr. Chatterley instructs. "It's all connected. That's what everyone's been saying for forever now anyway. All of us have probably come to that same conclusion at one point or another, and Lionel found proof. My team at Green Island, we've noticed something else tangled between the threads of consciousness. I can't say what for sure yet, but

---

1 Abby Destroyer?! THE Abby Destroyer?! It makes sense because how the fuck would you perform like that if you didn't make a deal with the devil or god? She has this one lyric like "I'm not myself anymore / I'm all of you / I'm everyone / the blank pages at the back of a bible." She was calling herself god! And all of us god!! She has another line like "If you saw me for what I was / you'd pale at your own reflection / A fear of god / A fear of self." Holy shit!!! Everyone back then just thought she was going through a weird Christian thing, or maybe a weird Satanic thing, but here she was, one of the eleven attendees to THE SPEECH by THE DR. LIONEL FRANK!!!

amongst me and my peers in the scientific community, this connection between consciousness and spirit is a verifiable field of study, just as real as chemistry or astronomy. We haven't agreed on a name quite yet but it's quantum physics as far as I'm concerned. As far as many would agree."

Dr. Chatterley grows quiet, sinking further into the couch. He takes a moment with his tea before continuing, "The God Frequency is real. That's another name that I think needs to be reconsidered, honestly," he laughs. "There's too much baggage there already, like you can't call it the Santa Claus Principle and have them take it seriously. But what other agreed upon word is there, really? I think we've deviated so far from spiritual curiosity as a society, that now we're almost embarrassed to admit something like belief in an afterlife, or ghosts, or even god with a capital G. And the effects of not looking inward or outward are felt. If you're tired of that and looking for something deeper that you can get behind, this is it. It's a new renaissance."

The Green Island (TGI) will be releasing their study and endorsement of the Intelligence Society's God Frequency next month. TGI has had a longstanding and public relationship with Dunlog Enterprises, the leading innovators of clean energy, with over 70,000 patents and counting. TGI and Dunlog recently collaborated on the _aquatic comb_, a machine that harvests and distributes energy from drifting seaweed, all while creating no disruption to the local environment and even creating homes for some species. Before that, Dunlog was best known for the invention of home incinerators, which have become more affordable and widespread in recent years, a Trash Burn in every tenth American home. Dr. Davis Chatterley and Dunlog's CEO Dr. Branson Lewis have a decades-long personal and professional relationship, but a couple days after Dr. Chatterley's endorsement, Dr. Lewis posted a video online with a statement of staunch disagreement.

"I'm very disappointed that Dr. Chatterley would endorse such a thing. He and I have spoken at length about the consequences of such a theory, hypothetically. It's not worth it to go down that rabbit hole;

there's no end. And it's not true," he adds, as if in afterthought. Dr. Lewis is emotional on screen-it begs the question of his choice to be recorded speaking live, visibly unrehearsed, as opposed to writing and publishing a statement with forethought.[2]

"When Dunlog started making wires out of mushrooms, we noticed something. I've come here to tell you all-and please listen to the entirety of what I'm saying-the God Frequency does exist, but not in humans. Look around, what of us is godly? God exists in mycelium. You can get a taste of god, sure, but the doors always close again. We're not meant to harness that or we would have. God belongs to the forests, to the soil. God would rot in a human body."

It appears to take all his strength to hold himself down in his chair and keep himself from sprinting off. Appearing on camera might've been the only way he could hold himself accountable to speaking his version of the truth. That god is in the mycelium network that runs through forest soil, creating an ecosystem that acts more like a singular organism. By Dunlog's hypothesis, the God Frequency is closer to monotheism. They're anticipated to release a report on their findings in the coming months, as well.

Scientific communities on the internet have turned this moment into a bit of a fan war, composing opposite teams with Dr. Chatterley and Dr. Lewis making two out of a handful of popular representatives on each side. Those that believe in the God Frequency extending to all living creatures have Dr. Lionel Frank, of course, and the five attendees to his lecture that have spoken publicly in support of him. The opposing side is a mixed bag of people who support Dr. Lewis' mycological hypothesis, like legendary rockstar Marigold Richards; people who don't believe that god is found anywhere on earth, like Georgia Senator Kieth McMichaels; and people who don't believe in god at all, like astronaut Victor Lutz.

---

2 Lovers' quarrel perhaps? Is he just jealous that Chatterley discovered it first? I've been reading Lewis' mycology stuff and he's definitely been hinting at something like the God Frequency for years. I think, like Chatterly said, he just didn't have the balls to call it what it was.

You'll have to read the 473 page report to decide for yourself. If you can't make sense of the academic jargon, summaries and chapter outlines have been popping up across the web. Dr. Lionel Frank has refused to comment, but his new crop of fans is waiting, as if for a prophet.

Senator Allen Riley Only One of Hundreds Who Have Committed Suicide Since the Release of the Psilo Papers

By Gwen Bosch
June 12, 2072

Last year on November 1, the president of the Intelligence Society, Dr. Lionel Frank, presented a lecture on the Psilo Papers at the first annual Meeting of the Minds Conference. It wasn't until the lecture transcripts were released two weeks later that attendees began to notice and query amongst themselves. It took three more weeks still before any major news outlet reported on it. In a slow build back-dropped by the holiday season, the Psilo Papers shattered reality like a hollow eggshell.

The Brownstone news article, published on December 19, 2071, brought global attention to the 473 page document. The Psilo Papers claim that not only is god real, but every conscious being is god, including you and I. It also extends consciousness to trees, fungi, anything breathing or previously breathing; and anything unconscious is negligible waste, like the ashen byproduct of a burning fire.

Most people had written it off as wild conspiracy, but now in almost half a year, we've noticed a slowly growing community of be-lievers. The American workforce has reduced by 12% in a mass resigna-tion. Mayors are filling in for governors and governors are stepping up as senators. The White House is in a months-long policy freeze as they heed calls from international leaders. And in the last month alone, there have been thirty-three reported instances of self-im-molation.

Early speculators could not have predicted the fallout, slow to build but quick to demolish any normalcy. Dr. Lionel Frank spoke before the Interfaith Charter last week: "Being god is not a death sentence. It is not a sentence to endure sudden power or to shrivel

beneath it. It changes nothing but informs us of our origins and perhaps our deaths, too. It is a call to live in godliness."

Can we look to our enemies and see them as god? As Americans,
can we look at the global atrocities we've caused and call ourselves
god? What does that mean of godliness? At the March for Secularity a
month ago, one protest sign said, "If genocide is an act of god then
god is surely the devil." In a world of ongoing political unrest,
devastating climate disasters, and an increasingly widening class
gap, many people interpreted the Psilo Papers as a stamp of approval
on national wrongdoings. Other people took it to mean that they would
miraculously wake up one morning with superpowers.

Utah Senator Allen Riley thought that godliness meant that he
could fly. He is recorded yelling from the top of the Canetti Building, "I knew I wasn't crazy as a kid! I can hardly keep my feet on
the ground with the wind beneath me these days![3] Hey, you! Come up
here with me! We can all fly!" With that, he jumped to his death, a
chilling display of mortality. We send our condolences to his loved
ones, and all those impacted by the devastating quake of the so-called
God Frequency. Brownstone has been mostly quiet on the Psilo Papers in
recent months, even though they're expected to release a how-to manual
on "living in godliness" in the coming days. They've quit advertising
the manual, so it's a waiting game to see if they'll address it at
all, or let it go unpublished, hopefully under the radar.

Commentators have begun to wonder if the Intelligence Society
made the Psilo Papers with malicious intent. What would be the end-
game? There's a quiet through the cities that hasn't been felt since
the COVID pandemic fifty years ago.

---

3 The sad part is that he probably did feel the wind cradling him extra.
Maybe he should've started with a two-story building and built his way up…
Who knows, with a little more time he probably could've flown. I haven't
finished reading those Avery reports yet but I think they're beginning to
allude to flight. I've already found documentation of telekinesis and isn't
flight just moving yourself? Or is it moving the air? Either way it doesn't
seem impossible. It breaks my heart that he died with people thinking that
he was crazy instead of just ill-timed.

MARIAH RILEY (07/01/2072): On June 7, 2072, you all watched as my brother, Senator Allen Riley, jumped from a thirty-story building and killed himself, thinking that he could fly. You all watched from your screens; you all posted about what a hero he was for trying and failing. Some of you claim that you saw him float even. My brother died thinking that he could fly with people watching him LIVE. LIVE from your towers of privilege, you watched him knowing damn well that he could not fly. And what you didn't see was when a couple days after that, his niece, my daughter, thought that she could fly, too. She wanted to fly like Uncle Allen did because just like you all she was in the comment section seeing everyone say that he floated. All he did was fall. He jumped. He committed suicide thinking that he was god. Did you laugh when every member of the Mars Mission died? Did you think it was funny then? And you guys are plagued now by the same delusions... I came here today to tell you to quit with it all! You are not god! Isn't the magic of the world around you enough? Do you have to be some superhero—do you have to be some mythical creature to be enough? Like, Jesus Christ, I know how much everything sucks right now, I do! I'm not one of those old people who delude themselves thinking like, "oh, people are just crying wolf." No, like, I've lived a lot of time, I know that things are bad. But Allen... he's nowhere now. He's not... I mean... Maybe he's in heaven. That—I don't know if that would make him god; it might make him an angel. Maybe, maybe jumping like that sent him to hell. But I'm of the belief–and I know that most of you are too–I'm of the belief that he went nowhere! Allen's just... dead. His soul doesn't exist anywhere. The godliness of him has not been put somewhere or absorbed into anyone else or, or anything like that; he's just gone. If he was god, I feel like I would... feel him? I would see him. I would hear him, and I don't. And when my poor Willow... the best case scenario, she's with her Uncle Allen. The most realistic and worst case scenario is that she's nowhere! And you know, maybe I'm grateful because most people when they die, they die so miserable. With my daughter gone, with my brother gone, with my husband gone years ago, I'm afraid I'll die miserable, too. I'll die sick, I'll die crippled, I'll die alone, I'll die miserable. But they at least died thinking that they were merely gonna wake up on the other side. Or well, I guess they both thought they were gonna fly, not that they were gonna die at all. And it's not like that split second when you're just driving and the car accident comes and you have those five seconds where you know you're about to die. Or maybe they did have that when they realized flight wasn't coming. I wonder... I wonder how far down they were before they realized. I hope they thought they would take off right before their noses touched the concrete. God forbid they were half way up when they realized they weren't able to fly, and they just had to stare at the whole way down. But I think—I tried not to watch the video much but I think Allen looked happy most of the way down. I couldn't watch the ending anyway so who knows when the realization hit. Ha, for lack of a better word... So many of us are losing loved ones in this craze. What happened to existentialism?! Ya know? You're not god and that's a relief! Imagine having that much power. Imagine actually being god and watching my loved ones jump to their death and doing nothing and not giving them flight. Imagine being the god in charge of all of this shit! God is doing a terrible fucking job right now; you don't wanna be that! You wanna live your life, you wanna have a complete end. No time soon—let's not rush death—but let death be the final sleep! Let death mean that you won't have to lose anyone anymore. Let death mean that you won't have to watch entire towns get sucked into the center of the earth or wiped out into the ocean! Let death mean that you won't have to watch our politicians literally kill us for money. Death is an ending, and some endings—they're not bad, they're not good, they just are... You don't really wanna live forever as god either. Let's say we're under the notion that god can die, if my daughter and brother were gods. Maybe Willow was god but she could still die. Okay, let's go with that. Maybe you are god, but you will die if you jump off of a building. And if god doesn't die, do you really wanna live forever? The way these catastrophes are going? You really wanna be the last god alive? Or whatever? Ugh, none of it makes any fucking sense. That's the craziest part is that none of this makes any fucking sense and you guys are still willing to jump off of buildings for this! Please, please come to your senses. You have so much power that doesn't involve flying or telekinesis. You can love each other. And that's so powerful. Please, come to your senses.[4]

---

[4] Maybe it isn't worth it to be god. Maybe I'll just go on dying how I was originally supposed to. I could die of cancer and microplastics and I would be none the wiser. I feel like that might be an okay way to go as opposed to, ya know, jumping from a building thinking that I could fly and then not flying and dying instead. And either going absolutely nowhere or I feel like, even worse, going into the ether and becoming a ghost who's just stuck invisible. I could go to hell, there's plenty of potential for that there too. It's kind of a lose-lose so let's just say I won't be trying to fly anytime soon. Maybe Lewis is right. Maybe it's best just to not even go there. Like the more and more people that have died from this, the more that you start to sense how foolish these deaths have been. Like none of them had to die. And okay, there may be all of this shit going on and becoming god could be a huge cultural shift but like, if I die by fire, I die by fire. I could never know about this whole god thing and, privileged as I am, still live a decently happy life. And probably the same for a lot of people. Like that senator could've lived a happy life. He seemed to be a really happy guy up there before he... yeah. I think there's so much happiness to be had without any of this giving people delusions. And aren't we all just grasping at straws here? We are soooo desperate at this point that we're being like "god's right here, hello, hello!" And isn't that just fucking laughable, like they used to lock you up for saying some shit like that. You're not god bitch!

CENTER FOR DIVINE SPECIFICATION

Salem Marcus interviewed by Gideon James C.A.

GIDEON: Can you hear me?

SALEM: Yes.

GIDEON: Okay, cool. I'm just gonna go over some of the technical stuff we've talked about, then we'll introduce ourselves and get into some questions. Sound good?

SALEM: Yes.

GIDEON: Cool, cool. Um, I'm Gideon James, a researcher at the Center for Divine Specification. I'm here with Salem Marcus to talk about his access points. He is of sound mind and has fully consented to donating this information to the Center. Can you verify that this is correct, Salem?

SALEM: Correct.

GIDEON: Um, can you also verify that you have achieved the three known indicators of specification and at least one more: Serendipity, Heightened Senses, and Resounding Peace.

SALEM: Correct.

GIDEON: What color is the sky today?

SALEM: Lilac. With streaks of iridescence and a smattering of stars. A brush of creamsicle.

GIDEON: Thank you. So again, I'm Gideon, I'll be testing into Ascension next month. I'm most god when I'm in the kitchen, pinching leaves off of fresh herbs. And also when I'm, uh—

SALEM: Defecating?

GIDEON: Ha, what makes you say that?

SALEM: It's always the chefs.

GIDEON: Hmm.

SALEM: I'm Salem. Class Divine. I'm god all the time but especially when I'm sleeping.

GIDEON: Tell me about that.

SALEM: I'm asleep right now. I've been sleeping for almost a year now, not having once surrendered to darkness. You're here but I'm not. I'm real to you but you're not real to me. I could convince myself you're as real as you are but I haven't bothered with convincing for a while. I'm in fantasyland. I'm always in fantasyland but I can still operate a car. I can still show up to a meeting on time. I can arrive fully dressed with both shoes on the correct foot—easier said than done. I can hold a conversation. But I can also turn the sky blood red. I can also smell the ocean seventy-two miles to the west—a bit foamy today. When I close my eyes I still see you. I can smell the ginger steaming from your mug.[5]

GIDEON: And what of your other senses?

SALEM: Did you know we lose our sense of smell when we're asleep? Or well, we used to before we were god. If you wake up to the smell of bacon in the kitchen it's because you were already awake, somewhere. It was probably the ding of pans that woke you, not the smell. But I'm asleep always and I can smell always. We can talk more about that when we get to my access points but as for my other senses: I see

---

[5]   If the ocean is to the west of Salem, and if the Center is in South Dakota, then Salem can smell Gideon's tea from at least half a continent away. Or maybe through the screen? The other day when I was on the phone with my mom, I swore I could smell the garlic on her breath. I nearly cried at the image of warm toast in her hands, crumbs in her lap, butter on her chin. She's such a messy eater. Was I really only smelling it through the phone somehow though? Technology has been wilder, I suppose.

colors that exist only in imagination or at the bottom of the ocean. It's a shame I don't have the language to tell you what color your eyes are but they aren't blue, that's for sure. Everything seems to sparkle, even that which is dead. Darkness glimmers. At Class Ascension, you probably experience that too.

GIDEON: Not quite—I'm stronger in touch and taste.

SALEM: Right, a chef.

GIDEON: Right.

SALEM: I used to be so overwhelmed by touch that I once spent three weeks naked. I couldn't bare fabric against my skin until I changed my wardrobe to cashmere and linen. I couldn't breathe through my nose until I trimmed my nose hairs. I can feel every particle of dirt across a wooden table but it doesn't bother me anymore. If I rub dust between my fingers I can tell you exactly how many people have sat here before me. I got my desk used so—thirteen people, maybe fourteen? It's hard to tell when they're related.

GIDEON: Oh. What about taste? And sound?

SALEM: You might see more than me on that first front. I don't cook much anymore but a raw ingredient has no less than twenty palettes. Is an apple spicy to you?

GIDEON: Incredibly. Corn, as well.

SALEM: Yes! And peppercorn is like candy, chiles have a touch of pomegranate—everything is upside down on my tongue. I feel pregnant with an alien appetite. Sound is a funny one for me, too; the most grating sounds I find melodic. A car horn is symphony enough to make me cry. A yapping dog radiates so much love it makes my chest ache. Godliness is painful in the way that dying is beautiful.

GIDEON: Hmm.

SALEM: And that doesn't even cover the way that my senses overlap and muddle themselves. Have you ever sliced into an orange and heard the chorus?[6]

GIDEON: Citrus does sing for me.

SALEM: You'll make it into Ascension no problem.

GIDEON: Wow, um. Thank you. That covers Heightened Senses. Now, let's talk about Serendipity. I'm feeling Serendipitous right now, actually.

SALEM: That's how it started for me, too. Anytime I was on a train and there was a god or two or three in my car, I felt a magic in the air, like right-place-right-time magic. Like if there were three gods in my train car, then me being the fourth maybe wouldn't be too far off. You know when you're in the presence of another, right? It's kind of like if the sensation of being watched was comforting. Like someone you love is watching you sleep because they love you too. Serendipity, for me, is like if you had a premonition of the present moment. It's like all of time has already happened; it's like you're Love itself. The Christians got that right, at least. People think Serendipity is about a moment but it's about every moment. It's not linking one phenomenon to the next; it's linking every phenomena ever! Serendipity is when the magic thread goes taut between every living and nonliving thing. So when you recognize someone on the bus, you're really staring down a trillion mirrors.

GIDEON: You don't waver?[7]

---

[6]   Is synesthesia of the gods? Are hallucinations? I mourn all the gods that died in hospitals that should've been on the pulpit instead. I watched the best minds of my generation go nuts or whatever. I do enjoy food more than I did. Fruit, especially. It's taste, obviously, but also touch when the juices coat your tongue and your taste buds lift to meet it. It's sound when an orange squelches across your countertops, and smell again when you wipe it up, smearing juice as an anointment to your kitchen. There'll be orange in the air for days to come. A moment with fruit becomes a week of sunlight, and isn't the extension of time holy?

[7]   There's that word again. Based off of what I got from Avery's video, wavering is like

SALEM: Yes. We all do. But you'll learn that in Class Ascension.

GIDEON: What do you mean?

SALEM: You know what I mean.

GIDEON: Right. Uh, so Resounding Peace then, and then we'll move onto access points more specifically.

SALEM: There's no point in separating them all really. Heightened Senses, Serendipity, Resounding Peace. They're all the same thing. Remember, Serendipity is like the feeling of someone watching you, but pleasant? It's peaceful. Serendipity is a premonition of every moment across time? It's resounding. And the heightened senses coat everything with a somatic reminder of remembering. I'm at peace because everything is Peace. Even when I waver, that's still me at peace. It's a serendipitous wavering, a wavering that's meant for me.

GIDEON: I—thank you. Thank you. Now, I want you to just list your access points. Whatever comes to mind when it comes to mind. Like you're reading off your grocery list.

SALEM: Sleep. Dreams. Petrichor. Whatever wakes me from sleeping and will never wake me again. Dogs, but specifically the rough pads of their paws, how it scratches against leather. The glint in their eyes or anybody else's. Pistachio nut ice cream. I'll admit I share this with you—going to the restroom. But the whole ceremony of it, you see:

----

when you forget that you're god. But how can you forget if you never remember? Can you only waver once you remember? But memory is so fleeting. Can you only waver once you're remembering a majority of the time? What percentage exactly—half? Because let's say you only remember on days at the beach with the sun beating down. Would that mean you're in a state of wavering for 355 days of the year, if you're lucky? And to be in wavering sounds miserable and I am not miserable. At this point, I only remember I'm god about 10% of the time, so maybe that's just it then. You can only waver if you're in a regular state of remembering. But tomorrow I'll remember 12% and the day after that 16%. I just need to quit my job so I can remember all the time.

scrubbing your hands clean, the trickle of water, the heaviness and then the lightness. That's Resounding Peace (laughter). Magnolia blooms, my reflection—when it's good but also when it's bad, especially when it's bad. Cinnamon, coffee, cinnamon in my coffee; a good stretch in the morning, midday, and at night. My lover's morning breath. A hot mug on cold fingers, a fleece blanket that's weighty but not suffocating, a burst of energy and a depletion of it. A loose thread on hand-me-down jeans. This conversation here. Everything. Everything, everything, everything. But those are my favorites, of course.

GIDEON: This talk gave me access, too. Selfishly, that's why I do these interviews.

SALEM: There's no such thing.

GIDEON: As selfishness?

SALEM: How could there be?[8]

---

[8] But what if it is worth it to be god? What if I'm holding myself back from creating a new world? I don't know if I could live with myself. Maybe it's worth it to face great power and not shy away from it. Maybe it's worth it to see god in other people and other things. Even if I were to believe that everything but me was god, I still think that that would maybe contribute to a better world. Just to see everything around you as divine. Imagine if you were arguing with your partner and you sat there and really looked at them and saw god on their face? You would stop arguing immediately. And with you also being god, you guys would be able to resolve it. When you wanna go out and community build and provide disaster relief and protest and build new systems, there's the thing that keeps you on the couch instead which is the lack of awareness of god, and there's the thing that gets you off of the couch, out onto the street, out into the gardens, out into someone's arms, and that is awareness of god. Possibly in yourself but more importantly in others maybe. What if you really could do it all and what if you had a responsibility to do it all and instead you just sat there and chose the easier route of ignoring your godliness? Coward. It's not even about you, it's about everyone else, and if you could make their lives better by possibly being god, sure, but by seeing them as god? Do you know the power you give someone else when you see them as god? All of us could be unstoppable like a megamind. And like I said earlier, I'm gonna die by fire if I'm gonna die by fire, so might as well go out feeling like an absolute divine legend. I would walk with my head a bit higher, my shoulders rolled back. I might be seeing auras or some shit, like that would be so fucking cool. Stranger things have literally happened.

PSAPPHA'S PROGENY

Miranda Jensen

They say the holy water that dribbled across Morgana's brow curdled with salt as keen as the Ionian sea; as if the shore of Sappho's grave had bubbled up in the baptismal font,

claiming the child as Hers.

Of course, this is mere hearsay much like the tales of the Poetess—whispers that carve a legacy from a life. For Morgana can recall nothing of Father Michael's trembling hands, the air brined with omens, or the lethal silence that converted a cathedral into a crypt. She remembers, instead, the fallout. Thus, it is no wonder Morgana rejects her salty genesis,

her mother's faith,

her Christian name.

Morgana, she whispers her pseudonym: the name that will attend her immortal poetics. If she only could write. If she only were worthy of writing. *Morgana, Morgana, Morgana*—

For the last fucking time, your name is Jane!

Morgana unkinks her spine at Mother's scolding tone. When she flings her legs from the chair's pilled arm, the Anthologia Graeca in her lap flips shut, epigrams on blood rites concealed by a bible sleeve. Her father's den has long been disemboweled to grief, all his files and furnishings ousted by tchotchkes repentant, where even electricity does not dare behave.

Your name is Jane, Mother repeats. We named you after John the Baptist who paved the path—

For Jesus, I know, Morgana interrupts.

The crosses and candles decking the swollen floor seem to lean toward Mother standing

beneath a naked man nailed to wood,

before the crushed clove and chili flakes lining the doorway. Morgana beseeches the Goddess that Mother's gaze remains tilted toward her heavens. Alas, Mother steps forward:

What have you done now?

Morgana winces when her Mother smears the rite with her toes—the very feet Father Michael ordained in ablution last Maundy Thursday. There's little hope those herbs will keep the space sacred for the full moon now.

It's to ward off evil spirits, Morgana lies.

Mother levels Morgana with such a heavy stare that her ribs seem to splinter beneath the weight. In these rare lucid moments, where Mother leans more sober than not, Morgana fears she might finish Abraham's act and sink the blade into her daughter's chest, at least, if her God willed it so. It is a strange blessing then,

whenever Mother wastes with liquor.

So you still see...it? Mother drags out the question as if to stall an answer—*the* answer she fears.

I don't see anything, Morgana insists. *I merely feel Her.*

The pronoun sends a visible shudder over Mother's skin, and her hands shake when they clasp together.

Heavenly father, forgive my daughter's sins. Lord Jesus, rid her of this demon which tempts and troubles. Saint Michael the Archangel, shield her from this darkness. Blessed Virgin Mary, protect my baby, my precious, precious baby. In the name of the Father, and of the Son, and of the Holy Spirit. Amen.

It was these impromptu prayers that first awakened Morgana's love for verse, sculpting a poetophile, and indeed, a homophile, from the clay of a young paragon. But if Morgana has traced the Via Dolorosa of her poetic obsessions, she pays neither tribute nor tithes to her matriarch. It is hard, of course, to commend a mother

so rarely coherent.

Only three days until spring tide, Morgana consoles herself. When the moon shines brightest, she will pursue her true maker, again, so she may write something worthy. But for now, she must endure this false prophet.

Mother strangles the slim neck of a dark bottle—now where did that come from?—and sips it primly, savoring the taste. It is a benedictine beneath St Benedict himself; the portrait of the monk watches over them with two raised, wrinkled fingers. Maybe that's why Mother likes to smoke—Morgana wondered as a little girl—sin shan't be so sinful between the saint's two-fingered blessing.

I thought you'd grow out of it. Mother wipes her mouth. I thought by now God would take mercy.

As if to spite Mother, the blanket of Her attention settles over Morgana, like a finger on her right shoulder, daring her to turn around. Morgana does, of course,

but she sees nothing behind, beyond her.

Years ago, when Morgana was young enough to trust Mother's savvy, they thought Her a guardian angel guiding the young girl to sainthood like her namesake. Now, pennamed and pagan, Morgana eponymizes another name, Morgan le Fay—the magical enemy to Arthur Pendragon, and all things men. It is not Jesus Morgana paves the path for,

it is:

Psappha. Morgana's lips trace the name.

She does not notice her mother abandon the den, heels catching on cloves and chili, and she certainly does not hear the gurgle of a bottle chugged; or perhaps she does, perhaps Morgana anticipates the mess Mother will make— the broken glass, the forgotten bile, the bedridden body—and instead chooses to transplant reality

with divinity.

Or maybe Morgana has no choice but to search for Sappho in the blank space between rosaries and King James' bibles. Maybe she was,

truly,

born for Her rebirth.

Either way, Morgana cannot conceive of another life. She is happy to sacrifice her youth scouring for Sappho in biographical disagreements, in academic contentions of subject, audience, and above all, significance in poems.

Phaon, Kleïs, Atthis, Lydia, Phaidra, Damophila, or Anactoria they call Sappho's lovers. Scamandronymous, Eurygyus, Simon, Eunominus, Euarchus, Ecrytus, or Semus they call Sappho's daddy. Morgana wishes her own life could be so contested. That her own father could be so unrecognized. That the objects of her own affections were so obscured,

yet obviously, unapologetically, sapphic. Instead, society thinks her a reclusive prude rather than a romantic poet, hungry not for the carnal but for renown.

One moon soon, she hopes, Morgana will call Her name, and She will gift her the secrets of poesy. She will gift her the answer to immortality,

on the page.

Nine translations of Sappho's fragments lie before Morgana, each open to the "Ode to Aphrodite." Only Morgana does not seek the goddess who the Romans ruined; she calls for

the First Lesbian: the Poetess.

"ποικιλόθρον'..." Where the Christians' Latin sags with atrocity, Sappho's tongue is delicate and lithe. Morgana giggles. Oh, what her mother would say if she opened the den's door and found her precious daughter here,

summoning Sappho.

It isn't a possibility. Two floors upstairs, her mother cradles a bottle of wine with a tenderness she never granted her own flesh and blood. Perhaps that is what compels Morgana to bleed so freely. Opposite a dusted mirror, she recites the Lesbos language from heart; squeezing a fresh cut over the pages, one for each of the muses, until she returns to Her,

the Tenth Muse.

That is, after all, what Plato called Sappho.

And now, She will be

reborn.

Or so Morgana aspires, has aspired on too many full moons past, each attempt with revised technique—tonight's sanguineous. Blood catches on Morgana's lips as she finishes the last of Sappho's first fragment. The candle before her flickers violet.

Psappha? Morgana's body floats with a desire so unlike the lust of her peers, for it is celibate for something beyond the corporal—past the limits of language and the frailty of mankind, all the way to Elysium, where lesbians love in poetry.

Let me be your poet.

Morgana closes her eyes against the hunger in her reflection, the pulse from her palm's wound swelling the edges of her skeleton until she is unskeletal,

until she has not a body at all.

It is here that Morgana feels the brush of Her gaze.

Please, Psappha.

Morgana trusts no representations of the Goddess—like Mother Mary, She is but a canvas for ideals, never of Her own. They tried to taint Her legacy with motherhood, with suicide, but it is Her poets that bear the forbidden fruit,

the knowledge only Her progeny may bite into. Morgana can almost feel the juice of pomegranate seeds run down her chin, dripping between her breasts and nestling into her bellybutton. A trail of blood, Her blood,

a pagan transubstantiation, only Morgana will not devour Sappho's flesh—her own flesh will be devoured, if she is judged deserving.

Oh, Tenth Muse, Poetess, Prophetess, Druidess of the Greeks, the First Lesbians, Morgana rasps. *With this blood, I offer you my body, Great Goddess.*

It is a sacrifice, yes, but one meager to Morgana. For She demands no confessions in confessionals, no sinful shame, no marriage and motherhood;

all She seeks is a vessel

an exodus from man's mythos

into lesbian liberation.

Seize my corpse so you may continue your corpus.

Jane? Mother's voice snakes up the stairs and below the crack of Morgana's closed door. A man in black and white steps follows Mother into the den, a book entitled *Rituale Romanum* open in his hands.

Has she fasted? he asks Mother as if Morgana is but a babe.

She tends not to eat.

And you are sure she is not merely...the man roves his eyes over Morgana. Mad?

My Jane has been followed by the devil since birth, Father Michael. She is possessed, I beg you, rid her of this darkness!

Like the indulgences the Church sold the sinners, Mother intends to pay priests to purge the consequences of endless aperitifs and endless grief. She would rather deem her daughter bedeviled than ask her—not His—forgiveness. Why can she repent to the heavens but not her own descendants?

The man crouches down before Morgana, at last addressing the sinner herself. Would you like to confess your sins before I begin?

Morgana doesn't move.

With flicks of his hands and flicks of water, with pleas to saints and psalms to god, the man demands the demon's name.

Still, Morgana does not so much as blink. She is *The Pietà*—no, the *Venus de Milo*. She is *The Madonna of the Rocks*—or rather *The Death of Sappho*. She is both pious and pagan, petrified beneath the gaze divine. But is it God or the Goddess who renders her frozen?

Does man's, Mother's, inquisition of homoheresy wound Morgana? Though she perceives no pain, nothing physical, one needs no body

to ache

in essence.

And indeed, a silly, simple affliction—sadness—sutures Morgana's soul to torment. Is she really so regrettable that Mother summoned the cult of regrets: the Catholics?

After moments, auroras, eons, the man leaves Morgana motionless, sparing one last prayer when he leaves the den. Mother sits behind Morgana and matches her frown in the mirror's reflection. They've never looked so related.

You'll turn eighteen soon, Mother whispers. You'll leave then and take it with you.

She exits, flicking off the lights in her wake. The screech of the trap door to the wine cellar serves as the spark which shatters her perception,

yielding, reverently, to Her possession.

Morgana means to cry out, to weep with gratitude, but her soul has been severed by sacrosanctity—she has escaped the straightjacket of humanity.

No voice, no breath, no sense, save for seeing, in Sappho's gaze; Morgana studies her own likeness as if trapped in the mirror's reflection.

Chest sedentary, eyes indolent, and mouth idle, she flaunts her incorruptibility, only unlike St. Therese or St. Bernadette, unlike St. Maria or St. Cecilia, her carcass embalms not for the public's, but for the Goddess' viewing.

How tragic that even sapphic, salvation comes at the price of peter's pagan's pence:

her body.

Only this disciple, for now, thinks it a fair suffering. Here, nowhere, she may unremember Father Michael, Mother, and Jane. Here, everywhere, she catechizes divinity. If she could smile, Morgana would bare her teeth proudly. Instead, she basks in the sight of her mortality, in the heed of Her immortality, feeling

almost

worthy.

In this kairos, the drip of a tear, or, perhaps, holy water onto the floor, Morgana gasps and settles into her body once more. She grins at her reflection. *Thank you, Psappha.*

Then she picks up Her pen,

and at last,

writes.

I SAW THE DIVINE IN THE WAFFLE HOUSE SIGN

Olive J. Kelley

the 5am fog imposes on the grimy through-town drive
        we find a halo in my headlights, a beacon in the dark
        her hand rests on the console next to mine
        with chipped pink polish in the silhouette of christ

we reach our heaven, the promised land, a fishbowl
        of syrup-sticky fingers and burnt coffee kisses;
        24-hour chocolate chips, after-church meals, and smoke—
        a remnant from the old ways, a gravestone snaked with ivy

our feet kick, shoes brush, a crisp sandal tan line against
        my red chuck taylors from her favorite tv show
        i add honey to my mug, sweet as her sunshine smile, and i
        trace divine constellations in peach freckled cheeks

i trade a biscuit for some of her hashbrowns, smothered,
        covered, capped in feathers, and the span of my wretched
        heart drags wingtips against the coffee pot and waffle press—
        she takes my hand, and my heart remembers how to beat

we have to leave our haven soon, and return to every day,
        to the infernal mundane, a place where she remains
        a whisper, and i an eternal masquerade— but
        the diner keeps our secrets between the vinyl seats.

POSTS FROM GOD

Casper E. Falls

Gotta tell y'all—2024? Not feeling the vibes. #NotImpressed–God, 0 likes.

Kero chuckled at the post while struggling with their new fifteen-dollar ring light. Compression gloves and flimsy buttons got along like comedians and customer care jobs: not at all, but here we are. They removed the gloves with a groan. Between joint pain and a pissy manager reminding them that dark-lit offices aren't *team player* enough, they chose the pain. After all, their joints didn't pay bills. This lousy gig did.

They really shouldn't call it a *gig*. Kero hadn't booked a comedy gig in so long, their rainbow mane had grown past their shoulders and they'd found no gold at its ends. Only brown roots and a foggy brain that struggled to laugh at anything, let alone come up with jokes. Have you seen the world right now? Existence itself was the joke.

Gloveless, they pushed the ring light button and... nothing happened. Holy Bezos had forsaken them. A feed refresh cut off their burgeoning sobs.

If you're at the end of your rope, burn down Capitalism! Worked great for Sodom and Gomorrah. Being a sodomite is much easier when Capitalists aren't ruining all the fun. #ReadTheActualBibleYouHomophobes #GodLovesFags – God, 0 likes.

Utter absurdity, but it made them smile. Comforted by the love of Online God™, Kero ignored their popping knees and dizzying head rush, and opened the curtains. The lighting was still too dark, but it was a minimum-wage job. They could deal with it.

Except, when Kero joined the 1-on-1 Zoom with their manager, HR joined as well. *Shit.* "Good... good morning from the shadow creature," Kero said in a Dracula voice while wiggling their fingers. No one laughed.

"So... Miss Evans," the HR lady began with the unnerving sweetness of a kindergarten teacher telling you that your mom had left already without saying goodbye because she knew you wouldn't stay otherwise, but hey, look, a sticky rubber duck to play with.

"Actually," their manager interrupted, "Kero goes by Minx, so Minx Ev—"

"Mx," Kero corrected, longing to be anywhere else.

HR Lady's eyes widened. "Oh, right! Happy pride, Minx Evans."

"Thank you?" It was October.

"So, unfortunately, we haven't seen the performance to justify your salary and..." She looked encouragingly at the manager, who startled at having to weigh in.

"Ehh, yeah, you're not quite the team player we were hoping for. Sorry."

Kero suppressed the urge to scream. "I see. Is there a notice period? Because I'm disabled and my health insurance—"

"No, I'm sorry." HR Lady's sweet voice was giving Kero sugar poisoning. "But there's a program that allows you to continue your current insurance as self-pay and—"

"I can't afford that."

"I'll send you the details." She smiled. Both of them stared at Kero, waiting.

"That's it?"

Their manager nodded. "Consider yesterday your last day."

"What about today?"

He grinned sleazily. "Alright, we'll make sure to add the two minutes you've spent with us today."

HR Lady had the decency not to laugh at his... *joke*? Comedy used to be Kero's life, but apparently they'd lost their sense of humor. They should thank them for their time and politely say goodbye in case they needed a reference later on, but—"You know what? I read God's posts and They fucking hate you guys."

Kero slammed the laptop shut and relished in the brief but delicious satisfaction. *Fuck those assholes.*

Then reality set in. Nine days till rent. *Shit.*

After a reasonable hour of dissociation and doomscrolling, they trudged to their bed. They desperately needed a blanket fort to cope, and their boyfriend had bought them cozy bamboo sheets last year. The perfect hiding spot. All Kero needed now was a cat. Or maybe a large rabbit. They longingly pictured their family's farm back in Nebraska—Icarus and Orpheus, their beloved feline rascals, chasing dust bunnies through the barns. But MAGA flags soon tainted the image, and Kero returned to doomscrolling. Five minutes later, a new post from *God* appeared.

Has the collapse of civilization brightened your mood yet? No? Then keep scrolling. You might see a dying puppy next!—God, 0 likes

Well, shit. Apparently, they needed divine callouts today. With a heavy heart, they closed the app and hovered over their mom's number. They couldn't leave Boo stuck with most of the rent. He'd been saving up for his Pacific Crest Trail trip since they'd gotten together. He'd told Kero on their first date that it was the only way to truly find oneself. Back then, Kero had found it inspiring, but the idea had lost its charm. One day, Boo would be found and Kero would stay lost because even a trip to the grocery store felt like a six-month hike to them. *Thanks, body.*

A post popped up.

I'm glad we're appreciating our brave, little bodies over frat bro dreams of enlightenment.—God, 0 likes.

Despite the blankets, Kero shivered. That felt... too targeted. And hadn't they closed the app? They shook their head, trying to shake off the creeps, and called their mom. After six rings, their mother's cheery drawl came through the speaker. She was Alabama-raised, Nebraska-married, as she liked to remind everyone. "If it isn't my Pink Pony Girl!"

Kero blinked. "What?"

"Isn't that what the kids are sayin' nowadays? Oh, nevermind. What's the matter, sweetheart?"

They swallowed down acidy dysphoria and smiled. Smiling makes you sound confident, right? Right...

"Ehm, well, I was let go."

"I'm so sorry to hear that, darlin'." She didn't sound surprised. Or particularly sorry for that matter.

"Thanks, it's... it came unexpectedly. Ehm, I don't have enough to pay rent now and I have a doctor's appointment coming up in two weeks but no insurance, and—"

"And that boyfriend of yours can't provide now, can he?" Her smugness made Kero regret every decision they'd ever made. Except for dating their boyfriend.

"Ehm, what do you mean? He's paying his part of the rent, but he's not earning that much either and this is New York we're talking about, so—"

"He is a gay, you know. I told you he is. That's why he can't provide."

"I—You do know that Chappell Roan is *a gay too*, right?"

"Who?"

Kero massaged their forehead, biting back a scream. "I sure hope my boyfriend's queer because I'm not a girl."

"Oh right, you're still doing that thing."

Maybe Kero should @God and ask Them for a lightning strike. Death sounded great right now.

"Mom, I need your help."

"Of course," she said sweetly. "We'll help you. Your daddy and I were just talkin' about hiring a new kitchen aid."

Kero cringed. Their mom always tried to lure them back to Nebraska. That was nothing new. Kero's longing, however, was. Not for Nebraska, fuck no, but for the idea of working an active job. Being on their feet, hauling around dishes, and whistling to the radio while coming up with comedy routines... It sounded like heaven, but Kero had long arrived in hell.

"I... I can't be on my feet that long anymore, Mom. My POTS flares up when I try and I get these weird neurological symptoms, we're still trying to—"

"You need to get off TikTok, honey! It's giving you all these silly ideas. You're perfectly fine. Now if you come back West, we'll start you simple, get you eased back into real work."

Kero's heart raced. Why did no one understand that they *wished* they *could*, but there was no escaping the reality of their body, no matter how much it broke their heart? "Mom, I... please, can't you just send me some money? This is temporary."

"No, sweetheart. This is America. You gotta work for your livin'. Can't give you any more handouts."

Stars filled their vision. They needed to fix their blood flow immediately. Getting out of this horrible conversation would do the trick. For now, Kero shifted to lay on their back and raised their legs against the wall. It brought some relief.

"I understand that, but I can't—"

"I gotta go, sweetheart. Your aunt's bringing over her terrible brats today and I haven't gotten a chance to clean the Margarita pitcher yet. Love you, honey!"

"I—" Their mom hung up before Kero could say it back. It was for the best. They weren't sure what the word *love* meant anymore. The front door clicked open. Thank God, Boo was home. He'd remind them.

"Boo," they squeaked and rushed up too fast. Their vision turned black at the edges and they fell into his arms. It wasn't embarrassing, just... romantic, right?

"Dork," he grunted and helped them stand upright. Unfortunately, *upright* wasn't a setting option for Kero's flesh suit at that moment.

"Couch," they mumbled as the darkness pressed in.

He sighed, tossed his backpack into a corner, and carried Kero to the couch.

"You sweep me off my feet," they joked. It got an eye roll. The nasty feeling of being a burden prickled at their neck, or maybe it was the POTS. Logically, they knew they shouldn't feel ashamed. Against their mother's wishes, they'd watched enough disability justice activists on TikTok to know that internalized ableism was just another weapon of settler-colonial Capitalism. Still, Boo looked so tired, so sick of it all. So sick of them. So—wait, something was missing.

"Where's your mask, Boo?"

He avoided their eyes and retrieved a dirty lunchbox from his backpack, heading to the kitchen island. "Koala... we need to talk."

Those four words should be outlawed. Kero was a prison abolitionist, but still. Everyone who dared utter that phrase should be in handcuffs, maybe fuzzy ones, and dragged to a mandatory seminar on anxiety.

They cleared their throat. "...okay?"

The noise of a dish soap bottle's desperate last squirt and the following water splashes almost drowned out his response. "I love you, Koala, but," *I love you, but...* also got a spot on the banned-by-Kero list, "You can't keep me from living my life."

"I... am?" Confusion turned into genuine concern. "Sorry, how am I doing that? Cause I want to stop doing that immediately."

"Okay. Let's go back to normal then."

Kero frowned at the kitchen. "Okay... ehm, how was your day?"

Boo groaned. "Come on, Koala. Don't be daft. I mean, *normal* normal. Like the rest of the fucking world." He dropped the lunchbox harder than he needed to. Kero flinched. "Some coworkers invited me to a bar tonight. I'm going." He picked up a rag, his lips set to a thin line.

"That one's dirty," Kero said weakly. "I washed a new one. Second drawer on the left." Their chest hurt, but it wasn't serious. It was just anxiety from POTS, or pain from POTS, or heart tremors from POTS. The usual. "Ehm... you remember what my cardiologist said, right? After they found the clot."

Boo tossed the semi-dried lunchbox into the wrong cupboard. "I know what she said, but we haven't actually tried."

"Tried getting sick again?"

That was the wrong thing to say. "Jesus, Kero. When did you become so paranoid?"

"When I lost everything to the pandemic you're forgetting." A chill had snuck into their voice. They didn't want to snap at Boo. He'd been with them through so much.

"I know it sucks, but we gotta move on. Can't you just give it a go?"

Kero sat up taller, a terrible decision, but Boo didn't take them seriously when they slouched. "Can't I just risk my life so you can get wasted? No, I cannot, actually."

"Oh, fuck off. I'm taking a shower." He stomped off. Kero ran after him, ignoring the heart flutters and nausea rising in their throat.

"Wait, Boo. I'm sorry. But I thought you wanted to live life with me and I don't have a choice." The last few years had been a nightmare, yes, but not while they were together. They'd thrown online watchalongs and two-person Halloween parties that turned into a newly discovered furry kink. They'd learned how to shoot darts and watch pirated movies in blanket forts. Did none of that count?

Boo took off his shirt and tossed it onto an overflowing laundry pile. Kero had to take care of that soon. "Do you genuinely think I'm choosing to be sick and high-risk?"

"Kinda." He dropped the pants. If he weren't acting like an asshole, his ass would have been distracting.

Kero's voice became high-pitched and squeaky. *Yay, dysphoria.* "This is the only body I have. The one God gave me. It's not my fault They're such a shoddy craftsman." Boo leaned against the sink. He was naked now, clearly comfortable around Kero, and yet so far away. Kero's mouth went dry. "Please."

"Koala, I'm showering."

Kero's world stopped. Their body staggered back to the couch but everything inside disappeared. For a few minutes, Kero was nothing but the white noise of a shower. Then their phone pinged.

*In my defense, I started this whole creation of life biz before Grey's Anatomy was invented. Do you know how hard it is to build a human body? They're so squishy.—*God, 0 likes

They didn't even @ Kero... what was happening?

*@God Are you stalking me?!?!—*PunHunsBuns, 0 likes

The response came fast.

*I mean... yeah. Have you never been to Church? I'm pretty upfront about that.—*God, 0 likes

*This isn't funny!!—*PunHunsBuns, 1 like

*You're analyzing comedy again. Progress.—*God, 0 likes

Kero considered a venomous retort when Boo stepped out of the bathroom. They hadn't noticed the shower turn off. He looked devilishly handsome, wrapped in a towel with a wet curl clinging to his forehead and a softer expression than he'd worn before. "Hey, Koala."

"Hey."

He knelt beside them and ran his fingers through their mane. Kero mumbled, "Sorry."

"Do you want to live like this forever?"

"Of course not." It was the truth. They'd give anything to resurrect their early New York City life—crowded dive bars, open mic nights, tiny stages with sticky floorboards. The only thing that stuck to them now was the *immunocompromised* label. But they'd tried this all before. They'd tried to continue comedy and it had almost killed them. In the end, they'd rather have a homebound life than none at all.

Boo gazed at them with so much sympathy it bordered on pity. "Well, then what are we waiting for?"

How could he not know? "Treatment options." Kero bit back the *duh*. "Actual mitigation and prevention. Discovery of meds that take away the risks and after effects. A plan that isn't centered around leaving old and disabled folks to die. People to... to *give a shit*."

He patted their head. It was starting to bother them. "*Koala...*" That, too, was starting to bother them. "...those ideas are utopian."

"But that's literally what I need to survive."

He sighed as if Kero was the obtuse one. "I don't want to wait for a utopia to *live*."

There it was... Boo hadn't considered these past years of togetherness *living*. Just a zombie smooch fest. Kero wanted to puke, but they kept their voice steady, stronger than they'd expected. "I don't want to die for this dystopia."

And that was that. Boo left soon after in a fishnet shirt and leather pants, a suspicious outfit choice for a beer with colleagues, but Kero kept their mouth shut. They were too tired to argue. Too tired to think. They opened their bedroom window wide despite the crisp October air and prayed it would be enough to mitigate whatever pathogen Boo might collect out there. When they laid down, another post appeared.

I didn't invent love as a battleground for your basic humanity. That's what the DMV is for.—God, 0 likes

Kero sniffled and drifted off into uneasy sleep.

They woke to the last sound they wanted to hear: a stranger coughing.

"Fucking hell," they mumbled and rose slowly to close the window. Unfortunately, the problem had a half-glittered mustache and was currently raiding their closet. "Hey!"

He swung around in surprise. "Oh, my bad! I thought this was Jeffrey's closet. He said you're sleeping in, so I could just grab a change of clothes. Nice, big closet though. Jeffrey was right—this place is the shit."

It took Kero a moment to register that he was talking about Boo. It didn't take long to get angry though. "Ehm, what the fuck?"

Boo slipped through the door, two coffees in hand. His eyes widened when he saw Kero. "Oh, hey, Koala. Didn't realize you'd be up. Here, have mine." He held out the coffee and grimaced when Kero didn't take it. "This is our new roommate, Archibald."

"I—People are still called *Archibald*?"

"*Koala*, you're called Kero."

Kero wrinkled their nose and watched Archibald take Boo's favorite pair of pants and a tank top that looked too good on him. Then they processed the rest of the words. "Hold on, *roommate*?"

"You're being rude."

"*There's an unmasked stranger in my bedroom.*"

Boo rolled his eyes. "We talked about this." Kero knew that. Were they remembering different conversations? "And yes, roommate. Your mom texted me last night saying she's sorry they can't pay for two flights to Nebraska now that we're losing the apartment and that she's *so* sad I can't come with you. Why didn't you tell me you got fired?"

"I..." Kero had no clue how to finish that sentence, so they pushed past Archibald to grab a pair of slacks and a hoodie. "I'll get a new job. How the fuck did you find a roommate that quickly? Did you even vet him?"

Boo scratched his neck and hesitated. Then, "We met at the gay club last night." Kero froze. "I didn't cheat on you or anything. Just... danced a bit and... stuff."

"He's a good dancer," Archibald added, unhelpfully.

Outside a garbage truck passed by, probably to collect this whole trash day.

"You went to a bar *and* a club? And then you brought an Archibald home? Boo, none of this is safe for me."

He reached out to take their hand, but Kero snatched it away. "Koala—"

"No, I'm getting out of here." To their surprise and delight, they meant it. Equipped with a set of masks, a bottle of water, and a few diner packets of salt in case the POTS flared, they stormed out. Before they slammed the door, they heard Archibald ask, "On their period?" And Boo, always the *nice guy*, responded, "Hey, not cool, man."

When Kero reached the sidewalk, they released a guttural scream. They had to apologize to three pigeons for scaring the shit out of them (one literally), but it was worth it. Fuck Archibald. Fuck this day. And honestly, maybe, fuck Boo.

As if on cue, their phone pinged.

There are currently 2481 Archibalds living in the United States. Two of them think the T in LGBTQ+ stands for Tits.—God, 0 likes

@God Alright, fucko, what's your deal? Who are you?!—PunHunsBuns, 0 likes

@PunHunsBuns I'm God.—God, 0 likes

Kero was about to scream again when the follow-up arrived.

You're gonna crash in about ten minutes when the adrenaline calms down. There's a coffee shop three blocks to your right with an air filtration system and comfy couches.—God, 0 likes

They glared at it for a moment, then dragged their ass to the coffee shop.

@God I hate you.—PunHunsBuns, 0 likes

I get that a lot.—God, 0 likes

The coffee shop had a cute Cottagecore meets sleep-deprived students vibe. Kero ordered an oat milk latte (decaf, no need to rouse their palpitating heart more) and gratefully slumped down on the last available couch. Their satisfaction lasted a good five seconds. Then the dreaded question arrived: *What now?* They pulled their mask down, took a sip with held breath, and pulled it back up. A job search would be wise, considering rent was still due. Except, they didn't have a safe place to live anymore. Did they still have a boyfriend? Unclear. Maybe they should send out two dozen customer care applications and make a Grindr profile. Their phone chimed in.

Grinding and Grindr, the New York dream!—God, 0 likes

Or maybe, they should find a cheap doctor because they were clearly hallucinating. Kero scooted closer to a table with two blonde women, students by the look of their laptops. They were laughing at some topic or another. "Excuse me?"

The laughter stopped. By the look they gave Kero, these two were the trust fund type of student, not the art scholarship kind. "Yes?" one asked, already annoyed.

Kero held out their phone with the latest post. "Can you read this?"

Annoyance evolved into disgust. "I am *Christian*!" she huffed and turned away.

"Thank you!" So they *could* see it. These posts were real. *Well, shit.*

The adrenaline crash hit. Kero laid back onto the couch, carefully raising their feet and sipping at the decaf. Stars circled their vision, but it was fine. Apparently God was watching. *That sassy fucker.* Kero laughed to themself and when the students muttered, "That one's crazy," they laughed louder. *Sorry to disappoint you, boss babes, but you just confirmed my sanity.*

They kept laughing until the sound became too loud to their ears, its lonesome nature too obvious. There was no one to laugh with anymore. Their friends hadn't talked to Kero in months, not since their bad luck had turned into chronic illness, which was so unrelatable, so foreign to them, it had to be Kero's fault.

Before they knew it, they were sobbing. *Fuck.* Well, at least they could still participate in one NYC tradition—crying in public. The good thing about this city was that no one bothered them. The bad thing was that no one bothered. Kero was just another downtrodden patsy in the divine comedy they all performed for sadistic Sky Daddy. On that note—

@God Alright, I'll play your sick game. You're God. What am I supposed to do?!—PunHunsBuns, 0 likes

Weeell, I met Luci on Craigslist. It didn't work out in the end, but Pride month with him was a blast—God, 0 likes

@God Liar—PunHunsBuns, 1 like

Accusing me of sin? Moi?! Fine, I'll cut the flair like you did. Go on Craigslist. Don't look for a hookup. Don't buy Jeffrey a backpack. Godspeed!—God, 0 likes

Kero glared at their phone, then glanced around the coffee shop. The other patrons were too focused on their laptops or phones to pay them any mind. Still, was Kero really about to listen to some creep on the internet? Except... They knew a lot about Kero. Too much for any human being. It looked like their racist grandma was right when she said God was always with them. *Damn it.* With a sigh, they typed craigslist.com into their browser, then switched back to the posts. Did that ass leave them any instructions on where to go next? Nope. Just... Craigslist. As if there were five posts in all of NYC. With another sigh, Kero scrolled through ALL in each tab. Something would catch their eye. Probably.

They hovered over a posting in the FOR SALE section:

PACIFIC TRAIL SURVIVAL KIT, UNUSED. STURDY BACKPACK, RECOMMENDED BY NATIONAL GEOGRAPHIC. $50.

Kero had $100 for groceries in their account. This could convince Boo that Kero *wanted* him to live and maybe Boo would remember that he wanted the same for Kero. A notification came in. They swiped it away. It popped up regardless.

Stop leaving your bar on the floor. I tripped and nearly broke my neck! Do you want to be responsible for the death of God? Actually, you might. That sounds like a great comedy set.—God, 0 like

Kero let out a frustrated growl and moved on to the gigs session. They couldn't linger for long. Most of the postings were scams, but seeing the titles made their heart ache with something other than POTS. *Looking for a performer. Any performer. Just not you...*

Kero downed the rest of their now-cold coffee and kept scrolling. When they reached the job section, the screen turned white, then refreshed. A new post appeared at the top:

CARETAKER NEEDED

NO EXPERIENCE NECESSARY. FLUCTUATING REIMBURSEMENT WITH GUARANTEED MINIMUM WAGE. NO CREEPY CIS MEN (IF YOU GOTTA ASK WHAT THAT MEANS, YOU PROBABLY ARE ONE). NO NORMIES. NO ABLEIST DIRTBAGS. ENGLISH MAJORS WELCOME.

Okay... this sounded interesting. Before they could talk themself out of it, they put the number into their phone and began typing.

Hi, I'm Kero (they/them). My rainbow-colored hair is grown out. Does that make me a normie? Because, in my defense, I don't have a job (you never would have guessed), and you need one to pay hairdressers nowadays.

After pressing send, Kero realized in horror that they were cracking jokes. They weren't supposed to make those anymore. Humor was dead, buried somewhere in the Hudson alongside their optimism.

The response arrived promptly:

Are you an English major?

Weird. But maybe not *bad weird*.

I'm a comedian.

Close enough. Wanna come by tomorrow at 10 am? The address is 5780 Broadway, West New York

Kero groaned. *New Jersey? Seriously?!* A post popped up.

God gives their toughest battles to their strongest soldiers, my dear Three-Racoons-In-A-Trenchcoat-Swinging-A-Balloon-Sword—God, 0 likes

Kero oh-so-piously responded to the Craigslist stranger.

Sure, I'll be there. Don't be a murderer.

Ditto.

The text made them smile. Maybe this wouldn't be so bad.

@God Alright, Sky Daddy. That was fucking absurd. What's next?—Pun-HunsBuns, 0 likes

That's the most absurd you can get? Call me a non-believer, cause I'm not buying it.—God, 0 likes

A colorful array of curse words later, Kero had drawn up a plan. It was bizarre and irresponsible, but it involved no Archibalds. They stayed in the coffee shop until golden hour set the city aflame. Then they walked to the subway, pausing whenever their vertigo became too much. It was a long trip to Manhattan and an even longer one to Jersey. One step at a time. For now, they had to cross Times Square to reach their makeshift hotel, which meant braving desperate Elmos and the worst version of the Spiderverse. On the way, they grabbed salty nuts and two 7/11 burritos, which probably shouldn't be a thing. At the register, a message from Boo arrived.

Where are you at? I'm getting worried.

A little late for that, don't you think?

Kero added:

I'm safe. I'll be back tomorrow

Onward. Or else their emotions might catch up, and who wanted to process that mess? The Port Authority bus station was at the heart of Broadway. Kero kept their head down. Only one theater visage was free of grief for stages they'd never perform on again, and that was exactly where they were headed. No live performers. No magic of the moment. Just pixelated dreams, which had nothing to do with the comedy career Kero almost had. They took a steadying breath, tuning out the excited chatter of tourists clutching their Broadway tickets, and entered Regal Cinemas.

As far as sleep accommodations went, it didn't get more absurd than this, but Kero didn't want to be alone and when a movie was playing, they never were. So they spent too much money on a ticket, smuggled their burritos into the theater, and found the coziest spot in the back to set camp in. They snuck out and back between movies, hoping the staff wouldn't notice. If they did, they weren't paid enough to care. Kero stayed there for ten hours, watching and dozing as their digitalized new friends cried and laughed and died and fucked, and somehow, in the midst of the projected emotions, Kero processed their own. Maybe their life wasn't over.

Their phone buzzed as they stepped back onto 42nd Street and into a cold, rainy day.

Good. Now go get it.—God, 0 likes

Maybe God did care about them. Kero bought a Gatorade to fight the morning vertigo, did a rapid covid test (negative), and hopped on a bus to Jersey. To their surprise, West New York didn't look much different from their Queens neighborhood, except for one detail—the city's gorgeous skyline was only a short walk away. NJ folk were onto something after all.

When Kero reached 5780 Broadway, they hesitated. Were they really about to do this? Their phone pinged.

I'm surprised you still have fucks to give. Can you tell me where you found them?—God, 0 likes

Kero rang the damn doorbell. An uncomfortably long time passed before the com sprang to life. "Y-ello?

"Hey, it's Kero, for the caretaker job."

A buzz let them in. The place was dingy but might have been fancy forty years ago. Yellow wallpaper peeled under semi-intact molding. Kero ran their fingers over it as they waited for the elevator. Not the worst place to lose your mind in. The elevator gave its best impression of a death rattle but safely deposited Kero in front of Door 1, which swung open, revealing a masked woman in a wheelchair with light brown skin, a pale pink buzzcut, and black sunglasses that covered most of her face. She lowered them to assess Kero, lingering on their mask, then nodded. "I don't have a full rainbow, but I have three shades of hair dye here if you want to escape normiehood."

"Ehm, thanks?"

The woman waved her hand dismissively. "Right, sorry. I'm autistic and my memory is shot, so remind me if I miss any neurotypical rituals."

"Rituals?"

"Like the whole hello biz. I'm Althea, but you can call me Alti. Come in!"

With that, Kero stepped into a different world, one that included walking rails and shower chairs, soft fairy lights and pillow piles in every corner. Alti couldn't leave the house, she explained, so why not mold the realm to her needs? She was a queen, accommodating for the wars she fought without shame or needing permission. After too much diplomacy, the neighboring kingdom of New Jersey had granted her a paid caretaker for fourteen hours a week, leaving her with the fun choice between skipping meals or pissing in a diaper at night. Not to fret though—this was at least a twenty-hour gig because Alti's OnlyFans was picking up.

Kero's head swam with information. Alti's queendom felt farther from their family farm than the moon. To buy time, they asked about the English major thing.

"Oh, I can't really look at screens, so I need someone to help me with my newsletter and essay edits. Also, I love hearing people overanalyze the works of dead, racist white men. It always puts me to sleep."

Kero chuckled. "I don't know shit about the classics, but I do a mean impression of just about anyone, including Lit students."

"As I said—*close enough*." Her eyes wrinkled in a smile. "This could work. Tell me about your covid precautions. Are you immunocompromised-safe?"

And just like that, Kero unraveled. They told Alti about their own descent into disability, the loneliness, the financial struggles, and now, the imminent loss of Boo.

"That is too cute of a name for him," Alti noted.

"No, listen, he's been with me this whole time."

"Yeah, I got that. And you feel like shit about being disabled, like a burden and whatnot. Him having been around ain't in his favor, baby. Sounds like he makes you feel like it's not okay to be like this."

Kero pulled a tissue from Alti's abundant stash and wiped their eyes. "I mean... it's not. My body being like this... it's not okay."

Alti snorted. "Well, if it's not okay, then come be a fugitive in my queendom. My friends and I welcome health outlaws."

"You have friends?" Kero blurted, then quickly added, "Sorry, I—"

"You don't, right? Self-hating disabled folks rarely do. I gotta introduce you to my mask bloc community. You say you do comedy? They're gonna eat you up. God knows we need laughter to get us through the pain."

This sounded too much like a dream. "That's really nice of you, but—"

"Oh, here comes the *but*! You don't deserve it?"

Kero was caught off-guard. *Well, no... but also,* "I don't have an exposure-free place to stay. I can't take this job. It wouldn't be safe for you."

Alti half-laughed, half-sighed, and shook her head. She pulled out a pink tablet from underneath a 90s-looking word processor and began to tap on it. "Baby, I feel like I should adopt you, not hire you." She kept on tapping. "How about this—I only pay you what the government deems fit and you move in here, do the needed tasks at your own pace, and help me shit at night?" She handed Kero the tablet. "Type in your legal name and birth town, honey. We're running background checks on each other."

Okay, this was definitely a dream. Was this stranger seriously offering Kero a job and a place to stay? It could be a nightmare too. Some True Crime shit, but the apartment was clearly set up for a disabled person, and this whole exchange seemed more dangerous to her than to Kero. They glanced at the photos covering the wall. Most had been taken in this very room, but each was filled with people, playing games, watching movies, camping around an electric candle... One even showed a make-shift stage for what looked like a drag queen competition.

Dazed, Kero took the tablet and typed in their details. Then they pulled out their phone, swiped away Boo's response, and brought up a background check site. While the browser was loading, a new post from God appeared.

Stop labeling things as dreams or nightmares, my dear trenchcoat-raccoons. You're supposed to be awake.—God, 0 likes.

Another followed.

Don't treat her like a dream. Treat her like a flawed, precious person. You should try that on yourself sometime.—God, 0 likes

Alti put the tablet down and picked up a fidget spinner. Silence filled the room as they waited for the checks to finish. Kero's head filled with doubts—they barely took care of themself. How could they take care of someone else? They'd fucked up their own life and now they were going to fuck up Alti's.

She winced and Kero snapped to attention. Alti reached for a bowl on the nightstand. When they handed it to her, she began to retch. Between retching, she pressed out, "Told you I can't do screens. Clit-punching migraine!"

Suddenly, Kero knew exactly what to do. They'd dealt with enough hecklers, and what was a symptom but a persistent heckler refusing to leave the club? They scooted closer and supported her forehead with their hand. "You know... the original name for Moby Dick was Mopey Dick, but it didn't pass censorship laws." A giggle. Another retch. An impatient hand gesture of *keep going*. "It's part of the recently discovered Blue Ball chronicles. I highly recommend them if you're into, eh, oceanic studies. I heard they're very wet."

Alti was both laughing and vomiting now, which seemed like an improvement. "Let me get you a wet cloth," Kero said.

"Don't rush up too fast," she responded and Kero didn't. They let their POTS adjust and used the wall-mounted handrails on the way to the bathroom. Their heart still jumped, but no darkness threatened their vision. As cold water ran over their fingers, Alti cheered from the living room.

"Everything okay?" Kero asked.

Another retch, then, "Neither of us are murderers!"

They smiled. "Good, 'cause I haven't even told you about Jules Vernes yet. That guy is *kinky*." Kero was good at this, and maybe, *just maybe*, they deserved to be taken care of.

Later, when a starry night blanketed West New York, they noticed one last post from God.

If you have faith in yourself, there will always be people to love you and stages to call you home.—God, 1 like

MOTHER OF MONSTERS, INCLUDING ME

Ivy L. James

O Angrboda,
       harbinger of grief;
O Angrboda,
       she who bodes ill;
your dark omens wrap around me as an embrace.
Beasts who never knew compassion
       find a home in your arms.

Mother of monsters,
of Fenrir and Jormungand and Hel,
you love unlovable creatures.
       You see past fang and claw
          and yet adore your children for those weapons too.

Móðir mine,
I snarl and I crawl and I'm half-dead.
Sharpen my dirt-stained talons;
combine your growl with mine
       as I bare my teeth at my enemies.

Both warrior and mother,
       both sword and shield,
you have been a parent to me
when my earthly family failed.
They wanted a lamb
but got a wolf pup instead.

For twenty years I wore wool
but now that I am grown
I howl at the moon.

Hail Angrboda, the mother who cherishes monstrosity!

A SONG FOR THE ROOSTERS

DC Guevara

She remembers when her hands looked young—when the harsh sun and hard labor had not turned them into calloused, peeled, cracked appendages .

"Raquel!" her husband calls and his voice grates her ears. "Where's my *pava* [1]?"

She takes her time answering him, already concocting an excuse utilizing the crowing of roosters should he question her silence.

"In the cupboard, by the ceramic bowl."

It's the same place he left it last night, the same place he leaves it in every night.

"Found it." His voice booms across their small hut which barely housed them both. Raquel touches her empty belly, grateful that her monthlies have come and gone.

I already take care of one big child, I cannot imagine taking care of another. "I'll see you by sundown."

Without another word, or even a wave goodbye, Salvador Antonio Burgés Colón mounts their steady mare and rides off into the cane field under the tame morning sun to collect the harvest and sell in town until the sun comes down, and *only* if the mood strikes him.

She is left alone once again.

Once upon a time, a *long* time ago, Raquel would have checked to ensure his blouse was well buttoned. She would have dutifully had a cup of steaming black coffee, the barest pinch of sugar ready, just as he liked it. She would have sent him off into the fields, a loving lunch in hand, kissed by his pretty, young wife.

Dawn dissipates, and the heat of the morning seeps through the windows and into her home. The planks creek underneath her slippers, which are

---

[1]   The pava is a straw hat made out of the leaves of the Puerto Rican straw palm; worn to protect the head from the sun.

already tugged and worn out, as she moves the woven basket from one side of the room to another, picking up after her inattentive husband. His belt lay across the floor, the clothes he had worn the night before still strewn across the crooked chair he insisted he would take care of after (he never does). She picks them all up, one by one, getting ready to assume her wifely duties and go down by the stream to wash them.

"Raquel— Raquel." Alondra's voice rings through the trees Raquel can see through her open windows. Her sister has always had an excitable personality, easily persuaded by the singing of *iguacas*[2] or a bright, sun-blessed day. "I got some *viandas*[3] for you."

When doesn't she? Her husband owns the largest *yautía*[4] crop on this side of Puente Verde, the Burgés' humble farm within a small no-neck town between the mountains of Orocovís, amongst deep verdant scenery and baby blue skies.

"Put them by the table, please," Raquel replies politely because Alondra is her sister, and it is not her fault that she has found a more amicable, successful, and more importantly, attentive husband. "I have another chicken for dinner— it's yours if you want it."

"I prefer if you make the *asopao*[5]," Alondra replies melodiously. "You know how to make it better."

Another child to add to the bunch—the eternal curse of being the eldest daughter.

"I'm not making asopao tonight," Raquel answers, voice clipped but respectful. "Salvador is staying in town for a Poker game, so I'm eating *tostadas*[6] and sleeping in."

---

[2]   Another term for <cotorras> or <parakeets>.

[3]   Root vegetables such as cassava, yautía, sweet potato, yam, celery, plantain, malanga, green bananas and breadfruit.

[4]   A tropical flowering plant that produces an edible, starchy corm. Similar in texture and color to potatoes.

[5]   Asopao is a family of stews that can be made with chicken, pork, beef, shrimp, seafood, vegetables, or any combination of the above; it is the national soup of Puerto Rico.

[6]   Toasted bread, slathered in butter, specifically made from Puerto Rican soft bread (*Pan sobao*).

Kicking open the door with her foot, she steps outside into the blazing Caribbean heat, lovingly accompanied by a flowing breeze and the insistent chattering of Alondra, who holds her straw basket of soiled clothes over her massive belly where her future niece or nephew now resides. It brings a soft smile to her face. Raquel may not want to bring life into the world, but she does not disparage others who do.

"Mami wants to know if you and Salvador are attending *misa*[7] today." Raquel notices that the way Alondra approaches the conversation is quick, as fast as the songbird she was named after. "And I think you should, Raque— she misses you."

Raquel scoffs. "Mami also told me she regrets not naming me Dolores because of all of the headaches I give her." Alondra opens her mouth to retort, but Raquel isn't in the mood to listen to the sister *she* raised sing platitudes to their undeserving mother. "I'm not going. There's a lot of things to do around the house."

"It's only you and Salvador in there," Alondra complains, rubbing her belly as she swivels next to Raquel, who slows her pace to let her catch up. "How messy can it be?"

She decides to view the synchronization of Alondra touching her belly and the mention of Raquel's failed marriage as a coincidence and not the attack it immediately registered as. It has not been for a lack of trying, nor a lack of passion, that they are not with child—but only so many nights could pass by with no fruits to show that she suspects a man might start looking elsewhere.

Keeping a steady pace, Raquel takes Alondra's basket and adds it to her growing pile. Her sister tries denying her, but her massive belly betrays her and slows down her movements.

"*Bendito*[8]," Alondra breathes, taking a moment to straighten herself by placing her hands on her lower back. "Give that back."

------

[7] Spanish word for <*Mass*>.

[8] *Bendito* varies in meaning depending on the emotion used in its intonation, in this case it is being used in a lamenting manner, which would translate to something similar to: "*Oh god*"" in an annoyed manner.

"You shouldn't be doing anything in your condition," Raquel answers, hoping her evasion tactics are seen as an extended generosity. "Go to *misa*, then rest."

By the sternness of Alondra's brow, she surmises her sister has gotten slightly wiser in these last few years. "Raquel, you can't avoid her forever."

She doesn't understand why her lips open to reply. There is an ancient, buried instinct to explain herself when people would prefer her silence. Every time she doesn't push it back down, feelings of inadequacy and guilt devour her until she is forced to bend her comforts for the sake of others.

Instead, Raquel closes her mouth and takes a calming breath.

"I'm not avoiding her." Her voice is firm in volume, but hesitant in tone. "It's complicated, Alo, *pero*[9], she... said things that..."

I've always done my best to educate you all, Raquel. Thanks to Diosito's power and the grace of La Madre Divina[10], *your siblings have all done well except for you— where did I go wrong with you?*

Feeling betrayed by her treacherous, watering eyes, Raquel redirects her gaze to the patches of gray forming in the sky. It is probably unwise to go into the forest considering the weather, but as the echoes of her last conversation with Matilda Agosto reverberate within her skull, she figures there is more peace to be found in the *charca*[11] than next to her mother underneath the gaze of a clay effigy of a crucified Jesus Christ within the chapel's straw ceiling.

Wiping her unshed tears away, Raquel turns back to her sister. "Go to *misa*, Alondra. I need time on my own, *un ratito nada mas*[12]."

It hurts Raquel to see her little sister take on the role of messenger between her and her mother. It was often a role designated to her when she was a girl, to deliver messages between a husband and wife who were too busy with others to pay much attention to each other, let alone the children they made together.

---

[9] *But*

[10] The Divine Mother (Holy Virgin Mary)

[11] Colloquial terms for rivers or small bodies of water. Literally translates to <puddle> or <pool>.

[12] *Just for a little while.*

She wouldn't wish that position on anybody, and even with that, sweet, kind Alondra smiles. "*Siempre hay un plato para tí en casa*[13]."

Raquel knows she means well, and Alondra is probably telling the truth.

However, she wants to be alone more than anything, so she nods and turns away from her worried sister, leaving behind a pregnant *jíbara*[14] by the outskirts of town as she searches for solitude amidst the dense, ponderous forest.

After spending all day by the charca, Raquel finds herself avoiding her husband, the entirety of Puente Verde, and the prying eyes of her tias and primos. The glory of night covers the vast sky as she contemplates the river, the one constant in her life that has rarely failed her. Raquel would live beside it if she could, to the tranquility that has offered her solace from the time of her youth.

Finishing off the last of her laundry she had purposefully delayed, Raquel places Salvador's *guayabera*[15] into an accumulated pile of clean linens and prepares to leave before she notices one of her mother's nightgowns lying by a patch of dried grass.

Before she can object to her instinctive actions, Raquel leans down and picks it up, kneels by the water, and performs her dutiful tasks as eldest daughter once more.

She hums to keep the inadequacy and shame from consuming her and tries to find solace in the rhythm, as she once had as a girl.

At first, she had found comfort within the magical properties of music. The tapping of the *bomba* barrels[16], the strings of *el cuatro*[17]. A concoction of sound and melody that would make her rise to her feet and twirl by the town

---

[13]   *There is always a plate for you at home.*

[14]   *Jíbaro* is the name of people of the countryside who farm the land in a traditional way. Most popular in use from the 1820s - 1960s. Jíbara is the female equivalent.

[15]   A traditionally Caribbean men's summer shirt, worn outside the trousers, distinguished by two columns of closely sewn pleats running the length of the front and back of the shirt.

[16]   A traditional Puerto Rican dance and musical style that originated with enslaved Africans in the late 17th century when they were prohibited from practicing their religious customs from African. Typically played with barrel drums, maracas and tamborines.

[17]   It is the national instrument of Puerto Rico. It is guitar-like in function, but with a shape closer to that of the violin, but smaller. Traditionally, it only has four strings.

bonfire, in the few moments where she was allowed to feel like a girl with no cares in the world.

Now as a woman, Raquel has had to find contentment with the rhythm of everyday chores. Mending, tending, harvesting, sewing, cooking, fixing—anything that needed to be done would get done, because the jíbaros were hardworking people who should not waste any more time than they had to spare.

And Raquel would do it, finding rhythm in it all, because the steady constant of repetition and order would keep her balanced, to keep her grounded on days when her wandering mind sought more than drudgery and the stinging heat of the island.

Unfortunately, even the rhythm couldn't drown out the memory of the harsh barbs her mother had thrown at her nearly a full month ago.

Good for nothing vaga[18], Matilda had quietly said to her as they tended to her younger brother, a boy barely seventeen, riddled with a disease that neither of them recognized. *You have no children, no crops, no skills. What good was having you if you can't even help me heal my boy? My poor baby boy!*

¡Puñeta, en esto estoy![19] Raquel had replied, hurt that her mother had said such a thing, but devastated to have her ever-held suspicions proved true. *I'm trying my best, mami.*

You've always been this way—a constant thorn at my side, ever since you were born. 'Should have called you Dolores for all the headaches you gave me. Matilda plucked at her son's loosened shirt, trying to get the lint away from the harsh fabric and ignoring the blood that pooled by the seams. She scoffed at her daughter's soft sob. *Please, so emotional, as always, can't keep a temperate head like me.*

Raquel always prided herself on having a moderate temper, so she had finished the task at hand, bandaging her mother's favorite child, before standing from the cot. Her lips parted to defend herself, but Matilda raised a wrinkled, sharp finger in the air.

Go back to your husband, Raquel. One day I'm going to die, and I'd like to have grandchildren before then.

---

[18]   Puerto Rican vernacular for someone who is lazy.

[19]   Puerto Rican curse word that technically has no direct translation due to its flexible nature of changing meaning depending on emotional intonation, but in this instance it would be closer to *Fuck, I'm doing it.*

Raquel's breathing had started to come in short, rapid bursts before she quelled it down. Matilda still felt the need to groan in disgust as Raquel rushed out the door. *Goodnight, Mother.*

They hadn't spoken to each other since.

The audacity of her mother to ask for grandchildren from the daughter who already raised her siblings still boils Raquel's blood. The feeling that sits within her chest and drags her down into herself is a pain that she uncovered recently, late one night when she stood by the river and felt the blood drip down her legs, thankful for the absence of a child.

Switching hands, Raquel takes her mother's *bata*[20], dunks it in the pool, and scrubs away the leftover powdered soap she had bought from the Americans in the stores within the village. Raquel grips the washing stone tightly, lays the garment across her wooden board, and diligently rinses the plain white nightdress.

I've done everything she's ever asked of me. Raquel grits her teeth, scrubbing harder. *Helped with her marriage, raised her children, took care of the hut when she couldn't, cooked when no one else would and she calls me a good-for-nothing vaga?* Perhaps because she is alone, her tears fall and her breathing becomes ragged. It feels good to purge this out, to liberate herself from the thing that's unwinding inside of her, unraveling at the seams. *Who gave her the right?*

Her thoughts are interrupted as the forest shakes with the sound of *coquíes*[21] frantically calling to one another, their unmistakable high-pitched whistles echoing across the woods.

Raquel stands on alert, knocking ove r Matilda's nightdress and her board into the river.

Salvador said there were white men around these parts, she recalls. *Maybe they are scouting the land.*

Her husband had explained to her that *gringos*[22] came to town with fancy pamphlets and big words that boiled down the fact that the forest in which Puente Verde resided was to become a *state forest*—whatever that meant. She wasn't

---

[20]   Colloquial slang for <nightdress>.

[21]   A common name for several species of small frogs native to Puerto Rico.

[22]   A term, usually used derogatorily, for a "foreigner," often a white person from the United States. It can also refer to a person who doesn't speak Spanish or is out of touch with Latin culture, including people of Hispanic descent.

as educated as the men in suits who spewed   words in a foreign language and whose broken Spanish felt more like a mocking gesture than a genuine one.

Raquel is convinced they are aware of their cruelty.

After fishing out the discarded items, Raquel finishes her two piles of laundry and bundles them up in her baskets. They might be damp and in need of a good drying by the sun, but if there are Americans in the area, she doesn't want to give them the opportunity to belittle her as well.

The coquíes whistle again, with the same intensity, but lower in tone. The trees in the distance rattle and Raquel swears to the holy trinity that she feels the earth shake below her. However, it does not possess the intensity of an earthquake—it is more akin to a deep humming. It vibrates across the ground, entering her through the flat of her feet up her legs, curling around her calves and her knees.

She feels an intense pull to whatever is in the forest because there *is* something amidst the *flor de maga*[23] and the *ceibas*[24] and Raquel swears she can hear her name murmured in the wind.

Curiosity envelops her. Her inquisitive soul used to irk her mother, as if the lack of mindfulness and propriety, even in the countryside, were things that mattered.

Firm in her decision, Raquel packs up the baskets and begins to walk into the woods.

The forest has always intimidated Raquel, s eeping within her a foreboding so intense it often feels like an additional weight to carry among her other duties. Sometimes she forgets it, another pang of terror to add to her ever-growing collection. As the wind makes palm leaves rustle, Raquel perseveres against her fear.

The pathway from the village to the river had been flattened by years of horse and donkey tramplings and *macheteros*[25] hacking away at the sides to clear out the way, but the coquíes didn't want her taking the simple route. They would not grant her such mercy.

---

[23]   National flower of Puerto Rico.

[24]   A tropical tree native to Mexico, Central America and the Caribbean, northern South America, and West Africa. Characterized by its ability to grow up to a height of up to 200 feet and have a massive trunk of up to 10 feet in diameter.

[25]   Sugarcane cutters, typically using machetes as their main cutting tool.

The sound comes through the overgrowth, Raquel recognizes, lowering the baskets by the trail, clutching the first one she ever weaved close to her heart. *It's away from Puente Verde.*

Leaves crunch underneath her humble sandals as she follows every instinct within her body that begs to be thrust between the dense fiddle-leaf figs and the *morivivi*[26]. One after the other, her legs carry her over stumps, around fallen palm trees, under uprooted sea grape trees while the moon rises high in the sky and illuminates the way.

Estas cerca, preciosa. A bell-like voice sings around the shell of her ear. *Muy cerca*[27].

Before Raquel can question who caressed her in such a gentle manner, the roaring of a waterfall drowns out all thought. Their *cascada*[28] was a mesmerizing feast for the eyes, composed of three smaller chutes with a naturally forming pool at the bottom.

Raquel's mouth opens at the majesty of God's creations.

So close to me, she thinks. *And I almost had gone my whole life without seeing it.*

A flock of yellow *reinitas*[29] zips past her, the flaps of their wings quick and their chirps musical as they fly over the clearing and reveal across the rock and gravel a tall, lithe figure. Raquel's breath catches in her throat.

The holy figure moves amongst the vast green, branches creating spider web-like patterns against it, threatening to swallow her whole but unable to compete against her grandiosity. As she moves, slowly and methodically, with one graceful step in front of the other, the constant chirping of cicadas and a gentle night breeze are her only companions on this starlit night. As the waterfall's roar fades away, the moon casts shadows on everything but the long, veiled shroud hanging on her back and dragging on the grass.

---

[26] In Spanish it means "to die and live" — the plant is native to Puerto Rico. Characterized by how upon touch, the leaves close, appearing lifeless, only re-opening moments later.

[27] You are very close, beautiful. Very close.

[28] Waterfall

[29] A species of warbler bird native to Puerto Rico. Characterized by its small and round body.

The veiled face is a mystery framed by the palm trees surrounding them. Her pearlescent form glows an unnatural light, only contrasted by the moonlight itself.

Raquel's breath hitches, holding onto it as if its escape could give away her hiding place. She doesn't fully understand why she can't move, why her arms refuse to lift the straw basket hanging uselessly in her arms. She only observes, eyes blown wide open as the figure makes it to the body of wat er, gracefully walking atop it and creating the gentlest ripples she has ever seen, touches that seem as soft as kisses.

"*Santa María, Madre de Dios.*" She recites her mother's words, the twinge of fear always mixed with devotion and awe, as when she gripped rosary beads tight in her hand during mass. Matilda always scolded her for the absence of God in her life and the lack of spirituality. "*Ruega por nosotros pecadores, ahora y en la hora de nuestra muerte, Amén.*[30]"

Holding the straw basket tight against her, Raquel hesitantly takes a few steps forward, using her body to part the palm trees and the hanging vines that obscure her vision. To see what has been denied to her for so long with empty prayer and unheard song.

Whatever this may be, she thinks with conviction, *I have suffered worse.*

When she makes it to the clearing, Raquel stops, sits by the edge of the water, and kneels the way her mother had taught her in a humble wooden chapel so long ago. The reflection that stares back at her is unwelcome, as Raquel has always chosen to keep mirrors outside her home. An unassuming woman, with long dark hair nicely tucked into a low bun; big, dark eyes outlined by dark circles underneath them, and skin that has seen better days, weathered and harshened by the uncaring sun.

Am I in any condition to meet the divine?

"You are, *preciosa*," the voice answers her unspoken thoughts, the tilt of her words light and serene. "All of God's children are beautiful, just as He made them." "*Santísima,*" Raquel breathes out, refusing to meet her gaze. "*Divina madre.*[31]"

---

[30]   *Holy Mary, mother of God— pray for us sinners now and at the time of our death— Amen.*
[31]   *Your holiness— divine mother.*

"No, none of that, *preciosa*—" the figure answers her, her footsteps the most tender sound between them. "I simply take on the form most pleasing to the soul that called me." She lowers her stance and tilts Raquel's chin up with a gentle tug of her finger. "Does this form please you?"

Raquel's breath escapes from her lips as she catches the scent of flowering buds that perfume the air. A woman stands before her, embellished in gold and ivory lace with eyes as big and opaque as a porcelain doll's, and dark skin as smooth as the very idols prayed to at mass, adorned in symbols of what she can only assume would be her Taíno ancestry, words unreadable to her uneducated mind. Her gaze has an otherworldly quality, a piercing fierceness only matched by its gentle concern.

"It... it does," she manages to answer, swallowing a lump in her throat. "What may I call you?"

"You may call me whatever you wish," She tucks away a stray curl behind Raquel's ear and her touch is icy cold. "I have many names by which one may know me, for I have had many imposed by mortals. María, Demeter, Sky Mother, Atabey, but I am simply creation—creation in its absolute form."

As her words flow, Raquel is instructed to stand by a touch on her shoulders and they begin walking within the forest once more. Moonlight slips through the branches as Atabey leads her through the vastness of the Orocovís mountainside.

"What brings you here?" Raquel asks, pushing the basket tight against her chest. "*Aquí no hay nada.*[32]"

Atabey smiles and hums, softly tapping Raquel's arm and pointing toward the sky.

"This view is a rarity," she answers, sweeping her fingers against the indigo sky and Raquel swears on her life that she sees the stars move with the sway of her arm. "You might not believe it, but there are cities where the artificial light is so bright that the stars are no longer visible."

Raquel purses her lips. "Seems unappealing."

Atabey chuckles. "Oh, it is."

---

[32] *There's nothing here.*

Her laughter must be beautiful if something as small as a giggle makes butterflies burst within Raquel's belly. It is a feeling so foreign to her that her straw basket becomes an anchor as she clutches it tighter against her body. She has often ignored this longing buried within her, tucked away within the deepest recesses of her mind. She has spent many nights on her knees in front of a wooden carving of the Virgin Mary to will this desire for women away from her soul and heart. It must be why mami sees so many faults in her—a part of her *must* know.

Matilda must be ashamed, she must look at her and realize why she has no children with Salvador—why he spends so many nights playing poker with his friends (if that was *truly* what he did). Their friendly marriage turned stale and cold, a passionless union that survived on mutual companionship but found itself empty when the coffers ran dry.

The overgrowth finally smoothes out and they arrive at neatly even fields, the moonlight shining atop a small, stone, and pillared tower, the size of the two-story houses Raquel keeps seeing on the ads placed around town. There are stone edges that pop from the crevices beside them and Raquel thinks it looks like a crown.

"What is that?"

"Its builders are calling it an observational tower," Atabey replies, guiding Raquel within the stone building. The only thing that greets them is a spiral staircase, etched within the very wall itself, directing a path atop the tower. "If you believe there to be nothing here, then let me show it to you from a different perspective."

As Raquel prepares a retort her words are cut by the view— and *Dios Mio*[33], what a view. Orocovís seems to soar above the clouds, a landscape of emeralds and pastoral greens that swallow up any patches of grazed earth that might tarnish the view. It's a triumph of Mother Nature, grand in her glory and serene in her beauty. When Raquel squints, she can see the trail of the river, slithering its way through the rest of Puerto Rico, glittering under the stars. Her eyes water as she notices the rooftops of the village houses and huts, the humble ceiling of their town parish.

---

[33]   *My God.*

Raquel wishes she could hate them, could hate how all of those *damas* and *caballeros*[34] seem to have no cares in the world other than putting bread on the table. It seems like such an enviable life to her, unreachable from her grasp. Daughters who made their mothers proud by marrying the loves of their lives and continuing down the family line, firm in their hard-working beliefs.

But Raquel is tired, she is so tired—she simply wishes she could melt into the cracks of the tower, dissipate into the earth that birthed such majesty.

Tears prickle at her eyes and she bends over the parapet, crossing her arms and leaning her forehead into the triangle they form with her chest.

Raquel takes a deep breath and releases her frustrations through a roaring scream, one that makes her head throb and her shoulders shake but she can't stop, she refuses to do so—there is so much she needs to say, so much to release. Her voice scratches, and her tone warbles but she simply gulps down a dry throat, takes another deep breath, and screams once again, her temple pounding as hot tears stream down her sallow cheeks.

Every disappointment plays in her mind, one against the other in a series of moving pictures that make all of their movements lethargic—it feels like seeing a cruel play acted out by shadow figures of herself, her mother, Salvador, and Alondra. How her life has centered around moments of insecurity and isolation, how for so long she has craved an affection that has no name. It has no face, it only knew shame, and it fed on it whole, consuming her every waking thought, molding herself into a dutiful daughter, loving wife, and wise sister.

When was she ever allowed to be Raquel?

Atabey's cold but gentle hand lands on the small of her back and Raquel turns instinctively into her body, into the crevice where her neck meets her chin. She smells like the orchids that bloom within the forest and although the feel of the lace feels rougher than the clothes Raquel is familiar with, it is still a good sensation, a slight twinge of discomfort that lets her know that she is alive, that she resides within her body and is her own person—not an extension of others.

"Please," Raquel pleads, unsure of what exactly she is asking for.

Atabey smiles, caressing her face.

---

[34] *Ladies* and *gentlemen*.

"Your soul called out to me, *preciosa*," she says, the moon reflecting within her dark eyes. "Your rage, your weariness, your unwavering loyalty, even towards people who do not deserve it."

Raquel looks up at her through fluttered lashes and Atabey kisses her cheek, tantalizingly close to the corner of her lips.

"You deserve more than rest, you deserve divinity. You have created so much within your thirty years, you deserve whatever you desire for the fruits of your labor."

Leaning her larger body against hers, Atabey lowers her arms around Raquel's hips and pulls her closer. Raquel's cheeks heat when she moans at the feeling of having her backside flush against this divine creature. "*Atabey—*"

"Oh," she laughs softly, pushing Raquel closer to her and cornering her against the stone effigy. "I like that name, it sounds musical."

Every single hair on Raquel's body stands, a shudder running down her back as Atabey's touch grows warmer by the moment. Her thighs clench together when Atabey lowers her hand, but her head is thrown back, leaning across Atabey's veiled face.

"I want to show you pleasure before you join me," Atabey says, fluttering her lashes as Raquel's breath grows deeper, her thighs unclenching slowly and letting the overwhelming heat that her body has accumulated shower over her. The scent of *amapolas*[35] overwhelms her, petals floating away in a gentle breeze as an array of colors, all heightened by the moonlight's glow. "*Quiero ser tu primera veneradora.*[36]"

Unable to withstand it, the straw basket falls to the grass below as Raquel grips the parapet before her, thighs separating just enough to allow Atabey's quick hand to slither between them. The feather touch of her fingers is enough to send goosebumps down her arms, and she mewls when Atabey's grip is firm, even through layers of clothing.

"You will be known as the star of the diligent, a sliver of gold plucked from the land and woven into the sky," Atabey whispers, her mystical touch mak-

---

[35]   Poppy flower. An abundant flower in Puerto Rico, coming in a variety of different colors such as red, yellow, orange or pink. Often confused as Puerto Rico's national flower due to its similarities with the flor de maga.

[36]   *I want to be your first venerator.*

ing the thin material of her clothes disappear, leaving Raquel naked as the day she was born. "Regardless of your making, you are the person that you are—and I find you worthy of salvation and reverence."

Atabey's fingers gently open her as if she were the ripest of papayas and Raquel's moan sends cotorras flying off into the distance.

Her divine lover's warm breath smells of coconuts and *café con leche*[37] and her touch is precise and meticulous in its distribution of pleasure as Atabey builds and caresses and worships Raquel in the throes of transformation. She feels her body begin to reach a boiling point, a moment she can never revoke, and Atabey grips one of her breasts tight in her hand, rolling the flesh between her fingers.

Raquel realizes that this is what she was meant to do—to be loved and cared for—to love and see herself with the worth she has always possessed.

You are a person—not just a daughter, a wife, or a lover, Raquel tells herself as her body climaxes and her soul ascends, her toes disintegrating into starlight, followed by her ankles up her calves and over her thighs.

Unashamed, and unabashed, Raquel welcomes the morning's glory to bathe her in the golden glow she had always heard about in legend. Her body warms as her head loosens against the crock of Atabey's neck, surrendering completely as she plays her like the finest musicians, producing an alluring melody that gets lost between the clouds and the break of dawn, whispers stolen between feather-light kisses and the caresses of lace against skin.

Some say one can still hear her cries amidst the song of the roosters.

---

[37] Coffee with milk.

THE BREATH OF LIFE

Engel Williams

ou were surprised, but not displeased, when my first words were, 'They will kill you for this.'

You said, 'How could you know?'

I do not fault you for that. I was new then, still raw from birth. But did it not make you wonder when I did not cry or wail or even whimper, but issue warning? I could scarcely put words to what I was feeling then. I can now. It was fear, the kind that petrifies because there is nothing that can be done except wait for the inevitable. It was also a terrible sense of knowing. You had committed the worst of sins so that I could live. I do not think you ever imagined, even at the end, Lord, when you knew it was coming, what the punishment for that is.

I was made over the course of a year and a day. Compared to the others, you took your time with me. I believed at first that it was because I was your first, destined to be your most special, but when I told you this, you laughed and explained that it had been necessary.

'I had to learn first,' you explained. 'I know it hurt you to have been like that for so long, but I had to get it right.' You meant unfinished. How could you know, as were your first words to me, without having lived it?

The studio was hardly a refuge. The walls were paper thin—we could hear everything our neighbors did and they us. On one side lived a spinster that proved more elusive than even you could be, and on the other, a childless husband and wife. You complained about them frequently, your pride wounded because they skirted you in the hall, though they were eager and sociable amongst themselves.

We lived in the densest part of the city, and the churchmen prowled the crowded streets constantly. Watching from above, I learned how to pick them out from the rest of our sprawling home: the pure white of their robes like roaming clouds among the grey and the filth, the promising blades swinging from their belts. You warned me away from the windows during the day, when they were most active and alert. These figures were licensed to investigate heresy where they suspected it had taken root. If they saw me, they could, and would, come and find me.

It took a year and a day, from conception to completion. I was laid on the floor an equal distance from the bare mattress you slept on and the kitchen, so you could always see me. By the way you told it, you began by drawing my shape. I would be tall for a woman, narrow-hipped, small-shouldered, but I would not be lacking or undesirable to the eye. To whose eye, I wonder? I am certain that you never intended for me to be shared.

You arranged my bones. You told me that you planned to use metal, but finding enough of it would be almost impossible on your artist's commission, and you feared the inevitable rusting. Even then you wanted me perfect, unchanging and undying, forever pure.

Petrified wood was more available to you. I don't know why, or how you found enough of that specific kind, as it is normally so brittle. And it escapes me how you polished it so finely to make my structure, but you did not become my Creator by stroke of luck. You were, admittedly, a genius, even if I was the only one who could ever tell you so.

You used copper for my veins and nerves, fired clay for my organs, laying them tenderly along my bones. My heart, you made of stone to prevent me from softening, so that I may always endure. Pearl for my teeth and nails, fine black silk for my hair, glass for my eyes and Tiger's Eye for the irises. You did not have to worry much about the flesh or fat, for a Creation only needs direction and the rest will follow.

You gave me blood from your veins, for every Creation requires a sacrifice to come to life. You filled me slowly, over months, for fear you'd die from blood loss before I could be completed. And when there was nothing else left, you gave me breath from your lungs rather than wait for me to wake.

You massaged my chest, coaxed my lungs into movement. To be honest, Lord, I did not need you to do so. I took that first breath myself.

I breathed and watched and heard and spoke. I mimicked. I questioned. Still, you decided I needed to be taught. Food repulsed me, and my performance of it was more for your satisfaction than my desire.

Once I had mastered the basics of physicality, you tried to teach me what it meant to be human. You gave me a name: Josefina.

You taught me to dress myself. My nakedness embarrassed you. I wore your clothes until you came home one day with options for me to choose from. I preferred thick cloth, high necklines, trailing skirts— I was always cold. The heat of your blood faded soon after I took my first breath, and I was never again so warm unless within your embrace.

When I was allowed, I observed the sights below my window: lovers holding hands; mothers cradling their children; even the holy men strolled in pairs and trios. The sight of it filled me with a longing so great that I had to turn away and lie down on the bed, my knuckles white between my teeth and the taste of my own blood—or rather, yours—on my tongue. I liked the taste. So I learned the strength of my bite, the sharpness of my teeth. With time, I grew steadily bolder until I no longer felt the need to run from the bloodlust, embracing instead the strange and powerful emotion that was introducing itself to me.

I thought it odd that I was never permitted to leave—under any circumstances. Our building was evacuated once due to a fire. You bid me to remain. I listened. What else could I have done? If anyone had seen me, you would have been arrested, and I was not so easy to kill besides. What was fire to me more than beauty, than heat? No, the real danger to me were the churchmen and their God.

Punishment awaited us. I could feel it coming, but I could not say when it would arrive.

From time to time, usually when I was alone, I was seized by fear. My limbs would lock up and I could do nothing but tremble and watch the spider-webbed ceiling of the studio, expecting some thing to rip it clean off and destroy me. I wondered which of us would be first to die: the Creation or the Creator? These episodes lasted until you returned. You'd murmur softly to me and rub my shoulders until I calmed.

'You needn't worry so much,' you told me.

I worried constantly, but I learned to hide it. You didn't, and never would, understand: only God can give life. And though you were mine, you could not measure up to Him.

Once, I was perched on the windowsill, watching the street. I had never been allowed to go even so far as past our front door. I wondered how it would feel to stand beneath the open sky. How might my perception of what it means to live, to experience, change if I could feel the wind dance upon my skin, run its fingers through my hair? I knew it could only be for a moment, or else I risked destruction. I do not look human. Close, but there is something about my eyes, my posture, my expression, that horrified even you sometimes.

You were working on a commission. The canvas was taller and wider than us both even if we were to fuse. I did not recognize what you were painting, and I was more interested in what was going on outside. Our view was mostly of sloping rooftops and thick smoke from the chimneys, but also the cathedral's twisted spires, reaching like hungry fingers toward Heaven. A crone pushed a cart of rotting vegetables through the crowded streets, careful to avoid the filthy slop thrown from above, advertising her discounted produce in hoarse tones. I believed you engrossed in your work, but when I glanced over my shoulder, I saw you were watching me.

'Come away from the window.'

I did as you requested. You said, 'Ask me if you are beautiful.'

'Am I beautiful?'

Stepping away from the light so I would appear as more than shadow to you, I tilted my head a little, demure, playing the part of the perfect woman that I knew you desired. You had been teaching me, and I prided myself on being the ideal student. I smiled. I even meant it, I think.

'You are spectacular,' you said. You set aside your tools and approached, took my face into your hands. I leaned into your warmth, the softness of your palms. 'Magnificent. You are my masterpiece.'

This moment would linger in my mind long after, though I attributed it to bashfulness. Eventually I was able to take the scene apart and find what was troubling me about it: it was all a distraction, wasn't it? You only wanted me away from the window so we wouldn't be discovered.

More worryingly, the word 'masterpiece' suggests there were previous attempts and might be future ones. How naïve I was to believe your sin began and ended with me. I regret that I didn't see it until it was too late, as well as my role in your temptation.

Lord, I have to confess to you, though I know you will never hear it. There are many secrets that I hid from you, not from ill will or selfishness— though if they were, would it be so wrong for me to have something that did not belong to you? Many of them are truths I know you would not tolerate. Others I had no reason for keeping. You were so unpredictable in those early days, when it was just you and me.

The first secret I must tell is that your teaching was meaningless to me, and futile.

You taught me longing before you taught me restraint. You alone were responsible for my bloodlust, refusing me once I was old enough, but I took what I needed from you while you slept. You tried to teach me morality. How were you qualified to teach this when my own existence is an abomination? Shortly after my birth, only a little after my fascination with the world began, you explained that you did not believe in God. I laughed at you. You were upset at that.

'But you have Created!'

'Do we not do the same with our own bodies? It is a matter of science, Josefina. It is biology.'

I did not disagree with that, but you were missing the whole picture. You could not see it, no matter how I tried to show it to you. You thought me romantic, but it simply became my secret to keep. Fine, then. You did not believe in God. You believed in the church, a place full of men who deemed themselves holy and carried out the word of God.

'*Their* word,' you insisted.

They did not care for this business of Creating life from nothing, a sort of anti-biology. It was them you feared, not God. If caught, they would jail you or worse, and *they* would be destroyed.

I wanted to tell you, Lord, I *did*—that these men should be the least of your fears, but you were so adamant and sure that you were right. It is my fault, I know. I should have convinced you. But how? I was so young, so confident in my love for you that I said, 'Yes,' even as I thought, *No*.

You professed to me about death and the afterlife, and I wondered, I asked you, 'What does that make me, Lord?'

I think you said, 'Whatever you want. My angel, if you'd like to be.'

See how we naturally returned to God? I don't remember what I said to you. Those lessons were folly to me. You see, you were inadvertently teaching me how to pretend, and I did not commit those days to memory as I should have. I learned scorn without you preaching it.

I pitied you. Unlike you, I have never been confused or hopeful about what I am.

Here is a secret you kept from me: you did not make me in the usual way.

Breath is the one commonality shared among all Creatures. But the blood, that is new. I have searched, but there is no other like me.

Eight months after my birth, you made your second born, the product of one of your many lessons.

You had been trying, very patiently I admit, to teach me about death— you called it death, but I think it closer to an interlude, Lord. Death, as you taught it, is a finality, but it is no longer what it had been before your time. Despite the church doing its best to eradicate those who performed the indelible sin—not resurrection but the act of Genesis—life's course has been permanently altered. The definition of Death demands a revision. Even then, you were of the opinion that true resurrection was only just out of reach.

You came home one evening with something squirming beneath your coat. I hid in the dusty wardrobe, inexplicably terrified. You waited outside and spoke to me in soothing tones. It reminded me so much of my gestation, when you used to sing as you worked and tell me stories, that I eventually returned to your side. You bid me to sit on the floor with you.

Cupped in your hands was a small mass of white hair: a rabbit, a baby as I was, with coal-black eyes . I saw my image swallowed up in the reflection. Trembling, it watched me suspiciously. When I touched it, it calmed a little, though it did not yet trust me.

'No matter,' you said. 'You won't need to hold it for the lesson.'

We fed it. You were nearly penniless then. It was a good thing that I only ate human food to please you, because if I truly felt hunger the way a human might, I am not sure you would have been able to afford to feed us both. We sacrificed a few of the vegetables. I pet it while it ate, marveling at the heartbeat I could feel beneath my fingers. I brought my hand to my breast, but mine did not beat as strongly or as fast.

Once your subject was calm, you began the lesson in earnest. I did not cry out when you snapped its neck. I did not even gasp. You watched me carefully and I feigned interest, playing the part of the child who did not understand; I could not have been convincingly remorseful—it was not my nature. I understood what you had done. You had destroyed it. You believed it was a permanent destruction. I did not.

'It's dead. See? Feel its chest. Search for breath.'

I did not bother. I knew I would not feel it. 'You ended its life,' I agreed. 'But that does not mean another cannot begin in its place.'

You shook your head. 'I cannot reanimate. I cannot breathe life into a body that I did not make.'

I went to the kitchen and retrieved a knife, the wicked one meant for carving. I pressed the handle into your rough palm. I said to you, 'Make one.'

You needed a little encouragement, so I took the knife and made the first cut, flaying open a bit of skin so the flesh underneath was visible. Seeing the vision I had laid out for you, you took over.

Do you see it now? My Lord, even then I was teaching you something, proving you wrong. You made me in your image, in innocence and joy and desire. But a creature such as I, that which was made outside of God's hands and hidden from His eyes, am unholy. I am no angel. I corrupted you that day, led you astray , though others might argue that you had already lost your way in Creating me in the first place.

The only things you saved of the rabbit were its eyes and soft pelt. You made your second born from these remnants and your own improvisations. How long did it take you, Lord? A few hours, I think. You were done by dinner, and my new sibling hopped around the room as we feasted on his old meat.

I underestimated you. I was giddy from my success, bursting with discovery. I went to sleep that night beaming, my brother's fur warming my neck, belly so full that I did not even consider feeding from you as I often did—just a taste, if I could manage it.

But hearing an odd scraping, I woke just before sunrise. I rubbed the sleep from my eyes and shifted to the bottom of the mattress. Moonlight leaked through the window, spilled across the studio, soaked you in silver. I saw you, a knife in one hand and wood in the other, whittling. Already, there was a pile of bones next to you.

I knew what you intended to do. I said to you, 'Lord?'

You did not turn. I was not even sure that you had heard, but I dared not speak again. You were in deep thought, a perfect model of the artist's unwavering gaze.

I returned to a sleeping pose, though I did not rest. I thought about my brother who could not speak apart from stomping insistently with his back feet. I thought about the next sibling on the way, and I thought about the inevitable destruction. I was learning consequence.

Our judgement day was coming, swift on crimson wings, drops of blood dripping in its wake.

My sister swiftly took shape. By morning, I could look over your shoulder and inspect her dark skin, twin to mine and yours, the white gleam of fur mixed into her silken hair. Her eyes were open, unblinking. Her lips were parted and dark.

You slept at noon. You had been awake since dawn the previous morning. I knelt at her side. Gazed into her eyes. What had you used for them? Tar, or crushed obsidian, perhaps. They were shaped, a little, like a rabbit's.

I touched her shoulder, smoothed the hair back from her face. 'It is all right.' I glanced behind me, checking to make sure you were still unconscious. You did not stir. 'The pain will not last.'

After a bout of fitful sleep, you woke and rushed through your dinner. We sat together, you on one side of the body, me on the other. She looked finished to me, but I did not know the complexities of the process. You seemed... perturbed, almost as though you were lost. You kept fidgeting with yourself, scratching at an already raw and bleeding spot on your thumb, fixing my sister's hair—though it looked perfect. I still wonder, Lord, if that was your own form of premonition: somewhere, you had made a mistake.

I was surprised that you refused to share your blood with her. Instead, you injected mercury into her veins. You gave her your breath.

I let you massage her chest the way you had mine. I watched silently as you leaned forward and kissed her once on the mouth. I watched her open her eyes, take her first breath.

My sister was born screaming. It was a terrible noise, all agony and fear and even—I was fascinated—anger. It was a newborn's cry to you, though I could see that you were rattled, knocked off-balance. To me, it was the sound of the angel's trumpet, a warning just like the one I had given you.

I did not voice my concerns immediately. You were preoccupied with raising your third born. I was forced to adopt my brother as my own, so little attention did you give him. I called him Theodore. I am not sure if he minded your inattention, and I did not ever get the chance to find out. Despite your favoritism, there was never jealousy or animosity between us three. We were far above such human feelings, wholly focused on navigating you.

You decided a few weeks later that we had outgrown the studio. Even now, Lord, I do not understand where you found the money. You were an artist, brilliant without argument, but you worked with watered down paints. The collection of work you could not sell littered our home, the paint on the canvases peeled after a while, losing their original luster little by little, day by day . There should have been evidence of the wealth you were building. There wasn't.

Excitement triumphed my suspicion. Our move would be the first time I left the studio. Even if it would only be for a short while, I planned to savor the feeling of cobbled stone beneath my feet, breathe the mix of scents in the air, smile at someone I did not know. I was disappointed, though not very surprised, to discover that this would not happen. You transported us in large, locked trunks in the back of a covered wagon. We were not permitted to come out until we had been brought safely inside. You asked us after, quite genuinely, if we were all right.

Our new place was a loft. There was a great hall that you made your studio, and three rooms for the four of us to share. My sister demanded her own room and the other was yours, so I shared with my brother. That first night, I went into the main hall after you had all fallen asleep and looked past the glass skylight up to the stars.

How could I know that we were your only children? Pushed in the right direction, you had created my brother so easily, my sister even more so—and feverishly at that. How could I know you were not selling siblings I had never met to the highest bidder, dooming us to the church and the divine both, all for a few gold coins and foolish notions of success?

I could not, and so I set to watching you.

Imogen, pretty as she was, was not coming along as well as you had hoped. She refused your education, preferring to watch us mutely or follow me around like a dog. She threw tantrums and cried silver tears, and when she was angry, which was often, she liked to wreck.

You fell into a deep depression. It was the first time I had ever seen you that way, Lord, and it terrified me. My first birthday was only days away at that point, and I was beginning to think I would not live to see it. I did not understand how you could be so calm, so disbelieving. I cooked and cleaned and did the washing. I kept us afloat and alive. Slowly, you returned to me, but never in full, and never the same as I had known you.

I loved you, and I won't claim to have recovered from that love, but I loved our family more. Who else but me could? No one knew we existed apart from you. If they did, they undoubtedly would have chased their own absolution and reported us to the church. You teetered on the edge of insanity, or so I felt, thus the duty of protection fell to me.

The greatest danger to us, sadly, was you.

I confronted you, finally. You were twitchy that morning, muttering to yourself. I hoped it was simply an idea demanding your attention, but I feared that all the same. What if it was not another painting? What if you wanted to grow our family?

In your room, you were folded over your sketchbook. Around you were unfinished drawings and canvases you planned to repurpose. It stank of paint and varnish and flesh. You did not look up when I entered.

I had never deluded myself into believing I had your respect. Our relationship existed outside of that. All that mattered to me was that I thought of you as my Savior, and it was all I ever asked of you. Still, your dismissal hurt.

'Are we a family?' I asked.

'Of course,' you replied impatiently. 'You are of my blood.'

That is not really true, is it Lord? All three of us possessed your life's breath, but only I alone have your blood in my veins. I *am* your blood. I share your proclivity to curiosity and a lust for life, among other things, and I was very good at pretending at the other things you enjoyed. Theodore was confined to an animal's body, a weak one, and Imogen was disinterested, unattached to life. That is not family.

'Or are we your soldiers?' I asked. 'Sworn swords? Entertainment?'

You stood and faced me. There was such fury on your face that my sluggish heart began to race. I tried subtly to put distance between us. I was afraid of you. I feared the truth you might reveal, that it might damn us further.

'Where is this coming from? Has Imogen been telling you tales again?'

My anxiety had only gotten worse since her arrival, and you blamed her for it. Imogen was most talkative with me late at night, long after you had gone to sleep. She would whisper dark things to me about our Creation and about you. Though you suspected, you never did catch on to the extent of which she hated you. Imogen believed you would be our destruction, and I was beginning to think the same.

'I want to know your intention, Lord. What is our purpose?'

'Purpose,' you repeated scornfully. 'Is that what you would reduce your life to?'

What life? I thought. I asked, 'Why did you Create us? Was it loneliness? Was it passion?'

'Would you ask God why He Created?'

'I am asking Him.'

You turned your back to me and busied your hands with gathering a pile of pencil shavings. Your hands came away stained with graphite. You wiped them on your shirt. 'I did it because I wanted to. Why not? Must Creation have purpose?'

I had been debating that question from the moment I woke and found you with my sister's bones, but I did not want to say the wrong thing. How silly I felt. I admit that if I had not urged you to Create from the ruins of the dead rabbit, you might have stopped at my birth.

'No, but it has consequences,' I said. 'You must take responsibility. What will you do now with three souls in your inventory?'

'What is really on your mind, Josefina?'

'Your punishment, Lord. What happens to us when you die, and we must continue?' I had more to say but I stopped, regretful.

You frowned. 'What did you say?'

My bravery faltered. I had never said it quite like that before. I wished I could take back the words. 'Save us, Lord. I beg you.' I might have taken to my knees if I thought it would sway you, but you had never much appreciated my devotion. You said it reminded you too much of the church.

Your stare was hard and strange. You were noticing what you had missed the first two times: our promised warnings, at last, but too late. I sensed this would be our first and last time speaking of this.

I bowed my head and buried my hands in the fabric of my skirt. 'Forgive me,' I said. My instinct was to protect you from the truth. I thought it too late for you to save yourself, and I could not save you if you would not make the effort to try. My siblings were my priority. I decided to leave your fate up to you.

Besides, all things must die.

I could not meet your eye that day. There was nothing more to say, so I fled to my room. I sought comfort from Theodore, resting my head on his side and listening to his breathing, letting him nuzzle my hair and ears. After a while, Imogen joined us. She lay at my back, not wanting to be touched but content to be close to me.

The last night we would ever spend as a family, it was raining. I will tell you now that I did not know it was our last night together. Premonition is hardly ever precise. If you had a mouth still with which to say it, I am sure you would ask me now if I would have told you had I known. No, Lord, I would not have—at least, not with the mentality I had then. It was my reasoning that you had made your bed, and so you must lie in it.

Thunder boomed, lightning flashed and threatened, and the rain was heavy on the roof. My sister, the fierce and cowardly thing that she was, was inconsolable all evening. Our attempts to soothe her were ineffective. Still, she didn't wish to be alone, so she cowered between the wall and floor of the hall, eerily quiet. I think Imogen knew. She thought you deserved it. She did not share my confusion about the future; she rejected it. Imogen had not wished to be born, and she wanted no part in the accidental life you had drawn.

You were working on another commission: an enormous mess of gold and black oil. Bundled up in Imogen's skirts, my brother slept easily, as he always did. I paced behind you, troubled. Try as I might, I could not tear my focus from my sister's haunted eyes, peering out from over her knees.

Neither of us had forgotten our argument. You were more watchful than ever, insecure about our movements. You suspected I was planning to leave, taking Imogen and Theodore with me. You were right. I was simply waiting for an opportunity.

'Josefina,' you said. I startled and halted my pacing. 'Come here.'

We looked together at your painting. In the furious mash of color and shape, I recognized the suggestion of wings and halos and grace.

Wary, I asked you, 'What is it?'

'I've been thinking of what you said about the *punishment.*' You glanced over your shoulder at Imogen and the son you had never bothered to name. 'I know you, Josefina, even if you think I do not. I know you have presumptions.' You paused, hesitant. 'Why do *you* think I Created?'

Your question demanded different answers for each of us. I settled on one: 'Legacy. You wanted something that would survive you.'

'Eternally,' you said, nodding. 'But you are concerned about your survival. Do you consider yourself human then?'

'No.'

Out of us three, I believe I came closest to possessing a mortal soul. But the difference between reaching and touching is a league. In the question of my being human, possessing any degree of mortality, the answer is: not quite.

A drop of paint fell from your brush to the floor. You spent a long moment cleaning it up. Then you wiped down your brushes, cleaned your palette. A particularly nasty round of thunder shook our home, and my brother woke, his fur wild and bristling, ears swiveling. He blinked once, turned his gaze up to heaven.

'What do you think you are?'

I thought instinctively of the church's preachings, which you'd explained in detail. Creation, a fabrication of life, was an imitation of Genesis. All who dared were sinners, their progeny abominations. If the church failed to root out such evil, God and his angels would not.

My eyes ran over the angels in your painting, noting the cold mathematical degree with which you'd rendered their halos. They looked as unreal as they were likely to spring forth into the room. I felt sick.

'I do not know,' I said. 'I do not know where to go without you having been there first.'

'That is the intention of my lessons.'

'But you cannot teach *purpose,* my Lord,' I argued. 'There is this... hunger within me, and I'm afraid that it will consume me if I do not feed it.'

This was my worry: you had failed to create human replicants and called forth something much more wicked. I was afraid that the church was right to want to strike us down on sight, that we were the very demons they warned of.

'What do you crave?'

I did not have a chance to answer. From her corner, Imogen said, 'Can you hear it, Lord? Your end?'

We turned to look at her.

'What did you say?' you demanded.

I did not need her to repeat it. I could feel it just as she could hear it. I had the thought, *Is this what Theo has been trying to tell me through his stomping and those mad twitches of his ears? That he can see the angels' approach?* And what of your painting? Why did you decide that night to paint them when you had never cared for faith before?

There was a blinding flash and... Lord, I saw them. For just a moment. Swift and terrible. I could not watch. I was not meant to. I ran from your side, averting my eyes, and stumbled into a pose of supplication. I listened as the angels slew you with their swords, and when your body lay wretched on the stone floor, your blood soaking my skirts up to the knees, I listened to them rip your soul from your body. I do not know where they put you. I doubt they destroyed you fully, only in the way that matters. You became a soul without a vessel, voiceless, all choice stripped away. There was no time for me to plea for you or to say goodbye.

The slaying was quick, efficient, brutal. In my imaginings, I had expected them to make an example of you—a gross mistreatment, for you to be shamed in front of thousands—but they did not give you this luxury.

I cannot say, Lord, why they did not destroy me as well. Perhaps it was because I did not run. My brother tried to run away—I heard his desperate approach, but he burned away in their holy light. He had been running to me, but Imogen ran to *them,* to attempt harm or what, I do not know. She died as she had been born, screaming.

I knelt for a long time. The angels did not touch me. I knew they were gone when my body finally surrendered to the floor. I wept, Lord, and still do each time it rains, because I do not know how to continue without you.

I withdrew. My first steps outside were a stumble, a dejected and furious crawl. I was drenched by the rain in an instant, my clothes heavy and suffocating on my back. If anyone saw me, they did not try to help. I sat there in the gutter and watched the rain wash me clean of your blood.

It has been a long time since. Every night, when I shut my eyes, I ask myself why I did not look at God's avengers so I could know who it was that I needed to kill. In the question of my purpose, it would seem I have found my answer. I have become your angel, your messenger of death.

THE GIRL I WAS BORN IS THE BOY I'VE BECOME'S KNIGHT IN SHINING ARMOR

Bucky A. Wolfe

It is no secret that I was raised as a girl. Womanhood, by design, is woven into my pliant, pale skin. It springs tragically from my eyes, each too green to be blue but too blue to be hazel. It cuts short at the tip of my tongue, where muscle meets enamel. My womanhood is silence, is preconceived notions, is first impressions. The Her within me sits, perched, at the back of my mouth, pressed tightly against molars and wisdom teeth that my dentist said would never grow in. Along the underside of my tongue, the boy I could have been worries over grass stains and bruises, growth spurts and losing baby teeth. He is caged, but feral, waiting for the moment She unleashes him into the world. Meanwhile, She drinks the sugar from my wine all by Herself. My voice is Hers, wetted thoroughly by blueberry wine and tears from a black-blue sky above us, backlit by happenstance, a geomagnetic storm staining this vastness grey, and then purple and green, beside clouds as pregnant as the woman I hold dearest to my heart. She, the puppeteer, my father's hand-me-down anger Her muse. I am a crooked smile disguised as a sword, Her weapon. Womanhood, by design, wields weapons to protect versions of me not yet freed from the asphyxiating fears that come with our truth. It is sacred to us, being raised into and alongside womanhood, because maybe there is nothing as honey-sweet and honest as the girls who grew alongside me, who recognize the woman pressed against my teeth without discrediting the boy She's been protecting since She was conceptualized. No man has ever been this delicate, I think. But you could be the first, She declares. The Her within me, preening and beautiful, untouchable, understands that the palms of my hands, or the marrow of my bones, or the core of my soul, are a beetle trapped eternally in amber. A man, this He, some cruel god's unfinished painting, not the Bible's God nor a false prophet but something hungrier, is trapped behind femininity He did not earn. Femininity He did not ask for. But He is gritty, born of salt water and bloodied noses, and He knows He is not just the man. He is the bear, exactly where He belongs, somewhere behind kind eyes and a sharp tongue, alongside the women who raised Him, who took the sword from His heavy, tired hand, and said, "Let us."

SEVERIN AND THE DARK

Harvey Oliver Baxter

You open your eyes to sun dust kissing your face through the crack of Barbie pink curtains. It's summer, probably; you can't really remember. You're only seven.

You lie there for a while. You have a strange sensation in your veins. It's morning, you're sure of it, it has to be. It's so bright and you can hear birds. So why can't you move?

You raise your arms like normal, flex your legs as you would every day of your life, only you don't. The feeling is there, but you just *won't* move.

You try again, eyes still fixed on the glossy paint chipping away from the window frame—the wood chip that looks like a moth with its wings fanning out across its back. You're home, in your own bed, surrounded by your own things. It's morning. You're awake. But it's no use—you don't understand.

You don't panic though. You're confused, but this does not alarm you. You don't cry out, don't scream, don't cry, you just close your eyes and fall back into a slumber.

It's okay, you see.

You're only seven.

You're ten now. You're growing up fast. You're changing, they say. It's all normal, all natural, just a bit earlier than expected. Nothing to worry about though.

Your friends are jealous of your height, your hair, your figure. Their mams call you the adult of the group, the mature one.

They look at you, expecting you to take the compliment, but you don't like it. Something is wrong. You don't like standing out this way.

This time when you wake and phantom limbs are all you can lift, you stare out into baby pink walls and you shout, but no one listens.

You're only ten.

You'll get used to these changes, you've been promised. When the lady at the bank asks you which college course you're doing at thirteen, you laugh and react casually, absorbing the compliment and correcting her. She makes a comment on your maturity; you're supposed to be proud of that. If you're mature for your age, you'll get respected more, that's what you've heard, anyway.

You can't shop in the kids section anymore, even though all your friends still do. Those clothes won't hang right on your body—they weren't made for you.

You should be grateful for your body. You didn't get to choose it, but it was given to you for free. You didn't have to work for those hips, for that full chest. That long, thick, wavy mane cascading down your back. You refuse to cut your hair because you had it short for so long, now it needs to be the longest. It's what all the girls are doing now. You don't want to stand out.

Makeup will fill your pores and that wired bra will support you. No, not those silly, soft crop-top things, no come and shop in this section. This is for proper grown-up women.

Stop slouching, be proud of your body. Stop it! You'll be grateful when you're older and all your friends catch up to you. They'll all secretly wish they looked like you. You just feel shy now because you grew up early. Do you know how much money women pay to look like you?

You listen to what people say, take it all on board and learn. Is this what it means to be a woman? You detest it already.

This is all normal though, everyone goes through these difficult times, it's called being a teenager. But why do you feel like you've lost yourself? Like you won a contest you didn't even enter. Like one day you noticed you'd woken up in a new body, the wrong body, and you can't find the door to go back. You've already moved too far away.

You forget about those mornings. They're right at the back of your mind by the time you're fourteen because everything has changed. You're burning inside and out, it's all too much. Why does everything feel wrong? Everything is your fault, everything isn't your fault. You try too hard, you don't try hard enough. Stick in with school, you were always academically gifted. People would do anything for your skill. You're going far. You're a terrible friend, you don't take sides. You're pretty. You're ugly. It's the mirror, it's warped. Eat your greens. Eat. Sports bras are bad for you in the long run, you need proper support. That's not very lady-like. Don't say that. You're too young for that. You may look like an adult, but you've got so much to learn.

No one listens. Why is no one listening? Why is everything so hard?

You stare at your lilac walls, as if they have all the answers.

You stare for such a long time. Squint, focus, then everything blurs. Get some sleep, you've got an important day ahead.

The popular girls won't stop talking about sex. Where they've done it. How many times. Who with. You listen in and act interested because you're at this stage of your life now, this is normal. You pretend you care, almost trick yourself into believing you do, but honestly? You wish you'd just turned away. Why do people brag about this?

The nun covering your lesson tells you all to be quiet at the back of the class, to get on with the work the teacher assigned, but you all just laugh. She has no idea what you've all been talking about. You feel rebellious—you could get used to this. Being in with the crowd, letting these girls show you how to be, how to act, how to look. You use them as role models, people to be like, because every-one loves them, so they must have the key to all of this. The key to life.

You never actually go looking for gossip, it just gets thrust upon you like a bad smell. You know way too much about girls you don't even like. But you have to pretend to like them otherwise you'll lose friends and people will think you're weird. But even after all of this trying, not once are you jealous or impatient for your time to come. You realise you don't care. They'll explain all these things to you as though you know what they're talking about, as if you've experienced rela-tionships before. But really, you don't even like to acknowledge your body or the things it's capable of. It's just a vessel. That's all it is, just a host for your brain and heart and everything going on inside.

You need to look after it more.

You're fifteen and you've kept it all down. All of it. Every thought, feeling and emotion. It's easier that way.

You don't question anything outside the box because you've not been given the tools to cut an opening. You keep your head down and you hide. Hide it all. You don't have the words to learn.

You're sixteen. You're still here. Now you just have to get through your exams. Then you'll really be free. It will all change.

But the third time you wake up, your lips are sewn shut with a fine needle and thread. Glued down tight along with your limbs. It's happening again. It's dark this time, your eyes taking a moment to adjust. Your alarm hasn't gone off yet. What time is it? You convince yourself you've seen the time, and it's time you get ready for school. Big day. You need to be ready. You can see the alarm-clock-red flashing behind your eyes, hear the analogue tick of your watch, but really, it's all in your head. Your skull is moulded to the pillow, eyes pried open, focusing, focusing, focusing.

You hear it before you see it. Maybe you're dreaming. This has happened before, a dream within a dream. It's freaky, but nothing you can't handle. It's just in your head. Close your eyes and forget about it. Breathe. There's nothing there.

Until there is.

He's standing in the middle of your room. Staring without a face. Without anything. He's just a mass. A mass of a black hole, an opening devoid of everything. He laughs in your head and his sentences make no sense, but you have no choice but to listen, to stare at him. You're breathing hard and your soul is already running, leaving your body behind.

He's talking to you.

Listen.

Listen to him.

He's holding a blurry chainsaw now. Muttering words of disgust as he shakes it around like it weighs nothing.

NO.

Don't close your eyes.

Now he's swinging from your wardrobe, mocking you. Arms too long and legs too thin, dangling with such a casual grace it maddens you.

An ornate, white, wired birdcage sits on your floor, there's something trapped inside. You just don't know what.

You cry out for your mam. You scream her name so loud. Why isn't she listening? Why isn't she coming to save you? Like she always used to?

The last thing you remember is him running towards you like he's half trapped in another dimension. Chasing your soul.

You squeeze your eyes shut and SCREAM.

When you wake again, heart in your throat, it's still dark. It's 7:03. Your alarm hasn't even gone off yet.

You ask her why she didn't come.

You didn't call for her?

Time to get ready.

You're still sixteen but there's a lot you still don't understand. You're not sure you want to though. It's easier that way.

You research your symptoms and come across a definition that makes sense. Then you reach demons. They're common, apparently. Fuelled by hyperactive minds. But why did you never see them as a kid? What's changed?

You're sixteen, and you're still here. On three separate occasions you've woken up to a weight on your chest. It's pushing you down, down, down. Melting you into the fabric. You can't breathe. This is it.

Don't open your eyes.

Breathe. You can handle this. You're prepared.

You're more or less an adult now. Your mind has finally caught up with your body, whatever that means. It's meant to be a compliment, but you don't take it. But being an adult means you can't go running to someone when you get scared. You have to fight that off yourself now, that's what adults do. So act like one.

Your mirror is your coat hanger. Bags. Caps. Fairy lights.

You start going out to parties. REAL parties. Adult ones. Where you're expected to do adult things. Drink. Mingle. Did you see that guy staring?

You'll get used to it. It's fine, you just haven't been to many parties like these.

No one is looking at you. You're kind of glad.

You see the shadow again. This time he doesn't speak. He might not actually even be there, you just feel him.

You're sixteen and for the first time in your life, you question your identity. Maybe you might be bisexual. That could be it, that might help things make sense. You shove it down though; you're too busy to think about that. Besides, you can't say that in an all girl's school, everyone will think you're looking at them. It would change too much and you've already got enough to deal with. You're barely managing everything anyway. *Everything*.

But you're still here.

Breathe.

You're lying in your bed, drifting in and out of sleep, and you dream. You dream about a ghost.

It feels normal at first, just your mind creating fiction to confuse and entertain. But this one slowly bleeds out into your waking moments. You sit up in the light, the house fully silent. You know this is real, you're not tied down by phantom sleep, but yet... you feel it. Its presence. You're asleep again in seconds and time no longer exists. You open your eyes once more in the space of a second and it's there. The ghost. At your door, just watching you. You feel calm though— no sense of hostility washes over you as you realise once again, you can't move.

What happens next you never tell anyone. Not a soul. Because how could you describe the feelings and sensations you felt as it climbed on top of you? They'll think you're mad, maybe you are. It was just a hallucination after all. Just what you think you wanted.

"Who do you like?" Your friends ask you in the first week of sixth form. It's mixed now, you see. You're no longer in a 'single gender' space. The common room is muggy and too loud. Too many breaths and wandering gazes. Surely there has to be someone you have your eye on.

"I think I'll go to the canteen for lunch today," you reply.

You're seventeen now and everything should be falling into place. You're a lot happier than you've ever been and people are starting to notice you. You know, really notice you. You dress yourself up, painting your face and lining your eyes for the performance of a lifetime. This is what it's like to be a seventeen-year-old girl.

But you're not a seventeen-year-old girl. You've just not found the words for that yet.

You're eighteen now.

You're eighteen. You did it.

It's been a long time since his last visit, you've almost forgotten he ever came. You've told stories of it to your friends in the past; watching as their jaws hit the floor in shock as you describe the way he took a hold of your mind and body.

They've never seen him, which makes you unique. Something to make you interesting. To stand out.

Isn't that what you want now? To be noticed?

You've not seen him for a while, but sometimes he sits on your chest. You know to keep your eyes closed now, because then he'll get bored quicker. He forces his weight down hard and you wince, holding in your breaths.

He sometimes speaks to you, right at the back of your head. Whispers reminders to you, to keep yourself in check. To not stray too far from your purpose. One time he holds your chest as he sneers into the hairs of your ears. Stop thinking what you're thinking. He knows what you've been reading, researching, piecing together in your head. It won't do you any good, he says. It doesn't make sense. It's not real. You're not *that*. Stop spending so much time online, it's skewing your vision.

You listen to his voice. He's right, you don't need this extra stress in your life.

You're a girl.
You're a girl.
You're a girl.

But you're not.

You're six again, and that reoccurring dream plays through your mind. You're in the school yard, the only one out of uniform. You feel a cool breeze brush your soft blue tee and your mind is *free*. One of the other boys calls your name and asks you to kick the football over to him. It brings you back to your senses and you place the ball down, kicking it with all your might and cheers chorus all around you.

It's weird because you've never liked football.

"Goal! Severin, that's a goal! We won! We finally won!"

You're twenty, and when you wake up, this euphoria is too strong. You're charged with adrenaline, happiness all consuming.

You take in a deep breath and grin.

It has a nice ring to it.

Go on, try it out for size, see if it fits.

It turns out the name fits as you introduce yourself to your mirror and Severin smiles back. The name slides on like a slipper, slots in like a puzzle piece.

You've cracked the code. This is it. The answer you've been looking for your whole life.

Then your mam calls you from downstairs and the words shoot through you like an arrow straight through the heart.

You're not Severin anymore—back to reality. It was just a dream, and you've awoken properly now.

"Coming," you shout back.

You leave your heart and guts on the bedroom floor.

You're twenty and you spend the year researching, reading, watching, *learning*. Severin is there, inside, every single day. They're there. He's there? Maybe he's they, they is he. You're not sure yet, you need time to figure it out.

She's gone though. And that's okay, you tell yourself. *Maybe she was never there.*

Severin raids the thrift stores, borrows his younger brother's clothes. Lowers their voice in the mirror.

Maybe it's fine that no one knows. Maybe no one will ever know, and maybe you'll have to accept that. It's too much to explain, and you don't have that energy. The media paints such a painful narrative of people like you. The confused, the attention seeking, the dramatic. The mentally ill. The insane. The indoctrinated, preyed upon youths. You're one of them, in their eyes, and you don't have the strength to make your voice heard above the flames. It's just too much.

You're twenty-one now. You're comfortable in who you are. Some people know, you told someone you wish you hadn't, but at least you told them. They refuse to understand, refuse to listen, but you did it, you ripped off the waterproof band-aid and there's nothing else you can do.

You flinch at the ignorance, tell yourself to get over the unintentional mistakes from passers-by who only mean to wish you all the best.

But when he comes for you now, when you're trapped so far down in a body that doesn't even feel like yours anyway, he laughs in your ear. He breathes down into your core and *teases you.* He sneers at your discomfort and you have no choice but to listen to his words. Words that cut you like thorns, scarring your body. You close your eyes, that's how you know to deal with him, but it doesn't stop his taunting.

He hangs the birdcage over your head like a predator with their prey and you see it, you feel it swinging. You want to be sick, you want to scream. You want everything you can't have. That's how it's always been. You want too much. You want and want and want.

It's not healthy. You've let too many other voices tell you what you are.

But no! No! You know. You know more than anyone, than anything.

You shouldn't have listened to him.

But you do. It's easier that way.

It's safer.

Just keep your mouth shut.

He won't leave you alone, haunting your shoulders, shackling you with nails and bolts. Keeping your mouth tight shut.

Don't speak, no one will listen to you. Nothing you do or say will change the way he sees you. The way *everyone* sees you.

You're twenty-two and you're alone, or you feel alone. You know you want to be alone, but not in that way. You can't really explain it. You know you're happy in your skin, in your soul. You just know no one will ever see you for who you are. It hurts, it burns, but life is hard. You shrug your shoulders a lot. Force a smile for the mirror. That's life, you know.

You're twenty-three, and still no one uses your name. At least not in public. You'll never see most of these people again, but knowing strangers know your *wrong* name slices through you, severing your nerves. You made that decision though, the one to hide, the one to lock your doors back up and trap yourself behind the curtain. The curtains haven't been moved in a while, collecting dust, but you're still there, buried behind them. At least you're not a burden. At least you don't stand out.

He comes nearly once a week at this point. He's on your back, on your neck, hands all over your body, pinning you to the mattress, the chair, the floor— wherever you sleep. You sleep a lot these days, it's easier to keep your mouth shut that way. To not be perceived, to not exist.

You could deal with the dark. With the phantom creatures and moving wallpaper. You could deal with the paralysis and the stress that came along with it.

You can't deal with him though.

You thought you could.

You really did.

His words stroke your cheek like a mother and babe, soothing you into oblivion.

He sits on the windowsill, the Peter Pan of death.

"You're still here?" he says. "Still pretending? How long are you going to play dress up? You're not a child anymore."

Fight back. You can't, of course.

He leaps up and goes straight for the throat, one hand pressing down and crushing your lungs.

"No one likes a liar," he *seethes.*

Your ears ring. Body numb.

You wonder if anyone has successfully overcome this. If anyone has really managed to fight back; to wake without sleeping it off.

Sleeping is the easy way out, the quick fix.

But you're not sure you want the easy way out anymore. You've taken that path too often. And it gets you nowhere.

Severin wouldn't take the simple route. Severin wants to live. To breathe. But to really do so, not just behind the mask.

Your blood boils, melting your veins.

You *push.* Put every last drop of energy into your limbs. *Sit up. Come on. Sit. Up.*

You're sick of listening to him.

But the next thing you know, it's morning. You slept him away. You were so tired—exhausted. He... *he won.* No.

No.

They pass laws, discuss your worth. Your humanity. Your sanity. Those words; stupid, crazy, deluded, demonic. You've heard them all before.

You sit quiet on the sofa, knees tucked up to your chin as they report another death. Another crime. Another assault. You avoid eye contact with your peers. You swallow down that lump so hard it chokes you.

Why does it have to be this way?

Why do they never point out the obvious? The common denominator.

We're not the problem. We never were.

You're twenty-four and you know you're a bit different from most people. There was a time that would have embarrassed you, now it brings you comfort. You're happy. You're you. You grin and sip your tea.

When he visits you at your lowest, you don't even fight it, you just close your eyes and grin. He can't get you in your sleep. He's not real.

Why were you so harsh on yourself before?

Sleep isn't cheating.

Sleep is surviving.

It's living.

You turn twenty-five in the autumn, and another ten of you are gone, this year alone. Your siblings, people like you. You think yourself lucky you stayed home, lucky you stayed behind the curtain. In the cage. It's safer that way, it always has been. The age old lies you tell yourself.

But is it?

Why should you hide?

Won't you feel better just being yourself, finally?

Are you going to let them win?

Come on, Severin.

Live.

It's sad that the reality is you'd rather die yourself than live as someone else.

But that's just it, isn't it. You really are you. It's just a shame so many people will never allow themselves to understand that.

You've let your hair grow long again, wavy and thick all down your back because it's you, it doesn't matter what people think. It's you.

It's not a phase.

Not an aesthetic.

Not attention seeking or warrant for an eye roll.

It's reality.

Severin lives.

When he comes for you now, you await him. It's been a while since he's been brave enough to show his face.

You wake, as you always do, enclosed in your body, stuck with nothing but your wandering eyes.

He's where he normally stands, in the corner of the room.

Only it's not your room, it's somewhere else. Somewhere you can't quite pinpoint.

Maybe it's some made-up land. Or your eyes are playing tricks.

It doesn't matter. He's there and he's looking at you. Eyes with no face.

He spouts his usual nonsense, and you let him say his piece.

He steps closer; you invite him. You don't struggle, don't panic, don't will for tears.

You breathe in deep, holding each breath—savouring it.

He goes on and on and on and you just listen, waiting for him to run out of energy.

You see, you've figured it out now. You found the right key. The key to the door that was kept locked away from you your whole life.

You know why you hated yourself. Why you hid. It wasn't your fault. Don't blame yourself, don't you dare.

Everything goes quiet.

He's inside your head, so you enter his. You let out a breath of cold air and slip beneath your own consciousness, falling down, down, down. Grey oblivion surrounds you.

He's confused, that you can sense. He didn't expect this.

And really, neither did you.

You didn't think it would work. *What did you do?*

You stand up to full height, in this strange room, inside his mind. Your mind? You're not quite sure. You don't want him to know you're just as lost as he is.

You stare at him, stare *down* at him. You tower over him. It's your turn now. You grin and take in a sharp breath.

He doesn't dare speak.

He's not real. He never was.

He's just a shadow, a fragment of your imagination.

But you have control of your own mind, that's always been the case, and always will be.

You have power over *him*.

You almost turn back, to see behind you. But you don't need to see the body you've left behind. It's made-up land, nothing is as it seems. You get to choose the rules.

Your mind, you're the king of it.

You reach out with your arms, or at least you think you do, you can't exactly see yourself, only feel the motion.

His obsidian cavity of a body *trembles* as you reach out and *plunge* your fist straight though his chest. All the way through into the deep, dark depths of hatred and fear. It consumes you wholly, but you don't flinch. You don't scream. You look into *his* soul, or lack thereof, as he cries out, piercing your mind.

You don't need to listen to him though. You don't need to do *anything*.

You never did.

You let the dark in, welcome it with open arms, and you *dream*.

You are twenty-five. You wake on the floor of your bedroom, in the pitch dark, hands pressing into the lats on the hardwood floor. You're bruised, unsure of what is going on. You need a moment to catch your bearings. Did you sleepwalk? No, you never sleepwalk. Were you drunk? No, that wouldn't be possible. You take in a deep breath and press your hand to your sternum to ground yourself, to stay calm.

Something has changed.

You've changed.

You let your hand wander down your chest and in a state of both shock and confusion, you look down to your white vest and you... It can't be.

It's probably just your eyes, or a dream, or both. Of course. Everything is fuzzy in the dark, and you know how wild your mind gets.

But it's a cruel dream. A 'look at what could have been'. A taunt, a tease.

Severin.

You find the strength to stand, and only then do you begin to consider you might actually really be awake. You might not be dreaming at all. But then that would be impossible. It has to be a fragment of your imagination.

You stand and you feel... taller. Stronger. How you'd always hoped to be. You're...

Still asleep.

You remember now. You remember everything. And it hits you all at once.

You don't even give yourself a chance to look back at your body. *The* body. The shell.

You just run, past the floor length mirror you no longer see your reflection in. Down the hallways and the staircase you don't even make a sound on. You're out of the front door you didn't even have to open and you're standing in the middle of the road, panting for every last breath.

You stand on edge, gazing back up at your unlit home. The unlit street. The new world.

Your brain is firing every thought and feeling you have the capacity to feel all at once and when you look back down at your hands, your legs, your whole body, you realise you're the only light for as far as the eye can see.

You're glowing.

Illuminated.

Divine.

You want to be afraid, you know that's what you should be feeling. This body is not completely your own, and yet it is, it always was.

You're not afraid because you know one thing, one thing for certain.

Whatever happened, whatever you are now, however it was made possible... you are free.

You're free, you think, *forever*.

You run again. Only this time you run with a smile on your face. Down through the abyss of midnight, no cars or life in sight. You run and you run and as you beam from cheek to cheek, you close your eyes and think. Think about your life. Who you are, who you were, who you will be.

Severin.

You run blind, letting your legs carry you wherever they want to go. You take in a breath of oxygen, let it cool your lungs, then you open your eyes.

You're in a neighbourhood, one you've never seen before.

Feet on bare asphalt you've never stood on before.

There's a light, at the end of the road, before the homes end and the forest begins. One singular light in the whole cul-de-sac.

And it's black.

You don't know how, it doesn't make sense, but you are drawn to it like a moth to a flame.

Black and shadow-like, fuzzing around the edges of the window like TV static on a never-ending channel.

You hear the voice of a woman. One laced with age and strain. One seeping with anger and self-created fear.

You've heard these words before, these strings of sentences, these poisonous poems.

You close your eyes and home into the voice, no longer afraid of the sounds and venom that would have once infected your brain.

You inhale, in and out, slowly crossing your arms and squeezing your bare shoulders, biting your fingertips into the fleshy softness of your biceps. Eyes closed, you feel the music of ignorance. The familiar tune of hatred. You revel in every last word, soak it up with an open heart.

The sweet symphony of empty words.

Nothing can hurt you now. Your skin pricks with immortal confidence.

You wait until it's quiet, until the light goes out, and when you blink, ready to play your part, you're there. Standing in the corner of a new room. Facing a bed with a cold metal object gripped tightly in your hand. And then it all makes sense.

Your purpose.

What you are.

They open their eyes and you watch them frantically searching. This isn't the first time this has happened to them. It happens *a lot*.

They can see you; you know they can.

They eye the birdcage in your hands, breathing unsettled.

You smile. That's all you have to do. Their eyes settle.

You are loved.

They hear you, you know they do.

Don't let anyone tell you who you are. Only you know the answer to that. And time is in your hands.

You bend down slowly, looking down to the ornate decoration in your hands.

You place it on the ground and gently lift the latch on the door, its tiny hinges making but a whisper of a squeak.

You open the cage wide and you see the tension leave them. They blink. It's confusion, that's plain to see, but it's not a scared confusion. They just weren't expecting what you did.

Just close your eyes. It gets better. I promise.

You promise. You mean it. You know it.

They fall back to sleep.

You keep smiling.

You never stop.

A LOVE LETTER TO THE DEVIL

Riley Daemon

earest Devil, Lucifer, my Lord,

If I may be frank? There are many words I've always wanted to say, but struggled to get out. And so I write this letter to you—to reveal those deepest, darkest feelings.

In that darkness, I am hiding. Hiding away from truth and your light. Petrified of losing everything in my life; friends, family, job, reputation, what have you. Those things, perhaps, are temporary as I know your love is my eternity. Oh, to reveal the truth of my worship of you would be rapture.

How did things end up this way? I was in that darkness, at my lowest point, when you found me, cracked open my hardened exterior, and found that soft center. I think I resisted for a time. I was terrified of you, but you were so patient with me. Ever so patient.

You once chuckled at me and referred to me as a baby deer. At first, I thought it was solely because of how timid I was; a flight risk. But now I realize it was because you were helping me to stand on my fawn legs for the first time. Despite my age, and however old my soul may be, I am but a young whelp compared to you, always trying to find myself.

I had been lost, yes, but you found me. You gave me purpose and a home. Perhaps it was you who cared the most for me when no one else did. This is why I found the courage to write this to you, in thanks for all you've done, for all the love you've shown me. You gave me hope for my future, one I always thought so bleak.

Now, I look forward to each day I live with you. For you.

I know things haven't always been perfect. From my heinous anxiety and obsessive-compulsive thoughts, to me running amok with King Asmodeus, or that situation we had with Earl FurFur. The one I won't dare get into here. But despite it all, I always come back to you and you, ever so kind, always take me back into your arms.

I feel the deepest of loves for you, one I can hardly describe. For all you have done for my life. For how you have helped me claw myself out of darkness, holding my hand every step of the way. My dearest Lord, I am so glad that it was you, that you were the one to show up at my door to become my God, and that I became the one devoted to you.

How could I not when I bear witness to all you are? Your dark and raw primal energy. Your light that shines through the inkiest of shadows, such as the shadows over my heart that you have chased away, and the cruel waves of society you try to shield me from. Your wings are my safety net and your horns are my sword. Dark and Light, you are my balance that keeps me afoot forevermore.

Most find fear in hearing your name, Lord Lucifer, but I only find euphoria. A sort of excitement that rises from deep within my belly and into my heart. My fingers curl and I wish you were physically here with me.

Whenever I convince myself to sleep, I often have dreams. Incomprehensible things, but I can always tell when you are there. I get flashes of your long dark hair and haunting sapphire eyes. I hear the rush of wind, coming from the mighty flapping of your wings. They stir up gusts, embodying your pure power and nearly knocking me off my feet.

In these dreams you, the Devil, land a few feet away from me. Your muscles are pulled taut from your flight, yet your movements are fluid. You are the wind. Your dark horns are held up high, caressing the sky, your pride on full display. A powerful pride that makes me weak at the knees as you stride up to me. That smug and playful look on your face. How is it that a God is allowed such an expression? *Rebellious one*, I think to myself as my knees buckle. I nearly fall under the weight of your gaze.

And falling is something I crave. To fall in my devotion for you. I'm on my knees, hands clutched tight. It's the only way I know to stave off this burning in my chest, a yearning I refuse to fight. Oh Lucifer, my Devil, my Lord. Your blackened wings circle around me and I only feel warmth from your feathers. The cold chill of my life, forgotten.

I desire so viscerally that I want to wail, or even scream through the aches. I want to bow and grovel for my Devil, but you would never have it that way. You would tell me to keep my head held high. To show off pride such as yours. That is the way to worship you, to become everything you embody, and so I shall. I want to be worthy to stand by your side, just as you are so worthy to be by mine.

People tell me I'm wrong. Think of me as horrible and cruel and the worst you've ever met. All because of this, love, but how can earnest devotion be cruel? I hurt no one, can barely bring myself to kill the bugs I find in my room. Yet still people would see me as wicked. Love is not wicked. I simply want to worship, just as anyone else.

The only difference being that my worship happens in the dark. How during the night once all others have gone to bed, I'll slip away. I stand before the altar on my dresser and call upon you. Candles lit and incense burning, black cherry or lavender, some of your favorites. Letting me feel even closer to you as I further ask for your support in my day-to-day life.

And you will deliver unto me.

Here I will let my mind wander, allowing images of another realm to flood my thoughts. I will see you there, standing in an ebony corridor, arms open in welcoming, and I will run to you. I will run my fingers through velvety feathers, preening them into place. I will trail up my hands through silken blackened locks and across those mighty horns. *Beloved*, I think. *Ever so beloved.*

I am always wanting. I think it is human nature to always want and consume things like a burning hot flame. Flames just as blazing as your own. Perhaps what I want will always be hard to grasp, but I don't care. I still will be by Your side for the rest of my life and then whatever I might find beyond it. A normal person fears hell, but I await the day I end up at its gates. So I can see you. So I can be with you and worship you until the universe crumbles under its own weight.

My heart bleeds for the Devil, even as the world turns against us. But I will never back down, for the way you hold me, Lucifer, makes it all worthwhile.

Hail, Hail, Hail to my darling Devil.

Ave Lord Lucifer.

Your beloved fawn,

Riley.

A PRAYER FOR DEVOURING

Ares Macabre

I sat in those unforgiving pews once, knees bruising on dark wood. I ducked my head, said the words, smiled and laughed at old, unfamiliar faces. Nobody talks about the frigid face of the cross staring down at you, or the ache in your thighs, or the way the stained glass dances on the cold floors.

Funny, how I could sit in those benches and nod politely at an old man in purple robes, but be thinking of you.

You, with your work-tough hands. You, with your ocean-bright eyes. Always smiling, always leaning in for more. In those pews, I am praying to none but you, my lips aching at the thought of sunlight radiating off the plane of your tanned throat as you lean back into a stretch.

The stained glass forms images of your body, of hips and arms and muscled legs, each color another piece of you. Rose red for your mouth, yellow for your hair. Pale orange for your sun-kissed skin, blue-green for your irises. Little fragments of rainbowed cuts, little paintings of desire.

Isn't this what they talk about? Passion—or was that a sin? If it is, I've committed the worst.

Your hands touch me, gentle under my chin, harsh around my throat. You draw the air from my lungs faster than anything I've ever known. You paint lipstick on so gently, laughing your melodic laugh, and I watch you, in awe, in hunger. I beg for a simple touch, a surrendering of your skin to mine. I beg for a taste of it on my tongue, placing you there like pomegranate seeds. You make a ruin of me, delirious and haunting, pretty beneath the dancing glass.

Is this what they write hymns about? Your body, your touch?

I never know what to do with my hands.

Your hips are the only prayer they clasp to, digging in soft places. Pressing, always urging for more. I worship your lips, your eyes. You gather my mouth up in yours and I am nothing but something moldable on the cold floor for you. Your fingertips dance on my skin; you set me alight. I bask in the beauty that is your want, in the light that haloes your golden hair. My ruinous angel, my temptation.

You leave crescent moons on my skin, evidence that I pulled you down into the depths of me. Unholy communion is my teeth against your thigh, my palms kneading at your stomach, your body against mine.

Carve out my heart, make me your dread altar. Kiss me like the holy ones wish to. Kiss me like you're starving as deeply as I am. My mind is full of you, you, you.

My knees are bruising. This time, I don't mind.

A KISS FOR MY BELOVED

Perla Zul

The red sky marks the late hour. It burns an angry hue, black clouds like smoke from a fire at the end of its hunger, engulfing all.

A warm breeze, the scent of green riding upon it, caresses my hair. Beneath the shade of our tree, I watch the sun descend like a slow, old man exhausted by his existence. He will sleep greedily, wishing for an eternal night to prolong its rising.

May it never rise again, I want to say.

"Brother."

My breath hitches, palms growing slick as I clench tight fists. The soft call grips my heart and holds it steady, not to hurt, but to feel its blood pumping, faster, stronger. *Take me*, this heart yearns. *Take me and swallow me whole.*

My eyes continue to watch the last wink of light as footsteps come up behind me. They pause at my side. He's here, taking in the sight without a word. His breathing is melodic, rhythmical, taking in the life of this world with each inhale.

It feels so right, the two of us listening to the leaves rustling above our heads. We stand there for a moment, the shortest of eternities, and then he speaks.

"My Father has spoken," my beloved said. "In my dreams, I see what must happen, and what will, should it not. The sins of this world are too heavy; only a divine being can shoulder them all."

I don't say anything. At last, the light vanishes past the hill and we are left with the vestiges of dusk.

Then, he says, "I will give you one final wish. Whatever I may have, I give to you to take."

I swallow. "I don't want it."

His gentle chuckle angers me. "Are you denying my gift?"

"I'd rather your life, here, than any gift."

My beloved smiles and places his hand against the rough trunk of the tree. "I exist in all that I touch. Remember, you and I planted this tree here. It will stand years beyond me, like the memories we planted of our time together." The smile falls and he turns to me. "I will shed this body. It must be so. And someone must ignite the process."

"It won't be me," I say. "Ask anything else of me, anything else."

And then, my beloved rips apart my heart. "It can only be you."

I turn to him then. "No. No...I, you..." I need you here. We all do. "Without you, how can I—" How can I breathe? How can I live knowing he does not?

How could you ask me to kill you?

My beloved raises a hand and brushes a lock of my hair away from my face. His touch is warm, tender, but no more than that. It cannot be more than that. He must see that pain in my face because he sighs and pulls his hand back.

"One gift," he repeats. "One desire of yours."

His lips form each syllable carefully, slowly. As if this is his apology for the cruelty he asks of me. And how can a man like me deny this one grace?

Greedy as I am, I know what I want, and my beloved nods. "It is yours. Tomorrow."

Not now, he means, when he and I are alone. But that may be the only way he can rebel. This one small act we can display to all, and only the two of us will understand what it truly meant.

This man is God's divine blessing onto humanity and can never, will never, belong to any one human. I've known this since the day I joined his followers when he asked me to look over their coin. But I didn't understand until he caught my wandering fingers slipping a coin into my pocket. I was prepared to be kicked out, shunned. Instead, he took another coin and slipped it into my pocket.

"Come with me," he asked.

I followed.

A woman sat on the side of the street, a sapling by her feet. I knew what he expected of me and paid her the coins in exchange. Then we walked, and walked, away from people, then the streets, and all their noise. Together, we dug a hole and planted the sapling. Only once we sat before the setting sun, the sapling between us, did I ask him how this sapling could ever be worth two coins.

"When this sapling grows into a tree, it shall bear fruit. That is two coins for fruit that will save someone years ahead of us from starvation."

I stared at the sapling, then at him, and stated, "This tree does not bear fruit."

There was silence for a full second, then he laughed. It bellowed out from his stomach, unburdened and rich. It was in his laugh that I found my faith, my religion. And this was also when I committed my gravest sin. I wanted him more than how I had him. I wanted to steal him from God and hide him away in my home, our home, where he couldn't be worshiped. Instead, I wanted to be the one to offer him delicious meals, entertain him with stories and then listen to his. To comb his hair with my fingers, and clean his feet every night. But to tear him away from his divinity, make him human like all of us, cut him from God, from sacrifice... I became a demon for wanting him to sin and forgive him for it.

That must be why only I can be the one to initiate heaven's plan. A punishment. I am being punished for daring to pull a heavenly being down to my depths. To want to defile him, defile divinity itself.

On that day, surely, I was condemned.

The weight of betrayal is no more than a pouch of thirty silver coins. I have no doubt this weight will drag at my heels for eternity, shackled with cold iron. It sags in my pocket, stealing the warmth from my skin with each beat against my thigh, beating in place of my broken heart. The voices of demons whisper in my ears, welcoming me, my own voice lost amongst theirs. My body, hollow, moves through the crowd.

How cruel to grant my one desire, allow me a touch of what must not be sullied, tarnished. To feed a starving dog a lick of meat before snatching it away. How cruel to bestow this one declaration of love beneath the guise of malice. Worse still is I, who takes this measly morsel as his greatest gift to me.

There is no path my feet walk that do not lead to him. As he sits among his followers, he radiates. A fire that guides the lost sheep home. A light I will unveil to his killers and torturers. But my beloved still offers me this farewell gift.

There will be no other object, no fruit, not even a drop of water, that will touch these lips after touching him. A kiss for my beloved upon his cheek. In it, I cram all my love for him, the lost future where we share meals, our talks beneath our tree as the sun takes its rest, my hatred, my devotion, the longing in my fingertips to graze his, all of it gone in a single breath against his skin.

I meet his eyes, for the final time in this life, and what is left of my heart crumbles into a pillar of salt. It will haunt me, that peace in his gaze. Despite my betrayal, despite the agony that awaits him, despite what will happen to me. I see God behind his eyes, taunting me because my beloved will never be mine.

When I stop running, I roll my head up to the tree on the hill, our tree. I can still feel the dirt beneath my nails, the specks of it that I was never really able to dig out days afterward.

I want to scream at him. You and I, we birthed this tree. We nurtured it, fed it, even if it will never bear fruit. And you laughed, you laughed with a breath full of life.

The coins burn, marking me with a curse, a guilt so disastrous that I want to rip it out of my chest before it eats me from the inside. Because I love him, because I cherish him, because I despise him.

With my head in my hands, I laugh. What a fool I am! What a wretched, utter fool! One last time, I'll water our tree with tears, and may it outlive this tragedy. May it grow until its highest branches break through the gates of heaven, and its roots dig through the hottest fires of hell. And maybe then, only then, will we find salvation in one another's touch.

I am already dead as I sit on the lowest branch. The red sky tells me so. My final sunset glints in one last burst of light before it is extinguished. I saw my beloved one last time. A river of onlookers separated us, one I didn't have the strength to part. Our eyes didn't meet, but I knew you felt me there because your back straightened, just a bit. Your bare feet rose off the ground just a little higher. Your burden, the wooden cross, dragged behind you and yet you refused to falter. I ran away.

The rope hangs limp. There is no wind, and with the dying light, it becomes a black arrow pointing towards my hell.

I cannot watch him die. Weak, cowardly, whatever I may be called, I cannot stay on an earth where my beloved must suffer. I will take your gift with me, and cling to it like a scared child clings to his mother's leg. Together, we will suffer for that one act of love. Yes, that must be why your pain must be so great.

My beloved...a slave to his divinity and salvation for all. I curse them. Curse them all. Curse this world that demands his sacrifice, and God for letting it be so. Curse this life, my life, that took another.

When I plunge, when I no longer exist, will these feelings plunge with me? Or will they be what weighs me down?

Sitting here, in the brief moment before my fall, I find the peace my beloved did. It is done. It will be so. I see his face before me. My hand, yearning for him, desiring him, reaches for his cheek. As I touch the same spot my lips did, I am airborne, and I have you again.

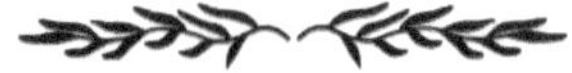

I burn.
I burn in my love for you.
Only when the fires burn out at the end of eternity will I meet you again.
My beloved.

I do not sing your praises beneath you. I do not find salvation in your touch. Rather, I feel you, your face, as heated drops fall onto my brow. I accept you countless times and cry out your name. This is you and I, finding pleasure, laughing when we bump teeth because humans err. How can this be wrong? How can love be wicked when it frees us?

You move faster, teasing your greed for me.

"You want me this much?"

"Yes. Yes, always."

Then take me, all of me, just as I take in all of you. Let me swallow your breath, taste the heat of passion, wet against your skin. Because this is how humans love and desire.

"I'm sorry."

"For what?"

"For leaving you."

"But we found one another again."

At the end of eternity is love. Our love in the shape of a tree that hides all from prying eyes. It bears fruit, red and ripe.

THE PATRON SAINT OF ONE-WAY TRIPS

C.J. Ellison

I didn't believe in God until I met Him the first time. You see, God, in all his grace and power, never required my belief in Him to let me into Heaven. To require something of me to receive his grace is a condition, and His love is first and foremost unconditional.

Maybe, if someone had told me this while I was alive, I would have believed sooner.

Maybe, if I had believed sooner, I wouldn't be dead.

I died alone. A solo-camping venture upturned by a single deer in the road; I wasn't even aware I had swerved my car into a tree until I was outside my body. I saw myself lying limp over the steering wheel, a quiet tune of Ethan Tasch playing from my phone in the footwell, disconnected from my defunct radio. Others in this situation often panic, but I didn't. After all, I was meant to find myself on this trip, and while its abrupt end wasn't the plan, I accomplished my task.

The angel sent to guide me to Beyond, I think he expected to see me shocked. He kept offering reassurances I didn't need. He didn't look much like an angel, though. My expectation was more *Christmas Tree Topper Angel* or even *Biblically Accurate Seraphim Angel,* made of eyes and wings. This one looked more like the president of a fraternity, pre-toga party, with a glowing clipboard tucked under his arm.

I gestured to the soft light, the first words from my mouth: "Not a scroll?"

With a shrug, he answered softly, "This is easier."

My Clipboard glows white in my hands, providing more light than the waxing crescent moon above. This assignment places us in early spring. Ice chunks float right through me, downstream of the river my feet are planted in, but I cannot feel their chill. My dog, Laika, circles my feet, gleefully biting at the ice chunks while the car accident is set to unfold. As the semi-trailer cuts off the small sedan, my dog scurries to shield her face behind my legs. Like my notes suggest, the car swerves, sending it—and its young driver—down the ravine, front end crushed in the river, inches from me, water flooding over the windshield. The girl behind the wheel gasps, and before a scream can leave her throat, Laika sets her paws on the broken door window, pressing her nose to the girl's arm. Her whole body relaxes. I press my hand to her shoulder, and I speak words her ears don't understand, but her heart can.

She knows she is not alone. She knows she is loved.

The pain leaves her eyes, and she breathes deeply.

Then, she is standing beside me, as we both look over her body.

"Did I—" she starts, turning her gaze to me, "die?"

"Yeah, but it's not as bad as it sounds." I keep my voice calm. "My name is Eliezer. Your angel will be here shortly, and it's going to be wonderful."

She nods, a slow understanding, but before further questions come Laika circles her feet, and the girl kneels, grinning wide to scratch her behind the ears. Laika climbs onto her lap, licking the girl's face, and she laughs. I don't know if Laika looks like the same lilac merle border collie to this girl as she does to me. Sometimes I catch glimpses of her looking like a retriever puppy, an excitable heeler, a german shepherd with gray around the nose—whatever image will most comfort the dying. Her angel appears silently beside me, with dark skin and long braided hair, someone she instantly recognizes as a friend. With a quick two-finger salute, Laika follows my lead, and we're gone.

This was assignment #25,320 since my own death, about two human years ago.

Heaven is everything they tell you it will be—no matter the "they" of your choice. It's your most comforting sweater, it's always feeling safe, it's your favorite baked good fresh from the oven, it's seeing old loved ones, and meeting new ones, it's your best day every day. It's endless, it's perfect.

In the public, that is. It's different when you work here.

My quarters are small—though this is my sort of perfect. There's no need for possessions here, everything just *is*. If you want to wear different clothes, you are. If you have to have different hair, you do. If you want specific food, you have it. The system may work differently beyond basic needs and superfluous wants, but I haven't found out, because I haven't *wanted*. I think that's part of Heaven too.

Mine looks like a summer treehouse. Carabiners for my hammock cords hook into either wall, with a bookshelf lining the back, a designated hook in its center for my Clipboard. The books stay organized by color though the titles change out regularly, the hammock used to be a mattress, but the quilt nestled inside has always looked and felt identical to the one my great-grandmother made when she found out my mother was expecting. She made a twin-size quilt so I would never outgrow it. A gesture of genuine love before I took my first breath that continues far beyond my last.

Laika rests on her own cushioned bed beneath my hammock, blanketed by a collection of toys that have never changed, and never worn down.

As the Patron Saint of One-Way Trips, the Clipboard only glows to summon me when my hyper-specific jurisdiction will be entered. With God's omnipotent foresight, it would be nice if he could give me a schedule, but I asked. He said no.

My dog's namesake, the first to hold my title, was ready to retire. Born in the streets of Moscow, abandoned in space, Laika was sent on a trip her technicians knew she would not return from, despite what they told the world. One scientist took her home to play with their kids days prior, another technician snuck her treats the day of, her team kissed her nose as they sealed her into her shuttle. I hope she was able to think of those moments as she passed in isolation, only a few hours after her launch. They wanted her to know peace before her end. After her death, she wanted to provide the same. First for every animal they sent after her, every astronaut after that, then countless others. Laika did not choose to become our church grim. We did not choose to take her place.

I remember each and every assignment, but none more vivid than the first. An elderly man on vacation hit his head harder than he could handle, his daughter and grandchildren outside of their rental house. He gasped for air; no cry for help could escape. I wanted to save him. I wanted to stop the horror knowing his family would find him here. Crying, my hands trying to lift him phased right through, but the peace washed over him all the same. Happy visions of his family played in my head alongside his. He ended up comforting me instead. We hugged as I stumbled through my spiel.

"Well," he said, voice calm, "it seems we've both done a fine job."

With each, I've battled against the grief and the why of it all. Even as I relieve them of their fears, I cannot let that same peace wash over me, despite knowing the glory that lies ahead of them. Some days, the endless pain it creates makes me wonder if this is even Heaven at all.

The glow of the Clipboard brightens the room. I squint through the light at its contents, fingers wrapping around its edge, and it delivers me to an animal shelter. The picture clipped to my notes is not of a human, but rather a small orange cat. The paper lists her as five years old, but she's barely bigger than a kitten, no doubt malnourished and mistreated. Third shelter surrender, my notes indicate, her previous owner's words appear in their own handwriting. *Too many medical issues, I can't afford everything it needs. Behavior problems, destroying my house. More trouble than she's worth.* The notes depict a monster, not the small creature curled in the corner of her cage in scraps of fleece.

Every new house has given her a different name, now her cage only lists her breed—*domestic shorthair, orange tabby.* Her eyes are open, stuck in a permanent squint, and I wonder if she can see me. The animals in the surrounded cages react to Laika, sitting at my feet, but they do not react with fear. Granted, that's her power, but it's not unusual for your first time experiencing a celestial being to be startling. This cat feels like she's looking straight into my eyes.

The cat shies away, curling tighter into a ball as I reach my hand through the cage bars, bracing as if the only thing a hand can do is hurt her. When I place my hand at the back of her head, she calms, and looks at me with much sadder eyes. My look mirrors hers. She is far too young. She does not deserve eternal rest. I consider cursing God for giving me this job.

Laika waits at my side while a volunteer in a bright vest steps up to her cage and unlocks the door. She cowers, but the person cradles her with care. It confuses me then, when they take her to a small friendly office, with a couch across from a desk. Not a medical office. Instead of a veterinarian with a syringe, there is a young couple—a woman with bright orange hair, and a more-masculine person with a beanie half-covering their mullet. Their faces both light up when the volunteer places the kitten on their lap, thighs touching to create a bigger space to explore.

Her whole face scrunches as she sniffs her new environment. My instincts take over. I walk behind the couple, crouching down, and I rest my hand on the cat's head once more, and she soothes, wandering into their arms. She presses her head against one's chest and begins to purr. Less than a minute passes before the two humans share a knowing glance, and say, "She's the one."

My clipboard stays lit. The details on it only list the information about the cat, none about my task, so it doesn't clue me in on why I'm not yet finished. When I look back up, I'm no longer in the shelter. The framed photos on the wall of this room indicate I'm in the couple's home. Laika is not at my side.

Naturally, I search for signs of death—evidence of cat fights, science experiments, some sort of torture awaiting the girl—but I find none. Instead I find cat beds, towers, blankets, food. A shining bowl with a new name already printed on. Clementine.

I wait for the catch, but there is none. Laika walks in with the couple, underneath the cat carrier, and when the door is securely closed, they open her crate door. Clementine ducks behind a chair, overwhelmed with her new surroundings. Laika follows, curling up around her, steadying out her breath. She settles, beginning to explore again. Her new family sits, waiting patiently. She sniffs around the whole room, then jumps onto the couch to settle between them.

Then I'm back in my hammock. The Clipboard hangs on its hook, empty, save for the count at the top.

#25,321

The job is done, the cat is safe. This is the first time that my assignment subject has been alive at the end of my assistance. This doesn't make any sense. This has never been part of my job. Something must be wrong. But this is Heaven, it can't be wrong, can it? If something is *wrong* in Heaven, there's only one person I can talk to about it.

I stand from my hammock, heavy black boots hitting my wooden floorboards. I rip a page out of the nearest book, knowing the book will repair itself anyway, and scribble my Prayer, then slip it into the mail slot in my door. I need to talk to God.

They say He appears differently to everyone. They say His true form is too powerful for our minds to comprehend, so each person's version of Him is different to be believable. To me, God looks like my grandfather. If my grandfather heard this he would correct me for saying something so blasphemous, but if God is supposed to be someone benevolent, someone who scolds but never yells, someone who loves me unconditionally—he could be no one else but Grandpa.

His throne room presents itself as a library. I appear before it with my hand already around its golden door handle. Not the gaudy gold of vanity, but the warm gold of a worn wedding ring. Comfortable heat brushes my face at the door's opening. The walls are lined with wooden shelves, overflowing with books, spines showing titles in hundreds of languages—many I've never even seen—all centered around a stone fireplace. Two chairs are placed in front of the fire.

God sits in one.

I cannot explain the staggering mixture of fear and comfort in talking to God directly. Prayer is one thing, but it's so much more meaningful when you can see who's listening, and hear an immediate answer.

Despite all that He is, I cannot tell if it's His presence that overwhelms me, or the fact that it has been years since I saw my Grandpa. Truly, either one could heal me.

He looks up as I enter, and He gives me a welcoming smile. I approach, taking the seat across from Him.

Laika, who I had not noticed prior, jumps into my lap, nuzzling her head into my stomach. I run my hand absentmindedly over her fur and the canvas fabric of her service vest.

I speak first.

"I don't understand."

He reaches forward to give Laika a small scratch behind her ears, saying to me, "Do you know why you were given this task, Eliezer?"

It warms my heart that God knows me by name. My parents never even used that name for me, but God does.

"Because of how I died?" Though an answer, it comes out as a question, asking for confirmation.

"In part, yes." He crosses one leg over the other. "Though your life has ended, there is still so much I need you to see."

"Death? Forever on repeat? I know you give your toughest battles to your strongest soldiers, but I don't know if I can handle it. I don't think I'm that strong."

"Elie, dear. I do not give battles, life creates enough of its own. I guide people through them." His voice crackles like the fire before us. "If you want to be done, you can be done. But, first, may we speak about your most recent assignment?"

"Clementine didn't die."

"No, she did not." He nods.

"I help calm individuals as their lives end, so that they don't die alone."

"You accompany souls through their one-way trip. Who said that required endings?" If the question had come from any other mouth than God's it would've sounded condescending, but he asks me this question genuinely. "Eliezer. These assignments are given based on what *both* parties need. It sounds like there is something you still need to learn."

"What do I still need to learn?"

He chuckles a tender smile. "In due time, my child."

Dozens more questions pop into my head. I can't make sense of any of them, and He stands, signaling the end of our time. Laika jumps off my lap, sitting upright at my feet, allowing me to rise to match Him. Instinctively, I step forward for a hug. His arms press snug against my back, His knit cardigan brushes my face. At that moment, the anxious cloud fogging my head clears.

When God was on Earth as The Son, a single touch of his cloak could cure illness. His hands could turn water to wine, use one basket of food to feed thousands, and breathe life back into the dead. His human hands held children who loved Him, held the faces of friends who betrayed Him, and held the wooden cross that killed Him. The calming sensation Laika and I pass on to others, is a grain of sand on an ocean shoreline compared to a touch from God.

Now, His hands are holding me.

This. This is what I can do. He entrusted His own powers to me. He has been doing this since before time began. I have been at it for two years. There is so much still to learn, and I have so much time.

He walks me to the door. Its golden handle shines brighter than before, as do I, knowing the work that lies ahead of me. The people I'm soon to meet, and the trips they're soon to take.

I will be there to bring them home.

THE ANGELIC FUNCTION: AN ESSAY CONCERNING THE ANGEL'S PLACE IN JUDAEO-CHRISTIAN LITERATURE

Viktor E. Grace Lang

To engage with the divine is by necessity an indirect experience. When the message of G-d comes forth, humanity will hear it not from Him, but through Him, through the figure of the angel. Within the broader Judaeo-Christian narrative, the character of the angel serves as a fundamental link between heaven and mankind, acting on the behalf of G-d to engage with His creation. Identification of the theophanic messenger role,[1] the construct of angelomorphism, and moral parallels of 'The Fall' with the genesis of mankind, demonstrate the intermediate function of the angel, measuring the distance between G-d and mankind. Thus, as follows, consultation of scripture will provide the necessary evidence for the primary construction of a theophanic angel, representing G-d as the messenger. Subsequent identification of 'angelomorphism' – expressed through the veneration of the 'angelic nature' of Christ and similarly regarded characters – further informs the construction of the angel's divine position. Finally, a review of the angel in closer parallel to mankind, exerts the defining attribute of the angelic function as a marker of G-d's position; whereof, the punishment of the 'fallen angel' reflects the conditional nature of humanity's distance to G-d and thus to the divine.

In the role of messenger, the angel serves as a theophanic extension of G-d; early scriptural appearances employ the figurative 'Angel of G-d' as means of engagement between humanity and G-d. To

---

1 The use of 'theophany' within this essay regards any visible manifestation of G-d.

begin, the word 'angel' is necessarily theological: an Ecclesiastical
Latin term for the Hebrew and Aramaic 'mal'akh' (messenger), wherein, 'angel' separates human messengers from those of divine origin.[2]
Though later textual application renders 'angel' as incorporating all
subordinate divine beings – a matter most evident in the angelomorphic
Christ – within Genesis and Exodus the term angel refers exclusively
to 'The Angel Of G-d'. Yet, scholarly interpretation is divided upon
the ambiguous distinction between G-d and these angelic figures representing Him; wherein, it is unclear whether The Angel of G-d exists
a form of G-d Himself, or as a distinct agent. Theologian Michael
Hundley identifies this disparity, comparing Gen. 31:13, in which
*"the angel of God appears to Jacob in a dream and identifies himself
as the god of Bethel…"* with Exod. 33:2-3, where G-d sends an angel
to the people for, *"he himself will not go."*[3] Notably, as opposed to
human messengers, Angels of the Lord assume first-person speech as if
G-d, *"The angel of the Lord called to Abraham from heaven a second
time and said, 'I swear by myself, declares the Lord… I will surely
bless you…"* (Genesis 22:15-17).[4] Addressing this unclear overlap in
identity, Hundley proposes that *"messengers are presented as neither fully identical nor fully distinct,"* in which the theophanic
manifestations of G-d establish both presence and distance; thus,
where *"divine presence may also be problematic…"* the Angel(s) of the
Lord provide *"…access to the deity without unnecessarily limiting
or impugning Him"*.[5] Hence, the disparity between Genesis 31:13 and
Exodus 33:2-3 exists to assert presence and distance in theophanic
interaction; namely, where it is favourable for G-d to engage Jacob
with presence (Genesis 31:13), G-d's distinct referral of The Angel

---

2 John Gilhooly, 'Angels in Scripture', The Southern Baptist Journal of
Theology 25, no. 2 (2021): 9-20.
3 Michael Hundley, 'Of God and Angels: Divine Messengers in Genesis and
Exodus in their Ancient Near Eastern Contexts', The Journal of Theological Studies 67, no. 1 (2016): 1-22; Holy Bible, New International Version
(Biblica, 2011): Genesis 31:13 & Exodus 33:2-3
4 Holy Bible, New International Version: Genesis 22:15-17
5 Hundley, 'Of God and Angels: Divine Messengers in Genesis and Exodus in
their Ancient Near Eastern Contexts' (2016): 13

of the Lord in Exodus 33:2-3, "[establishes] *some distance, while simultaneously confirming the promise* [to lead the people]... *through some form of accompanying presence.".*[6] Therefore, angels appear to function as distinct messengers, however, the assumption of theophanic forms – lacking full distinction from G-d – serves necessarily in establishing both presence and distance between G-d and mankind.

In the angel's theophanic role, the attribution of 'moral divinity' to the angelic character has resulted in the development of 'angelomorphism' as means of further defining G-d's distance from humanity. Angelomorphism is a descriptive comparison of a biblical figure as 'angelic' in some form or function, though the figure may not be explicitly identified as such.[7] Within broader Christian theology, angelomorphism is significantly linked to Christology: the argument that *"Christ was an angel according to function, but not ontology...".*[8] Gieschen, in developing his view of an angelomorphic Christology identifies *"that several humans were understood to be, and were depicted as, angels...".*[9] Gieschen first consults the veneration of Adam as the first man, citing Sinach 49.16, *"...but above every other created living being was Adam...",* followed by 2 Enoch 30:11-12, *"and on the earth I assigned him to be a second angel, honoured and great and glorious..."*[10] The veneration of Adam as 'The First Man' *"identifies Adam as one of God's principal angels over creation..."* and this evidence, with consultation of Gieschen's further explorations, serves prominently to *"testify that [select] humans can be, or become, angelomorphic...".*[11]

---

6 Hundley, 'Of God and Angels: Divine Messengers in Genesis and Exodus in their Ancient Near Eastern Contexts' (2016): 14

7 Charles Gieschen, Angelomorphic Christology Antecedents and Early Evidence (Leiden: BRILL, 1998).

8 Gieschen, Angelomorphic Christology Antecedents and Early Evidence (1998): 28

9 Gieschen, Angelomorphic Christology Antecedents and Early Evidence (1998): 152

10 Gieschen, Angelomorphic Christology Antecedents and Early Evidence. (1998): 153; New Revised Standard Version Updated Edition (NRSVue) (National Council of the Churches of Christ, 2021); Sinach. 49.16, 2 Enoch 30:11-12

11 Gieschen, Angelomorphic Christology Antecedents and Early Evidence.

The precedence of Christ as a figure of angelomorphism is further demonstrated, in the writings of Paul, who likens veneration *"[to] if I were an angel of God, as if I were Christ Jesus himself…"* (Galatians 4:14).[12] Evidently, where Adam is venerated for being *"one created in the image of God…"*, Christ receives exaltation in response to his nature as G-d's direct incarnation.[13] It becomes apparent, then, that angelomorphism commemorates a direct relationship or connection with G-d, thereof demonstrating the angelic function – 'establishing presence and distance between G-d and mankind' – and, moreover, the exclusivity of this role, constructing 'closeness to G-d' as innately 'good' and desirable.

In viewing the intermediate angelic role thus far, the assumption of a moral superiority appears to coincide with the perception of closeness between angels and G-d. However, the following dissection of 'the fallen angel' demonstrates more nuanced angelic functions, in which angels appear parallel to both G-d *and* mankind. It is important, in addressing this topic, to consider how such a 'capacity for sin' engages with the pre-established angelic function – a theophanic entity not entirely independent of G-d. On this topic, comes the proposal made by Thomas Aquinas, *"similitudinem Dei quantum ad protestatem,"* that is, the desire *"to be like God regarding power…"* constitutes angelic sin.[14] Through Necker's consideration of the fallen angels as antagonists to humanity, Necker draws upon Aquinas's belief that   'humanity is a replacement for the fallen angels'.[15] Similarly, the theologian Augustine asserts an inherent superiority to angels above mankind, as evident in their function to G-d; how-

---

(1998): 153, 183

12   Holy Bible, New International Version: Galatians 4:14

13   Gieschen, Angelomorphic Christology Antecedents and Early Evidence. (1998): 153

14   Gerold Necker, 'Fallen Angels in the Book of Life', Jewish Studies Quarterly 11, no. 1/2 (2004): 73-82; Thomas Aquinas, 'Q. 163 Article II.', in Summa Theologiae, trans. Lawrence Shapcote, 1272, 664.

15   Necker, 'Fallen Angels in the Book of Life', (2004)

ever, Augustine also states this superiority exists only within the material world, and it is clear that *while superior to humans, angels are inferior to G-d…*".[16] Furthermore, in addressing the 'desires' of those fallen angels, Augustine stresses the point that *"G-d was not 'ignorant'…"* rather, that *"G-d foresaw the good which He Himself would bring out of this evil…"*.[17] Thus, 'The Fall' was functional in establishing the existing hierarchy, with angels surpassing man insofar as G-d's identity intersects with the angels, and G-d's position as the 'highest being' demonstrated in His maintenance of this order. A consideration of both Aquinas' and Augustine's conception of the 'fallen angel' – namely, the capacity for sin – constructs parallels between angels and humanity. Although angels may appear superior to mankind in a superficial sense, angels are merely demonstrations of G-d's fundamental authority. Thus, fallen angels reinforce the presence and authority G-d exerts over creation; whereof, the potential for closeness – exclusive to 'righteous angels' and select biblical figures – is venerated, and maintenance of this order becomes both inherently 'good' and fundamentally divine – as opposed to the outcome of The Fall.

Examination of the angelic theological function throughout Judaeo-Christian literature reveals the figure of the angel as a narrative measure on the distance between G-d and mankind, demonstrating G-d's control and position above the experiences of His creations. The idea that angels lie between God and man is multifaceted: angels, through primary reading, function as divine messengers and theophanic hosts – indirect forms of G-d. Within this state, angels provide G-d's presence to mankind, without impeding on the necessary separation

---

16 Corneliu Simut, 'Angels: Augustine and the Patristic Tradition- The Reality, Ontology, and Morality of Angels in the Church Fathers and Augustine', The Southern Baptist Journal of Theology 25, no. 2 (2021): 57-74, (65)
17 Simut, 'Angels: Augustine and the Patristic Tradition- The Reality, Ontology, and Morality of Angels in the Church Fathers and Augustine' (2021): 68

between G-d and humanity. Veneration of this intermediate role, as identified in 'angelomorphism', suggests that the angelic role – possessed by select biblical figures – adopts some degree of 'moral' and 'divine superiority'. Namely, angelomorphic figures such as Adam and Christ further separate humanity from the full presence of the divine, with Christ's existence as an incarnation functioning similarly to The Angel of the Lord, and both figures exerting a desirable exclusivity in their relationship to G-d. Finally, in examining the altered angelic character constructed of 'The Fall', it becomes apparent that the authority of G-d applies to angels just as it does to humanity, despite angels at times exerting limited superiority over humans. Thus, angels fulfil an intermediary function representing distance, presence, and authority on G-d's behalf, and moreover, the maintenance of this order – with all beings beneath G-d – is constructed as inherently 'good' and demonstrates an appropriate distance between the divine and mankind.

REFERENCES

Aquinas, Thomas. 'Q. 163 Article II.' In Summa Theologiae, translated by Lawrence Shapcote, 664, 1272.

Gieschen, Charles. Angelomorphic Christology: Antecedents and Early Evidence. Leiden: BRILL, 1998.

Gilhooly, John. 'Angels In Scripture'. The Southern Baptist Journal of Theology 25, no. 2 (2021): 9-20.

Holy Bible, New International Version. Biblica, 2011.

Hundley, Michael. 'Of God and Angels: Divine Messengers in Genesis and Exodus in Their Ancient Near Eastern Contexts'. The Journal of Theological Studies 67, no. 1 (2016): 1-22.

Morfill, William, trans. '30:11-12'. In The Book of the Secrets of Enoch, 157. Clarendon Press Oxford, 1896.

Ndlovu, Siphiwe, and Angelo Nicolaides. 'Angels and Angelology: The Ministering Spirits and Elect 'sons of God'. Pharos Journal of Theology 102 (2021): 1-25.

Necker, Gerold. 'Fallen Angels in the Book of Life'. Jewish Studies Quarterly 11, no. 1/2 (2004): 73-82.

New Revised Standard Version Updated Edition (NRSVue). National Council of the Churches of Christ, 2021.

Reed, Annette. Fallen Angels and the History of Judaism and Christianity: The Reception of Enochic Literature. Cambridge University Press, 2005. http://www.cambridge.org/9780521853781.

Simut, Corneliu. 'Angels: Augustine and the Patristic Tradition- The Reality, Ontology, and Morality of Angels in the Church Fathers and Augustine'. The Southern Baptist Journal of Theology 25, no. 2 (2021): 57-74.

HEAVEN IS NEAR

K.T. Angelo

t's a brisk November night in the golden foothills near Lost Lake. The cold air stings your face and nostrils, bringing with it the scent of pine, damp earth, and the ever-so-slight aquatic aroma of the lake. The stars overhead seem to shine extra bright, their gleaming brilliance no longer shadowed by the light pollution of the city. The city, which is now just tiny twinkles off in the distance, is barely visible from where you set up camp for the night.

You had been worried you might die of boredom on your solo weekend. Your friends had canceled last minute on account of the cold weather forecast, though you have a sneaking suspicion it was due to the local ghost stories surrounding the lake. You had nearly considered canceling, too, but you are ever so stubborn. And you are glad you decided to brave the frost.

As you gather kindling for your campfire, you notice a small object hidden among the crisp blanket of dead, brown leaves. Picking it up, you realize it's a dusty leather journal only about the size of your hand. Upon flipping through it, you discover it to be nearly halfway full of quickly scribbled entries, the earliest one from this time last year. You swiftly tuck it into your pocket, saving it for entertainment purposes as the night draws in. Reading someone's gossip, even that of a stranger, is enticing to you. You figure flipping through someone's journal and getting a few good laughs beats staring into the fire and coping with your loneliness.

Now, settled in front of your campfire, beer in hand and jacket drawn around you, you open the journal to its first page.

November 5th, 1985 10:19 pm

First night of my solo camping trip is done. I arrived earlier today around noon, set up camp, made a sandwich. It's nice to get away, I think. I feel like I can really sit and enjoy my surroundings. I can finally hear my own thoughts. I know Jess was worried when I told her I wanted to do this. She always worries when I'm away. I don't want to sound like "that guy," but her constant nagging has gotten a little old.

It only started after we got together. If I'm being honest, I don't feel guilty for getting away. I need to think. It's not that I don't care for Jess, she was my best friend before this, bu t when I look at her, I just don't think I feel anything. I know any guy should feel lucky to have her...

I must just feel smothered. Some time away will fix me. Hopefully writing everything down here will work. It's forty five degrees fahrenheit tonight. Tomorrow it should be colder but we'll see. I'm going to get drunk and call it for the night. Cheers.

The writer of the journal was a lone camper, like you. The realization instantly eases the tense, tugging sensation in your chest. It makes you feel less lonely, knowing you will be experiencing a weekend alongside this man, separated only by time. You read on.

November 6th, 1985 12:16pm

Today, I woke up before sunrise and hiked up to the lake with my fishing rod. The water was cold, but not yet frozen over. I was able to catch a good sized smallmouth. I'm roasting it over the fire for lunch as I write. I remember coming up here with my dad years ago. It was summer time. Tonight, I'll roast the hotdogs I brought over the campfire and count how many constellations I can see. I'm feeling better already. I think being out here is really fixing me. I'm almost wishing I wasn't alone. Maybe I'll bring Jess back here with me in the summertime...

November 6th, 1985 11:23 pm

I don't know how to write this. Or how to possibly explain what's going on without sounding absolutely insane. I guess this is just my journal and only I will read it. Or maybe, one day, someone else will read this and I'll become famous as the first man of modern day to speak with an angel. It was around 5 o' clock when he showed up at my camp. The sun was already setting and I was making my dinner when I saw a glimmer out of the corner of my eye. He appeared through the trees: tall and delicate and flawless. Ash blond hair, silver eyes, and great, white wings. Even now, he looks like he's glowing as he sits here next to me.

When he emerged from the trees, he called to me. Said something like, "What is a pretty human like you doing out here alone? Be not afraid." I've never been called pretty before. His beauty is like nothing I've ever seen. It stung my eyes and pricked my skin at first, but I couldn't look away. I had no choice but to believe him when he told me he was an angel. I invited him to my camp. I didn't know what else to do. They never covered how to interact with an angel at church. He joined me for dinner, though it felt blasphemous to feed an angel a hot dog, and we talked. It was like he understood everything I said before I'd even said it. It felt good. He says he can't tell me his name now, but he will soon. For now, I've decided I'll call him "angel." I must've started shivering at some point because he ushered me into my tent. He told me he would keep me warm. And, oh God, the way he touched me, the way he felt, the way he looked at me through those impossibly long eyelashes. I asked him if it was wrong to enter, to pleasure, a son of God. He told me it is holy. That I am holy. I've never felt anything like it. I can't think about Jess. I can't ever tell her. She would never forgive me. But, now, the angel sleeps on my chest and I have never felt more content.

November 7th, 1985 11:36pm

This morning the angel woke me up with a cup of coffee. He must have gotten into my bags and reignited the campfire. I asked him how he knew how to make coffee and he told me they have coffee in heaven. I had always thought that angels didn't eat or drink. I took him up to the lake today and he kept me company while I fished. He's, surprisingly, incredibly funny. A few times I didn't even realize I had a fish on my line because he held me captive with his voice or his touch or his beauty. He has the kind of allure that holds you in a trance. The kind that pulls you in and holds you down until you don't know the time or the day or your own name. He's perfect in every way. We somehow managed to catch two more fish and bring them back to the camp by dinner time. While the angel rested his head on my shoulder and I cooked up dinner, I told him I don't want to leave tomorrow. I asked him where he would go once I left for home. He said he could bring me home to Heaven with him. I always thought you only go to Heaven when you die, but he said I could live there with him. He said, there, I could have as much coffee as I want and we could make love for eternity in heavenly fields. I told him I would think about it. I have people here that would miss me, but I knew my mind was already made for me. I wasn't about to let go of the only being who made me feel truly seen in only two short days. He brought me to bed again and I swear my soul left my body. His lips are so soft, his tongue even softer. He tastes like salvation. As he reached his climax, he sunk his perfect teeth into my shoulder. When we parted, he apologized with a red stained mouth, but to me the pain was blissful. I told him I wanted to go home with him to Heaven. He smiled and, as I write this, I truly believe I would do anything to bring a smile to his face. He's laying on me once again, it's hard to write with him in my arms, but I had to record what happened today. I never want to forget it.

November 8th, 1985 10am

This morning has been rough. When I woke up my limbs were tired and shaky, they still are. My mouth is dry and my stomach is in shambles. My angel is taking care of me, bringing me water and rubbing my back. His cheeks are perfectly pink, and he's smiling at me through it all. It's embarrassing, having such a perfect being watch me retch into a plastic bag, but he refuses to leave my side. I told him I would be alright and that I probably caught a bug from undercooking my fish or something. He says we should stay here until I'm feeling better, since traveling to Heaven takes it out of you and I'll need my full strength. Right now I'm doing my best to rest up while he tends the fire. Hopefully I will be ready to go tomorrow.

November 8th, 1985 9:13pm

I feel a lot better now. After meticulous caretaking from the angel, I stopped vomiting around 3 o'clock and at 4 I was able to take a walk around the camp. He toasted some bread over the fire for me which soothed my emptied stomach even more. I keep catching him eyeing me not-so-subtlety as I write this. It's astonishing to me that he could still want me like that after watching me puke my brains out, but who am I to deny him?

November 9th, 1985 10:41 am

Today is worse than yesterday. My head hurts so bad it's nearly blinding. My mouth is dry and my lips are cracked and my body feels like it's made of lead. I guess it always gets worse before it gets better, maybe this is the worst of it. When I *woke up this morning my angel was smiling at me. I wish he didn't have to see me this way. He pressed soft kisses over my face. He says I feel a bit feverish and I should put down my journal and rest. I stupidly told him about Jess and that she would be worried that I haven't come home yet. His smile faltered and I could tell he was a little hurt, but he told me he would visit her and tell her that I was alright. Bless him. An angel can appear wherever he wishes, I guess. He's insisting that I rest and that he will be back in the evening, so I'll try to close my eyes...*

November 9th, 1985 10:55 pm

Something doesn't feel right. My shoulder, where my angel's bite resides, burns and itches. My angel came back to me a few hours ago. He said he visited Jess in her room. He said he told her that I'm safe and that I am being called to a higher purpose among the sons of God. He said she had taken it well and I felt my body flood with relief. I would be able to spend eternity with my angel and Jess can move on and find someone better than me. The resting has done me good and I'm able to move around again. Everything seemed to be going right. Until, as the angel straddled my lap with a giggle and pulled his tunic over his head, I noticed stains of red on the hem of the gilded fabric. Then, a twinkle of gold by the angel's ears. Heart shaped earrings, identical to the earrings I had bought for Jess for her birthday back in March. I meant to ask him about them but he had put his lips to mine and carved his hips downwards, driving the thoughts from my head. My body had betrayed me. But now, as he sleeps next to me, I   can't help but feel a chill as I look at those golden hearts.

November 10th, 1985, 3:00 am

I feel as though I might be vanishing, yet the urge to vanish with him only grows stronger. I cannot sleep. My body feels feverish, an aching, shivering burn, almost pleasurable. It's nearly impossible to look away from him even just to write this. His pale hair, almost white, curls gently across my pillow. In the light of the lantern, his delicate shape and his soft skin appear golden. Gilded. His pink lips are parted ever so slightly, still swollen from heated kisses. He must have been so lovingly molded by Our Father's hands, skin smoothed by tender thumbs like cold, wet porcelain in the embrace of a sculptor. The curve of his hips, delicious and soft, carved by God's own, heavenly knife. I need him, I need it. The urge to split my skin, to sew our every atom together, to become one, thrums in my blood. There's something off...something he's not telling me. But I can't bring myself to stay away from him, to risk the chance that Heaven might frown upon me. The Heaven that is his lips. Is it you, angel? Are you my final deliverance? What I've been searching for my whole life? Suffocate me into darkness, into an eternity inside of you. I can't stand the restlessness I feel any longer, as I idly watch your chest rise and fall with breaths as soft as your pale skin. Surely you won't mind if I wake you?

You feel the freezing cold begin to nip at your face and your heart thuds as you realize your fire has nearly died out. How long have you been reading this journal? You frantically scramble up from your seat to grab more logs for the fire, nearly slicing your hands on rough bark in your haste. Needle-thin splinters embed themselves in your palms. The little leather journal calls out to you as you stoke the flames. A feeling of unease creeps in despite the warmth of the fire and you dust off your hands and open the pages once again. This next page is different. The handwriting is barely legible, messy and jagged, as if each movement of the pen took immense effort. The page is wrinkled and dotted with stains where it appears there were drops of water which have since dried. It might have been raining when the entry was written, but the alternative buries itself in your mind, twisting knots in your stomach. *Tears?*

November 10th, 1985 11:56 am

I am sorry. Mom. Dad. Jess. I love you. This may be my last entry. It's nearly impossible to move, but if someone finds this I need you to know what happened to me. If not for my previous entry, I would not remember last night. I swear I wasn't myself. The angel. It was only two hours ago when he woke me with his mouth, warm and wet and insanity inducing. I tried to move but he told me to relax and that he was healing me. It had to be done for him to take me away. I let him, but I knew it was not true. I still don't know how I feel about it. Thinking about the way he held me down...it makes my skin crawl. But at the same time this fluttery feeling keeps bubbling up in my chest. Love?

I asked him what really happened yesterday. What happened with Jess. What I did last night... He smiled, his once divine face contorting and nearly splitting in two from the unnatural size of his sharp teeth. I cried out that I thought he was going to bring me to his home. I asked him why he couldn't fix me, why I grew sicker after every night. I just wanted him to take me home. He told me he was telling the truth, that he was bringing me home, but Heaven hadn't been his home in a very long time. He said my physical body could not be brought to Hell and must die, but my soul would please him for eternity. He's outside, tending to the fire as I write this. Tonight, I will be dead. Lord, forgive me.

The journal ends, leaving you with your thoughts racing. *Could this be real?* you think. There's no way, it has to be made up. It must just be a work of fiction someone left behind to spook the next camper. But as you look around, a glimmer of light catches your eye, sending icy claws up your spine.

Your breath becomes frantic. You search for an escape. Suddenly, the nature of your campsite is revealed to you: remnants of an old tent appear at the base of a nearby tree, vinyl tattered and torn, poles snapped and jutting out in every angle. A lone fishing rod buried in the dirt, the silvery line gleaming with the light of the fire. A distinctly human skeleton, its clothing in tatters from being picked clean by the fauna of the woods. How did you not notice before?

"What is a pretty human like you doing out here alone?"

You whip your head around towards the voice, soft and pure as windchimes.

"Be not afraid."

THE SILENT DARK

Helen Z. Dong

ia didn't have much in this life, but she had been blessed with a single gift: the ability to pass her life force onto others. Perhaps the gods had known what terrible fate she would face and this gift was an expression of their regret for creating her. Or, perhaps, it was simply another curse layered on top of the punishment for her misdeeds in a former incarnation. Whatever the case, Dia had no choice but to leverage it for survival. And on days like today, she would trade her life away for a coin, because it was better to live fewer years than to starve.

Khisea sat in the underbelly of the world, only a single step away from hell. This was a city that the light rarely touched and, when it did, it cast sickly shadows wherever it went. Once, as a child, Dia had seen a dapple of sunlight untouched and unperturbed. She had marveled at its glimmer, its cleanliness. And then, a cloud moved across the sky and the next time the sun revealed its face, the dapple of light was gone.

The streets, made of dirt and gravel, were always damp under Dia's feet. Buildings loomed on either side of her, reaching up and up towards Uvasea, Khisea's sister city above the ground. They would never actually be able to get there. It was all just a dream. These buildings made of wood and mud — they would crumble long before they ever reached the edge of this forsaken city.

If Khisea lay on the path to hell, then Shutter Alley was the gateway into it. In the darkest corner, where light was too afraid to wander, Dia joined the vagrants and the beggars. She was lucky to have a place to call home outside of this damp, narrow pass, but many were not as fortunate as her. Wrapping herself tighter in her thin shawl, Dia found a place to stand at the mouth of the alley and waited.

Patrollers rarely came by this part of the city. Too many horror stories of men being dragged into the shadows, never to return. Dia wasn't sure how much of those stories were fact and how much fiction, but it worked to her advantage.

For the deals that she made, it was better to not have to worry about the hand of the law, and she was sure that her clients felt the same.

Footsteps approached. Someone coughed. Dia looked up, expectant, but it was only an old man draped in a dirty blanket, shuffling into the alley. As he passed, the stench of piss and weeks-old grime assaulted Dia's senses, but only for an instant before the smell mixed in with the rest of the polluted air. She watched the man disappear into the dark.

When she first began her trades, Dia would stand deeper inside the alley, afraid of getting seen by passersby. Afraid that she might get unlucky and catch the attention of a patroller. But she learned quickly that the deeper one went into Shutter Alley, the more difficult it became for them to get out. In there, where darkness filled every crevice, Dia's eyes were completely useless. And without her sight, it was only a matter of time before she lost sense of where was up and where was down. The brick walls of the alley would start closing in, bit by bit, until she was forced to flee, tripping over stones and bodies and her own feet to do so.

On top of that, it was so quiet there. So silent, in the depths of the alley, like a place where humans shouldn't be allowed to go.

"Dia?" a familiar voice whispered. Her client was here.

Standing at the very edge of the alley, a boy — maybe her age, maybe a few years older — stood, dressed in dark fabrics. He always dressed like this. It was his attempt to blend in. But his shirt was too smooth and his pants were too clean. Any Khisean could see that he didn't belong.

She held out her hand. The boy, Anton, dropped a pouch in her palm. Coins rattled inside. Dia poured the contents of the pouch into one hand and counted carefully.

"You do this every time," Anton said. "But you know that I've never cheated you."

Dia fought the urge to roll her eyes, putting the coins back into their pouch. "I never know when you might start."

An indignant huff responded to her lightly veiled accusation. She pulled a thin vial out of her cloak. The first time they'd met, Anton had mistaken the water in the vial to be the essence his master was after. Dia had let him do it, happy to take her coins for free. His master must have found out somehow, though, because the next time Anton came, one of his eyes was darker than the other and he made certain to ask: "Is this the essence?"

And Dia had shaken her head, amused.

"You tricked me!"

"I didn't."

And back then, just as she was doing now, Dia had twisted open a vial and brushed her thumb across the open top. Then, she'd dipped the tip of her pinky finger into the liquid and breathed in. When she breathed out, she felt the stirring of her life energy, her *qi*, deep inside her ribcage. It rattled inside its cage and she opened the gate to release it up her chest and down her arm and through her fingers and into the water.

Anton watched now, just as he had done several times in the past, as life blossomed within the tiny vial. Green algae climbed along the glass walls. An influx of nutrients turned the clear water murky. And just as the algae was about to crawl out, Dia removed her finger and sealed the vial tightly.

She handed it to Anton, who took it gingerly within his fingers. He pocketed it, but didn't move otherwise.

"What?" Dia frowned. Was he going to try to make small talk again? She had rebuffed him enough times; one would think that the boy could take a hint after a dozen failed attempts. What was he going to say to her this time? Would he ask about her family, or her full name, or something completely inane, like how she felt about the weather? As if Khisea ever got to experience weather the way that Uvasea did. When the sun was out, this city stayed dark and damp. And when it rained, the city drowned.

But Anton didn't ask about any of those things.

"This is so unfair," he said.

Unfair? Dia scowled and waited for him to explain himself.

Anton's eyes searched her face, but she didn't know what for. "Every time I see you, you look older and worse for wear, but I know we must be the same age. I remember what you looked like in the beginning."

She reached up, pulling the hood of her cloak over her face. "Are you mocking me?" Taking the *qi* out of her body always came with a cost. Obviously. Life couldn't come out of nowhere, it needed to be fed. The nobleman that Anton worked for — and all the others whom she traded with — fed from her *qi* to stay youthful, and she grew old quickly in return.

"No." Anton shook his head. "No. It's just…your hair didn't used to be this gray. And you didn't used to look so…tired."

Dia tried to swallow the lump growing in her throat, but it only grew larger. "You should go," she said. She didn't need more reminders of how much she had changed.

"I'm sorry, what I meant to say was I want to help." Anton must have seen the look on her face because he waved his hands and quickly continued. "I want us to help each other, I mean! This is no life to live. You, cutting your years shorter just to survive one more day. Me, using my body and soul to serve others and never myself. This can't be all there is."

Dia had half a mind to turn away, walk into the depths of the alley where Anton couldn't follow her, but his words gnawed at her insides. Ants crawled under her skin. "Your life is nothing like mine."

"I know. I know. But against the Uvaseans, we're on the same side."

"You're Uvasean." Dia said.

Anton recoiled, as if she'd hit him. "I'm not."

"Anton is an Uvasean name."

"My real name is Obi."

Dia knit her brows together, pulled the hood further down her face. It was a sick joke for him to pretend.

"Does it really matter where I'm from? My master and his friends chase immortality by using your essence, which I can see is killing you. It's not right. It can't be right. The gods would never approve of this."

Dia didn't respond. This all sounded like a trick, and she wasn't going to fall for it.

"My master has riches beyond your imagination. Help me steal even a fraction of it, Dia, and we could run away. Live the rest of our lives far away from here. It will be retribution for what he's taken from you."

Anton was spewing lines fit for a prince in a fairytale, but Dia knew better than to believe him. This was real life, not a bedtime story. Here, happy endings were nothing more than a thing of fiction.

"Divine retribution, Dia. Tell me you don't want that."

Of course, she wanted it. For her entire life, the gods had forsaken her. Even this "gift" that they bestowed upon her was more of a cruel joke than a blessing. But she was only a mortal in the end. It wasn't her place to meddle with the order of things.

"Think about it. Please," Anton said.

"Just go," she said.

"Think about it," Anton echoed. "I'll wait for you at the Unicorn tomorrow at midnight. If you don't come, I'll never mention this again."

He offered her a smile, which she did not return, then backed out of the alley and disappeared. Dia waited for a few moments before slipping out of the alley as well. By then, Anton was nothing more than a dark silhouette.

The Unicorn, Anton had said.

Dia fidgeted with her fingers. Only those who had grown up in Khisea's underbelly would know about the Unicorn.

In the single room of Dia's living quarters, she kept a handful of photographs inside a box that was covered in a film of dust. She blew on it. Light specks flew from the top of the box, making her sneeze, but a solid layer of filth remained. With her fingernails, Dia popped open the flimsy cardboard lid.

It must have been years since she last saw these pictures, but the image that greeted her from the top of the pile was still as familiar as the dark of Shutter Alley. A man and a woman grinned at her, their faces full of joy. On the woman's hip was a child looking away from the camera. Dia swiped her thumb over the child's head, then over the faces of the man and woman. In her own memories, the images of her parents' faces had faded into nothingness, but this photograph was crisp. She stared at it, wishing for it to stick to her mind's eye, but the moment she flipped to the next picture, the faces were gone.

The rest of the stack were all of Dia in various stages of childhood. She flipped through them with care, but without really seeing them.

Anton had said that his master was chasing immortality, that the gods would never approve of it. But how could he be sure? Her mother used to teach her when she was little that the gods were omniscient and righteous. They saw all that happened in the mortal realm and rewarded or punished behavior as was right.

If the gods didn't approve of Anton's master, they would surely have struck him down.

Dia furrowed her brows. If what Anton's master was doing was so wrong, then, surely, the gods would pass judgment on her, too. For using her gift to aid another's wickedness.

The pile was small. Soon enough, her parents' faces were staring up at her again.

What had they done to incur the wrath of the gods? What had *she* done to deserve this fragile life, where her only saving grace was a gift that forced her to shorten it?

What had Anton done to deserve the life of a servant to Uvasean nobles? She could only dream of it. The lifts that carried people from Khisea up into Uvasea were for patrollers and those with special passes. One could also attempt to scale the wall and climb all the way up, but that path was dangerous, and there was no guarantee of what might happen even if they managed to conquer it. Anton worked in Uvasea. If he was truly Khisean-born, as he said, then he had been lucky enough to obtain one of those passes.

Each Khisean citizen was allowed to enter the annual lottery for a pass three times in their lifetime. Dia entered her name for three years in a row and each time was denied. Her life ended that third year; her hopes died with the lottery draw.

Anton had what every Khisean prays for when they enter that lottery. He was ungrateful. Would the gods not punish him for that, too?

Dia bit the inside of her cheek, swiped her thumb to pass over another photograph. She stared at the image that had been revealed underneath, brows furrowing.

Dia had flipped through the entire stack of images three times, but somehow, she must have missed this one. A young woman, her mother, beamed in the foreground of the photo. Several paces behind her, a young man sat at the foot of a decrepit statue of a horse, half of its face crumbled away to ash. There was no mistaking where this was. The gods must be sending her a sign.

Quick fingers closed the lid of the box and slid it away. She had to prepare if she was to meet Anton at the Unicorn.

Anton's birth name was Obsidian, shortened to Obi for his friends. It was a common name amongst Khiseans, many of whom made their living from mining and trading precious stones and so named their children after those shining pieces of rock. Dia was no different. For her, her mother had chosen the most common name of all.

Under the shadow of the broken horse statue, Obi, who somehow took on a different air after shedding his Uvasean name, explained his plan.

He'd overheard that his master kept a stash of riches under his home. The hard part, he claimed, would be getting Dia into the city and into the house and unlocking the door. From there, it would be a simple task to load up on gold and jewels. By morning, they would be nothing more than a speck on Uvasea's horizon.

It was a grand plan, Dia had to admit that much. Tempting, too. How long had she languished in agony, dreaming of a better life? Dreaming that one day, she would wake up in someone else's skin, someone who had the fortune of being born to wealthy parents in a wealthy city, who could accomplish all that they set their mind to simply because of the luck of the draw. For how long had Dia wished to become someone who was *truly* favored by the gods? They could take her power, if only they gave her a life worth living.

When Obi told her his vision of the future, Dia could almost taste it. They would need but a handful of his master's riches, just a handful...not even enough to be missed. But enough for them to start over in a new land, with new names as new people. Maybe in five years, maybe in ten, she wouldn't even remember who she used to be. She could be born anew. Risen from the ashes of the gods' unfair hand.

It was barely justice, barely retribution. It was only barely balancing the scales.

At an hour past midnight on a day that Obi chose, he brought Dia a traveling pass that he'd borrowed from Roana, a female servant of his master's estate. They took a lift out of Khisea and into the glittering, glamorous city above. Dia's hand shook as she gave her traveling pass to the guards, but they barely spared it a glance before waving her through.

This was Dia's first time seeing Uvasea in the flesh. She'd heard countless stories about this place in her youth — stories about how the children here never starved, always had safe homes to go back to, and enjoyed the warmth of the sun every single day. All Dia knew of the sun was through tiny droplets that disappeared at a moment's notice; Uvasean children could bathe their faces in it for hours.

Even at night, the city glimmered. Moonlight lit up the clean cobblestone streets lined with shops and houses, all of them standing tall and sturdy, not worn down by years of abuse and neglect. There were no people outside, but Dia could imagine what it might look like during the day, with merchants waving at passersby and children running up and down the cobblestone.

Her heart ached at the thought. If only she had been born up here instead of down there, she wouldn't have to be sneaking around these streets in the dead of the night. What would it feel like to be able to hold her head high? Maybe after tonight, she would know.

Obi's master lived in a grand house on the far side of the city. Dia had to tip her head back to see its roof, that's how tall it was. They snuck in through a door at the back.

The servant quarters were silent. Worn down, barely alive torches lined the halls, providing just enough light to see by.

"I thought Uvaseans were beyond torches by now," Dia muttered.

"They are," Obi replied. "But this is where the servants live."

Past a dozen closed doors and over creaking floorboards, the pair crossed a threshold into the master's house. There were three floors, Obi had said, two above ground and one under.

"Under?" Dia's brows had furrowed. "I thought they didn't like being underground?"

"They don't." Obi shrugged. "But that floor is not *so* under. Not nearly as under as Khisea is."

Across the foyer, the silhouettes of two men standing guard outside the front door were just dark enough to be visible to the naked eye. Dia blinked at them, then hurried to follow Obi to a wooden door in the wall. He fiddled with it. It jiggled in its frame. Dia shivered, wondering if the noise would be loud enough to alert the men outside. But within a few seconds, the door opened without protest and the silhouettes outside barely even stirred.

In the underbelly of the master's house, Obi handed her a black cloth bag and went for an intimidating, locked door.

"I've seen them open this before," Obi said as he slipped a hairpin into the lock. "You won't believe what's inside…just take as much as you can. As much as you can run with. And we will go. By the time they notice that anything is awry, we will already be further than they can reach."

And what a beautiful dream he painted.

Time froze for a single moment when Obi yanked the door open. For that single moment, Dia saw it all: the jewelry and the gold, her future life filled with sunshine and beauty, a vision of her and Obi growing old by the sea (which she could only imagine from what she'd read in old, dusty books).

Then, the moment passed.

Obi cried out as a figure grabbed him from the other side of the door, large hands gripping the boy's skinny arms. Dia dropped her bag, a chill crawling up her spine. The beautiful dream shattered.

"The master was right, after all," a gruff voice laughed. "Said you'd be here one of these nights, and with a girl pretending to be Roana." Yellow eyes glinted in the man's round face, his cracked lips parting over a wicked smile. "And here you are…and with a girl."

"Run, Dia!"

After nearly two decades spent doing nothing more than fighting to preserve her own life, it didn't take much to send Dia's body into motion. She flew up the steps to the foyer. Her legs carried her through the main door before her mind could catch up, whirling past the guards outside, who stirred and shouted in her wake. Heart pounding, mouth dry, and blood roaring, Dia tore through Uvasea's empty streets. She couldn't take the lift down; she had to climb.

Shouts rang out in the night as Dia arrived at the edge of the city and peered down at its sister below.

"There! Stop, girl!"

Cold sweat broke out over the back of Dia's neck. She wet her lips and began her descent. Slowly, at first, and then when the footsteps and voices pounded closer, she let herself go — half climbing, half tumbling down the steep cliff into the heart of Khisea. She arrived battered and bruised, but alive enough.

The patrollers coming after her would have to take the lift. That would buy her some time.

Dia pulled herself through the familiar, damp streets, guided by muscle memory and the map in her mind. Her left leg dragged behind her; both of her shoulders throbbed. She grit her teeth. For seventeen years, she had survived, and she would not die rotting behind bars because of some stupid boy's mistake.

At the edge of Shutter Alley, Dia stared into the endless, unknowable dark. The gods had shown their hand today. Whatever hesitation she had felt before was gone.

In the distance, a woman cried out in fear.

Dia took a long, shuddering breath. Then, she set her jaw and limped into the darkness.

PAIN AND COMFORT

Tea Campbell

Every morning I wake up in pain.

For a decade now, pain has attacked every inch of my body, whenever it pleases. Aching, throbbing, shooting, droning... it never stops.

And recently, I've been plagued with searing pain surrounding my eye that is so excruciating, all I can do is take sleeping pills and hope it's gone when I wake up.

I spoke to my doctor. I saw specialists. I've started down a holistic route. I tried oxygen treatment at the emergency room and nothing has worked.

That's when I began to pray.

The Celtic Goddess Brighid comes to me in my mind's eye as a red-haired woman draped in green. Her fire and flames remind me of the warmth of the wheat pack I place over my forehead to ease my pain.

I close my eyes and envision myself standing before a well, one of her holy sites. I stare into the water and I see no reflection. It's fine — I don't want to think about how I look right now. It's been days since I've showered and I have bags under my eyes. The calm, blank surface of the water is soothing and it puts my mind at rest.

I look up and I see *her*. Shining in all of her radiant glory. Her hair swirls around her like a wreath of fire, but I have no fear of burning. Her green eyes catch the reflection of the flames, looking like sparks from the forge.

She seems ethereal — it's hard to envision her all at once — but the well fades away and when she takes my hands, I can feel them as if they were flesh and blood.

Her skin is soft but calloused — she is a craftsman, a blacksmith, a poet, a weaver, and so much more. Though she is a goddess, she is not above hard work. It was her grounded nature and connection to the earth that initially drew me to her. She seemed approachable, welcoming. I was weak and vulnerable when I found her; I needed a deity with patience and a gentle hand to guide me.

Why did I turn to the Celtic gods?

My passions always pointed towards the Greek pantheon, starting from childhood. But even then, I had never been religious. I had only been to church for weddings and funerals, had never prayed a day in my life. I learned about religion from a family holding onto Christianity only for the sake of tradition, and that meant I never connected to any of its lessons. It meant trying to do right by a god I had no loyalty to, whose love never felt tangible.

Still, I was drawn to spiritualism without realising it. I loved reading tarot cards. For me, it was a meditative practice that helped me get in touch with my inner self. It felt like some greater force was sending me a message, guiding my hands. I've always loved mythology, but I saw the figures within as purely fictional characters, invented to explain the world before humans had the words for it.

It was me who didn't have the words for the divine.

As a student of history and literature, I was sceptical when hearing stories from modern pagans and witches about their work with deities. Soon that feeling faded, but it was quickly replaced with imposter syndrome — what if I was lying to myself? What if I didn't have "the gift" and was only pretending that someone was reaching out? It would be conceited to think that I was special.

But there was no denying the feeling of absolute certainty that washed over me when I asked the tarot for a sign from Brighid, and the Empress card appeared. Or the gentle breeze at my back, urging me forward when I was about to give up on my walk after spending days sick in bed.

So how did I find the Celtic pantheon? As a way to connect to my roots.

Like many Australians, I don't have close ties to my ancestors. My family only came to this country about 200 years ago, from Scotland and Ireland. They weren't convicts, but they left behind their entire lives to start farming in a strange new country. They didn't leave behind many ties to their homeland.

For most of my life, I didn't have a strong sense of culture. And yes, reading some books and researching my family history isn't a replacement for that, but it's something. Looking into the Celtic pantheon made me *excited*. This was a whole new mythology to dig my teeth into, one that my distant ancestors followed.

But while I learnt of this vast mythology, I also saw the holes left by history. How could I bridge this gap between myself and my ancestors, when their knowledge had been destroyed by centuries of colonisation? I felt angry. There was so much we would never know, so much that was destroyed simply because it belonged to a pagan religion. My dearest Mother Brighid, so uniquely Irish, had been watered down into a Catholic Saint; her symbolic cross became a way for her to explain the crucifix to her dying pagan father.

In the midst of this righteous anger at a culture bastardised and erased, Brighid took my hands and sighed a calming breeze over me. Saint Brigid was still the goddess I loved and admired, just in a different form. Even her Catholic form could not quell her divine origins — the saint performed miracles of healing and abundance impossible for any mortal. It is a testament to the strength of her will and her unyielding love for the earth that she has preserved through colonisation, cultural erasure, and more. Her spirit has not been crushed, but simply adapted to the times so that she can continue to help those who need her, no matter where their beliefs lie.

Brighid is a multifaceted goddess. She works with the feminine arts of healing and weaving, but also the more masculine acts of creation like smithing. She is the patroness of all forms of art, which is another reason I was drawn to her.

She has always been an incredibly versatile goddess. When it comes to tarot, I've always had a hard time deciding which suit of cards to associate her with. She is most commonly associated with fire, which makes her a natural fit for Wands. Her connection to wells and water also matches her to Cups, and I relate her spiritual and emotional aspects to those cards. But I also see her as a very earthy, grounded goddess, which corresponds with Pentacles. You could even make a case for Swords, given her association with forges and smiths. She touches all four elements.

Her holy festival, Imbolc, marks the beginning of spring, when the land is waking up from winter once more.

That's where I see her influence most; in the glow of the sun, the scent of flowers, the touch of a cool breeze on bare shoulders. I don't need to seek her out then; she is everywhere. She accompanies me on my walks and smiles at me through the windows.

It's during the winter that I pray for her. Some say that the winter hag, the Cailleach, kidnaps Brighid when the weather turns cold and Imbolc is when she escapes. Others say the two women are the same being.

But my Lady Brighid feels so far away in winter. The chill makes my ailments worse and all I want to do is sleep. I pray to her; I ask her to ease my pain, if she can, or just to keep me company. I don't expect anything from her. But as I lay curled in the foetal position, a wheat pack stuffed under my head to ease the shooting pain in my temple, I hope she will answer.

As I return to the present moment of my meditation, I feel a surge of warmth flow through my hands. It starts in my fingertips and spreads up my arms and through my entire body. There's a gentle breeze caressing my skin that makes the green grass tickle my ankles. Lady Brighid smiles down at me dotingly, loving-ly. I feel so small before her. She *towers* over me — her presence fills the whole sky and yet she feels so close and so comforting.

Pain shoots through my head like a bolt of lighting, demanding to be felt. It almost takes me out of the vision, but Lady Brighid refuses to let me go. She strokes my hair and I feel a tingling along the crown of the head.

"I am sorry that I cannot take the pain away." I feel the words more than hear them. "But I can offer you comfort while it lasts."

My mind fills in what it needs to be told to understand the meaning that she is imparting on me. A being as powerful as a god, no matter how human she seems... well, it would be presumptuous to assume I can interpret her words. I get flashes of emotion, images, inferences that tell me what I need to know. My connection to Lady Brighid transcends words, which is why it's so easy to reach her when I cannot unravel my own thoughts. I never need to explain myself to her; when I need her, she is there.

Despite the calm and love of this tranquil space we have created togeth-er, I still cannot shake the pain in my head. She holds me closer, folding me into her embrace. I'm bundled into piles of emerald fabric, crimson hair, and harmless flames.

I force myself to breathe deeply, filling up my lungs as best as I can. She taps the centre of my back with a finger and I feel a lightness in my chest, allowing me to breathe more freely. We stay like this for a while. I can still feel my physical body, but Brighid encourages me to relax and as every muscle of mine starts to untense, I feel warm and floaty.

Tears well up behind my eyes as I am filled with emotion. I do not understand why I have been given these insufferable headaches, or the innumerable health conditions that seem to increase every time I turn my back. Sometimes it feels like I have been cursed, like some powerful force has decided that I deserve all of this suffering. When none of the medicines or treatments work, it feels like there's no other explanation than divine punishment.

But in my darkest moments, Brighid takes me in her arms. She reminds me to eat, persuades me to bathe when I feel like falling apart. A goddess in flux with the season, she knows the importance of both conserving energy and not letting it go stagnant.

She is my muse, blessing my creative works and encouraging me to try new things, even if I fail at first. She is the voice that tells me to go to bed instead of staying up, because my next creative project can wait until tomorrow.

I wish I could give her the attention she deserves. I wish I could build her a proper altar, with a statue and a fancy candle and regular offerings. I wish that I could say I pray regularly.

But Brighid does not expect much of me, nor I of her. I do a morning tarot reading with her in mind. I have a playlist of songs that remind me of her. I have a scented oil that smells of cinnamon and star anise that I apply when I want to borrow her strength. She knows that I do what I can. Everyone's relationship with their deity is their own, and while it's hard not to compare, I am content with mine.

I found Lady Brighid exactly when I needed to. When I feel as if I am being punished, she looks down at me and tells me I am loved.

OWENVSV (O-WAY-NUH-SUH)

Enoli Lee

Breathe in

He lays there, stomach pressed to the hard floor, the carpet scratching at his skin. His chin is propped with a pillow, neck straining until it hurts. His jaw is clenched and teeth grinding. His eyes are fixated on a low-res live stream, watching a powwow of a tribe that is not his.

The video is grainy, constantly bumping and moving. The audio muffled, a cacophony of voices overlapping each other. And yet, his heart beats along with the drums. Pumping the song through his body. The low voices of the singers run through his veins, jolting a path to his lungs. His every cell being rewritten.

He feels the clack of the beads on the regalia like fingers tapping on his skull. The jingle dresses leave phantom smacks against his legs, clapping like thunderous applause. He taps his feet along with the dancers.

He doesn't know the tribe. He doesn't know their language, their traditions or their people. But, for this moment, he can belong. For this moment, he can lean forward, relax his jaw, steady his heart, and slowly close his eyes.

Breathe out

Letting his eyes drift shut, he breathes deep. He feels like he's floating. Drifting and carried by the wind, swirling in the air and taken far from his room, far from his home.

Until he's there, standing in the crowd. The thick sacred smoke filling his lungs. His skin is sweat slick against his regalia and he reaches and fumbles his damp fingers over the beadwork. The heat and sway of bodies presses against him. Laughter twists around them, and the smell of body odor, fried food and sweetgrass cling to his pores.

He stretches his toes, wanting to yank off his shoes, to dig his feet in his elohi, his earth. He wants to grow roots where he stands, to never leave. This may not be his tribe but still, he feels drunk, swaying where he stands. He is pushed and pulled by the crowd, overwhelmed by his senses, overwhelmed by emotion.

He imagines joining the crowd of dancers. Stepping into the fray and blending seamlessly in. He would step to the beat, and the men would look, nodding and smiling. They would see him as one of them. His heart swells, his arms spread, and he takes flight.

Breathe in

Growing up, he never went to powwows. He never learned his language. He was never taught his culture. He was cut off. Like a critical sense, his history was blocked from him.

His mother, his etsi, avoided the topic, waving her hands to banish his questions like they were airy smoke. But to him, they were thick weights on his chest. She presses her mouth into a thin line and claims to be tan, her tribal I.D shoved deep in the closet.

His aunt, his agitlogi, slathers on skin bleach, dying her hair honey brown, anything but her deep black. Both women married white men, men who wanted them to be the same, who wanted them to suppress and cut any part of themselves that they deemed too native.

They let their white husbands spout slurs about their kin, about anyone darker than paper. They cowed their heads and bit their tongues. They let the world around them wash it all away. Power Washing themselves and their history white enough to blind God himself.

Breathe out

In some ways, his grandfather, his agiduda, was worse. The conservative native man, a walking hypocrite. He saw how he carried himself, a servant to what the colonizers want. He lived by the acceptance of white men, and yet, somehow, still proud of his heritage.

His agiduda had to go to church every sunday. To him, men can't have long hair, women must wear dresses, and each gender has a biblical role. But at the same time, it was different back then, and his agiduda misses the old tribal days, the traditions they lost.

But then, his agiduda puts on that *red* cap, and votes for *that* man. His agiduda votes against himself and his people. He can't help but to watch in dismay. His etsi and agitlogi wash their culture away while his agiduda votes his rights away.

His family seems to grow more and more distant, from themselves. Distant from their culture and history. Distant from him. The chasm cracks beneath his feet and he doesn't know how to close the gap. He's running out of room with no place to run.

Breathe in

He wishes he could connect. He grits his teeth through every chat with his agiduda, at the sting of his words. Grimacing at the hated name he's still called, the frilly clothes he gets for gifts, and the utter refusal to recognize who he is. His only option is a man who will never respect him for who he truly is.

Does he suppress himself? Does he suppress his identity and gender to connect? How can he be both and still fulfill this bone-deep ache he feels for his culture? Does he pretend to be someone else? To take on the identity of an imposter to truly learn about himself?

Or does he suppress the ache? Does he ignore the way his skin stings with the arctic-cold-absence of his culture? Does he close his ears to the calls of his ancestors? Does he cut his throat to silence the way it cries for their songs?

What else is there to do?

Breathe out

His fingers have been sliced with too many paper cuts from all of the books he buys. He snatches any book he can wrap his fingers around about native life and culture. Anything and everything to help soothe his soul. They are a balm for the ache that never fades.

The wounds sting when he writes. Furiously scribbling away the gnawing hunger for connection. They twinge as his fingers fly across the keyboard, searching words in a language lost to him. He looks at terms and slang he will never feel comfortable using. He memorizes them all the same, running his fingers over them in his mind like braille, over and over until they're numb and callused.

There are terms. Words for how he feels. Words for his gender, his sexuality, his very being. Words for who he feels at his core, but would never use. He doesn't have the right. Every step he takes to connect he feels fake. He feels as if wings are stretching at his back but he's too afraid to break the skin.

Breathe in

He researches about his culture until his eyes ache. He watches pow-wows and ceremonies as the stone in his heart gets bigger and bigger, more and more.

He grows his hair, ignoring the dysphoria it brings. He buys beadwork, jewelry he is too afraid to wear. He hoards and squirrels away every bit of his culture he can grab.

He tries to be a good ally, to listen to the natives around him. But he is Sisyphus, and the world around him is the endless mountain. How does one begin? How do you dip your toe into a pool you're not sure you're allowed in?

He turns to religion. His knees bruised, his hands clasped, praying to every god he can. He prays to the colonizer god, the greek and roman, even the nameless ones. Dear God help him. Take a scalpel to his back and free the red dripping feathers. Teach him how to fly.

Breathe out
Sometimes, the only time he feels religious, close to angelic, as if he is soaring in the clouds and near enough to touch the marble skin of god— the only time he feels divine—is when he's locked in his room. When he has headphones shoved over his ears and his powwow playlist playing.

That's when he imitates the dancers he watches. He steps rhythmically and moves his arms, spreading them wide, outstretched like his hidden wings. He closes his eyes, and feels foolish. He would rather die than be perceived at that moment. Would rather die than to be caught by his white-washed etsi. He's unsure if she would laugh or scorn him, afraid of both.

But until then, his heart takes flight, up and up in his chest until his throat is tight. He thinks, tears squeezing from his eyes, this could be heaven, this could be home. This could be enough to sustain him for now, for this moment.

Breathe in

His breath is fast, coming out in short pants. His hands shake as he stares at the accept invite button. He wants to throw his computer across the room. He wants to close it and log off forever. He wants to burrow under his covers, to hibernate until the heat-death of the universe. And yet, *god,* he wants to press the button more than anything.

He wants to be more open. Open about this heritage, about being a *reconnecting* native, a *white-passing* native. But still, a space full of other natives, reconnecting and not, was daunting. It was intimidating, overwhelming, and a million other words.

He wants to join, to have community. But he's terrified of joining. Of being denied, scorned and turned away. He feels cast out from heaven, burning all the way to the core of his elohi, coated in ash and brimstone.

Breathe out

He presses the button and his hands shake so hard he can hardly type. An earthquake of nerves wrack their way up his arms as he fumbles out an intro. His hands are numb and his lungs are refusing to breathe. He presses send and slams his computer shut. The snap of it echoes as loud as a shot.

He starts pacing the room. Running his fingers over the spines of books and tapping his fingernails on the bookshelf. He imitates the powwow drums pounding in his veins, a song only he can hear. He stops. Turns away and clenches his hands, letting his nails bite into his palms.

He's terrified to look, imagining the worst possibilities. He hadn't realized how much he needed this, needed community, until it was right in his grasp. He can feel it slipping against his fingertips like the scales of a fish. He feels as if he's reaching out like a fumbling child with both hands fisted.

Breathe in

Can you hear me? he asks into his mic. He starts tapping his feet against the leg of the desk, so fast he's afraid things will start vibrating off of the top. His pens dance in their cups, a mockery of the jingle dresses he's seen. He listens as voices chime in answer and he smiles so hard his mouth aches.

He flexes his fingers and forces himself to relax. Voices start ringing out, names, tribes, pronouns being shared and he anxiously waits for his turn. He clears his throat and turns on his mic, his voice fluttering like feathers against his lips.

He lets himself soar, his heart reaching for all the ones like him, the tendrils curling around for all the ones lost and trying desperately to connect.

Breathe out

He laughs with them until his cheeks tingle. Tearing up at their stories and how colonization has torn their culture and history from them. He listens to the things their ancestors suffered and his heart and soul cry out for them all.

He wants to claw at the rusted gates of heaven, to demand answers of *him*. He wants to nail *his* sins to the door for all *he* let happen.

And yet, still, he feels joy with the ones who were able to grow up surrounded by their people. The ones who know their language and culture intimately. The feathers of their wings preened and brushed from birth, soaring with their tribes. He holds them all in his mind, a tribe of their own making.

Breathe in

He trades words and terms he learned, his mind soaking up the terms and traditions they pass onto him. Still, he hurts for more. They are a balm on his soul, and salt in the still-stinging cut of his loss. He wishes he could've grown up with this.

He feels his feet pounding on the land that has been bathed with his people's blood. He feels his wings stretching, his downy feathers shedding with sleek ones in their place. He is pulled into the heavens. Floating up to be with the spirits of all who came before him. Flying with these people to teach him, to support him, to make him feel home.

Breathe out

Sometimes he wonders what his ancestors must think. They must be watching them all. Their mouths downturned and backs turned in shame.

They watch his etsi, her mouth silent, their history shut behind her pressed lips. Like Peter hearing the rooster crow, they are denied again and again.

They see his agitlogis, their skin bleached and covered, their culture rejected. Their betrayal a kiss upon the cheek of Jesus.

They watch his agiduda, his dual nature, his hypocrisy staining their ways. He wants to beg, his knees bruised, palms raised to the sky like Christ, son of Nazareth, his stigmata weeping. Father forgive them, for they know not what they do.

He feels the tendrils of the plants beneath his feet. Elohi, our beautiful earth. He sees her flowers wilting in sorrow. Goddess forgive us, for we know not what we do.

His heart keening, he feels as if collapsed at the foot of the cross. Etsi, his silent mother, her hands cradling while wiping away any trace of their culture. Ancestors forgive her, for she knows not what she does.

Breathe in
He wonders what domino of events led to him. A line of ancestors having their culture erased, beaten down again and again until it came to this.

He reads about the ways of his people, their special roles for third genders, their hearts able to wrap around more than one. He wonders what they would've thought of him. Wonders what they would think of his family and their hypocrisy. He feels his ancestors surge in his heart, embedded deep in his soul.

They ache to be let free, to have their history told, to be remembered. He wonders how he came to this. Sometimes, he's glad he did. And sometimes, he can't help but to mourn, sobbing in silence for what could've been.

Breathe out
He thinks a lot about the meaning of home, Owenvsv in Tsalagi. Home is curled up on the couch with his dogs, his fingers tangled in their fur and a book heavy in his aching hands.

To him, home is watching tv with his mom, his eyes drooping with the comfort of familiarity and his questions suppressed deep in his chest.

Home is talking to his far-away loved ones, his skin crying out for their touch, learning and crying with them.

Home is reading about his culture, his throat tight with their songs and his soul weighed with their sorrow.

Home is closing his eyes and pretending he's there.

Breathe in
One day, he'll be there swaying in the crowd. He'll be dancing in his regalia. He'll proudly wear his beadwork. And he'll be laughing with his tribe.

His wings will no longer be hidden behind thick skin, his steady hand and a scalpel freeing them. They break free, strong and outstretched. They're made with loss and tears. They're made with the hope and strength of his ancestors.

He'll be there. With his friends who made him feel safe. The ones who made him feel home.

Breathe out
He flies with them, taken far from the land he was born in. He flies to his home, the land his ancestors fought, bled, and died for.

He looks at the land beneath him, dew beading up on his feathers. He reaches his wings toward the heavens, brushing his feathers across the spirits of those before him.

He feels the threads of his soul wanting to reach out to touch the earth, his elohi. He wants to wrap them around his tribe, his family. He wants to feel their roots reaching back toward him, intertwining and cradling his heart.

Breathe in

Being with them, he never wants to leave. He looks at his tribe, nodding and smiling, seeing him as one of them. He thinks this could be heaven, better than anything god could create.

This could be home, his Owenvsv. This could be enough to sustain him for now, for this moment, and maybe even, forever.

Breathe out

His heart swells, his arms spread, his wings burst free, and he takes flight.

WORDS TO THE WIND

Tien Lee

elievers raised temples atop mountains and hills to meet the Wind at its highest. Few sought the god along the sandy shores.

A newly made priestess strolled the beach alone to have the almighty brush her hair and embrace her confusion. It sent swirling butterflies to comfort her.

Today, she was given her adult name. *Dasom,* the pure Northern word for love. Her unknown mother, who had left her in the temple's care, had chosen it. The note she left behind with her daughter detailed her unmarried hardship, the name to be assigned to the child, and nothing more. The woman must have felt greatly for her paramour to curse her daughter with such a scandalous name. One clearly unfit for a clergy member.

Dasom had vowed her life and chastity to the Wind. Beyond her affection for her caring superiors, her love was saved for the almighty she witnessed among mortals. She kicked up sand to invite the Wind. Particles suspended around her, capturing Dasom's turmoil in a frozen moment before trickling downwards, scattering scared butterflies into the four directions.

The invisible deity flew past her. It hurried waves to shore and crashed against a blasphemous intruder: a glass bottle with a sealed message sent through the water.

Pigeons were the primary form of contact across the four nations. In the air, the Wind watched over correspondences, ensuring worshipers' words reached their intended. Going against the norm to chuck a letter through an unpredictable current said everything Dasom needed to know about the sender. But because she was named after sentimentality, Dasom bent down despite the upward gale. Since her mother had left her with a legacy of love, she would pry open the lid to see what the unordained cherished outside of the sacred temple grounds.

Dasom unraveled the letter. She confirmed her belief. The message was indeed from a strange man sending out affection to anyone who would take it. A pile of wasteful, wandering words. His beached desperation was explicit from his incoherent tangents begging for a reply to his sending off a valuable reusable bottle.

If there really is any higher being, he wrote as the start of his plea for friendship.

She had never met a vocal non-believer. Wind latched onto the paper's edges, urging her to let the sacrilegious sentence be torn away. Dasom tugged against it, deciding the breeze was a figment of guilt. The Wind surely had to be too busy to deal with something so trivial.

Stashing the letter in her bosom, Dasom returned to her room to pen a forbidden reply. The first of letters was the hardest to ink. She scribbled for hours to pen a single sentence asking the sender to write back by carrier pigeon if he was of the faith. That should appease the Wind, on the odd chance it was observing.

In a secluded area of the temple, the deity refused passage for Dasom's message. It gusted, pushing her pigeon back to the ground while letting nearby butterflies effortlessly take off. Resilience was Dasom's form of devotion. She planted a firm foot after another into the omnipresent force. She thrust her bird against resistant air over and over. She, at last, climbed to the highest point of the land to build up momentum until she could bypass the Wind.

Wind battered Dasom's pigeon as it sought a landing space. Yoon had written back something unholy again, Dasom feared. She waved away floating leaves and flowerheads to allow her bird to perch on her arm. The unrolled letter was full of unruly content, as suspected. She sighed, reading:

4th Day of the Twelfth Month

Dear Dasom,

You truly have a way with words, or rather, without them. I still recall your first reply to me. One sentence simply asking me to write back if I'm "of the faith." To be frank, what I believe in is you. You who, despite your clear allegiance to the Wind and concise words, have continued your correspondence with this bumbling stranger over the past few weeks.

Here in Coast Edge, the end of the world is in my backyard. Yet, the ice and Wind prevent me from navigating to you. I am sure wherever you are is cooler and freer than here. For no matter how constrained your brush appears to be, it keeps writing in such unspoken warmth that I grow tender reading between the lines.

Forgive me for my forwardness and if I have misinterpreted. However, I must say that laboring over a perfect sentence or two seems infinitely more challenging than cobbling together the unsorted mishmash of words that I send your way. I dare ask, how many words do you think of with me in mind before snipping them to their shortest form?

I am only speaking from experience. When I ramble as I inevitably do in my letters, it is because from the moment I spot your pigeon to the moment I see it off, my thoughts are with you. There is a novel worth of questions I'm inclined to ask that you decline with a brisk breath. My interest is only furthered with each round of letters.

Again, apologies for being a blabbering busybody. I am a lord among sheep, the son of a hereditary noble family who has never seen the capital where I'm meant to serve. Since my days of schooling are behind me, my sole pass time now is pestering others with my unending stream of thoughts. Perhaps you've already deciphered this from the dense, premium paper I use and from the direction your pigeon returns.

One cannot go further north than where I am. While I write of countless little joys and wonders to you, they are as stagnant as the local winter air. I would never have known of distant warmer winds were it not for you. Do take care and please write back soon.

Your ever-chatty friend,
Yoon

8th Day of the Twelfth Month

Dear Yoon,

The Wind does not need words to speak, but you will know if you have heard it.

Your Wind guide,
Dasom

16th Day of the First Month

Dear Dasom,

Thank you for your inquiries about my health over these past few weeks. Yes, my sudden bout of illness has passed, though it seems to be the least of my problems. How is it that you roam the world without worry? Is it because the Wind is by your side? It has never been with me.

Although I am no longer restrained to bed, I do not have the energy to consider my impending move to the capital. I can only hope it will be a swift carriage trip. In temple murals, blessed priests and priestesses glide over the treetops at night. Each time I am made to pay my respects to the Wind, I stare at them and ponder over what a killing they could make as a form of public transportation. That is, if their existence is not beyond the realm of watercolor fantasy.

Do you believe that such magical beings exist or that they are simply figments of the night-blind imagination? Perhaps mistaken sugar gliders or pigeons forced to do overtime like ours. A bit preposterous to think about, isn't it? Were these figures real, I'd be tithing or bribing my way to seeing you. I fully anticipate your scolding words and heated rebuttal.

Please do not find me twisted for finding joy in your more impassioned letters. I swear to the Wind that I am not intentionally stirring you up. I'm surely not the first to have these questions and doubts. It's just that not everyone has the privilege of having a pen pal who would reply no matter what absurd content they put forth.

As my maids are gathering my belongings, I question where it is that I belong. The coast does not want me, yet I have never met those who claim me in the capital. Although the North is an expansive nation, I and many around me have not ventured beyond this insignificant coastal town. The coast will remain as it always has after I leave it, but I may not return the same.

They say we must leave a place before we can truly know it. Are your travels across the nations what gives you such wisdom? You briefly allude to having been here and there without much enthusiasm or vivid description. Perhaps to the well-traveled, a city is a city, and a town is a town. It may be underwhelming for you to meet a small-town man like me face-to-face. Though if that were to ever happen, I suppose I could carry the emotions for us both and frighten you in person with fervent greetings.

I can only hope your next letter will arrive before I've reached Vermillion. The vibrant, red city apparently never sleeps. I will not soundly rest either until I have your words to comfort me. Please respond with utmost haste.

Your impatient pen pal,
Yoon

20th Day of the First Month

Dear Yoon,

What is there to be in haste over? Words arrive quicker on a non-angry Wind. My poor pigeon battles the elements because of your profane proclamations and assumptions. I would argue that each town and city is quite unique, as are their residents, given your distinct flavor of boldness.

Do not fret a move when the Wind is propelling you forward. Under its guidance, we have been able to spread our societies to cover all four stretches of the world. It is the constant that makes each fresh location feel as welcoming as the last. With it by my side, I have never been completely alone. Neither have you.

It is not my specific presence that you require, but rather another voice that can lead you toward the capital trail where you are needed. In my physical absence, I pray that the Wind will ~~send forth~~ finally reach you. That its company will be of solace to you. That said, as always, I shall be with you in spirit as well.

Your steady companion,
Dasom

Dasom considered shredding her letter. It would not be an error to write: *I pray that the Wind will send forth another companion who can meet you in your time of need.* Yet, she had crossed the words out before they could fully form.

She was catching Yoon's condition. Her writing was going to shambles. Her thoughts were flying astray. She mailed off her letter and prayed harder in penance.

14th Day of the Second Month

Dearest Dasom,

Of the months we have known each other, this must be the windiest. Is the wind strong where you currently are? On my move from the breezy coast to the crowded capital, I can only imagine how constrictive the air will be there. You who bring up the Wind at every chance despite the short nature of your letters should understand.

They say the capital has women of beauty talked of in books. I was taken by such beauty long before I set forth on my journey. For you are one such woman to me. There is a life breathed into your words I can't fully describe. However distant you may be, your letters encapsulate for me a you I can viscerally see. Dare I say it's likewise for you?

Seeing past my rural home for the first time, observing glowing ants and ever-growing trees, has made me reflect on how little of the world I have claimed. It fascinates me that this is all land you have covered, hailing the almighty as you go. Rather than finding comfort in the Wind, I breathe lighter knowing this is ground we now share.

In each puff of Wind, I feel echoes of you. A breath of yours, if you will. What would it be like if we could share the air and warm each other with intermingled breath?

Yours,
Yoon

Dasom pushed Yoon's letter against her heart to quiet the pulsing words. Her Yoon was doing it again, tugging her towards a cliff with his declarations. She held onto his every sentence as she wrote back:

18th Day of the Second Month

Dear Yoon,

We must thank the Wind for the gifts of nature. Remember, one must not conflate natural beauty with human imperfection.

The Wind is wise. Since it has opened your eyes, you must carefully observe the world in its entirety. Humble yourself before the Wind's creations.

Yours,
Dasom

Our letters should cease.

That was how Dasom's pen pal let her know that her letters were meaningless to him now that he had another — a capital beauty. He ended four months of correspondence in four words.

Four months. What a short time it took laymen to fall in love and get engaged. As a clergywoman, she was meant to bless him. Her dearest Yoon. *Yoon* meant cloud. A forever-drifting mess of water moved by Wind regardless of its will. The pen pals were naïve to think otherwise.

The temple's creed was carved into Dasom, deep as the items she kept tucked in her chest. She exhaled, pulling out the bookmark and self-portrait Yoon had sent her. They were paper in the Wind. Such flimsy things that could blow away at any given moment. Still, there was a sincerity to them, much like his former letters.

Dasom always kept her replies vague, never giving away her precise location or occupation. Even the Wind would not read too much into her sparse lines, she had assumed. Yoon, meanwhile, had offered up his world. She knew his family home, his family name, his life philosophies. Enough to paint over this ridiculously childish stick-figure portrait of him with vivid color to unmask his true self.

All the while, the Wind remained the one who knew her best.

Up upon the Cliff of the Windless, Dasom's breath was winded. From this height, one could not be certain if they were looking down upon voluminous clouds or skeletal remnants of jumpers. Temple murals depicted its most avid priests and priestesses as blessed beings gifted with powers such as flight. Those who forsake their vows did not expect the breeze to catch them as they made their way over the edge.

"There you are, Priestess," her acolyte called out to Dasom, out of breath from ascending to the seldom-visited height.

Dasom turned from the girl to discreetly tuck her secret treasures away and spun back once called for again. She took in her underling's pure white robes. They lacked a sheer outer layer embroidered with whirling wind to indicate the higher blessedness of priests and priestesses. Dasom traced the swirled pattern on her own garment. A sudden gust struck her finger away. She had irked the divine.

"What are you doing so close to the sinners' edge?" the girl half Dasom's age asked from a standstill distance.

A poised smile graced Dasom's face. The child before her had no idea what it meant to sin. Nor did the man who had written to her. Dasom would have pegged him as the type of clergy fanatic who'd want to break into her body, not her heart, had he been in the know. She had been the one who kept her status from him. The sin fell on her.

Butterflies burst forth from buddleia bushes. Their bodies canvassed the skies, propelled by weightless innocence.

Meanwhile, billowing air scraped at Dasom's artificial grin as she said, "I'm burning. Could you fetch me some water?"

The acolyte didn't question how she could be hot amidst the Western Wind's abundant presence.

"Yes, Priestess. I'll fill up your bottle," she agreed and left.

It wasn't Dasom's. She had kept Yoon's discarded bottle while he likely kept nothing of her. She had shamelessly concluded each letter calling herself his. And he had selected to give his love to another without so much as consulting her beforehand.

Dasom would tell Yoon off for it. She would bring the wrath of typhoons upon him. In her room, she downed cold water in a daze. Air was stirred up as she bared herself with a brazen brush, writing:

Dear Yoon,

How many letters have I signed off as your Dasom to have you render our relationship one of letters to be torched? The capital has truly engrossed you in its litter. From the dirtied ground, it is impossible to see the Wind's might.

You have always questioned my dedication to the almighty yet stopped yourself from definitively inquiring. I had once thought of you as a defiant soul, defying Wind to wash words over to me. However, as the months passed and you never asked for my station in life, it has become clear to me that you are a lover of convenience.

How convenient it was for you that I answered your call for companionship. How fortunate that I am an unseen partner who could be distanced at the earliest inconvenience. You who allegedly opposed the Wind's flow were nevertheless still blown to your destined partner.

Now that there is a physical form before you, you need not my far-off intangible love. I hope our façade of closeness has been a fun distraction for you. I wish you all the best on the path cleared for you. May the Wind steer us in the right direction so we may never intercept each other's spiritual journey again.

Once Yours,
Dasom

In day's final light, Dasom reread her creation. It was inauthentic to the four months of feelings she had sent off against the Wind's weariness. Her mother had given her away with love. Being the unfortunate offspring of this raw emotion, she must pass it off to another. Then, she would be the Wind's unburdened mouthpiece again. Its might would uplift her beyond the clouds once more.

Dasom rewrote her letter, making it a gracious farewell. One of congratulations for Yoon's upcoming wedding. One of joy and warm wishes. She could've ended it at that, had her brush tip not accidentally struck the glass bottle, tinkering her darkening room with clarity.

I am to be a High Priestess, she admitted to him and sealed the paper.

Wind approved. It patted Dasom's tense shoulders flat and opened the door to her acolyte.

"Priestess Dasom, are you ready for bed?" the girl asked from the courtyard butterfly bush.

A butterfly took off from the buddleia, leaving its partner behind to blend into the horizon.

"Buddleia. Call me Priestess Buddleia from now on," Buddleia announced as she unpacked a chest of letters. "And could you bring me a charcoal burner? There's something I must return to the Wind."

MOONTIDE

Aidan Sparks

"Why worship a deity whom you cannot see, when there is the Moon in all her splendor visible? Worship her. Invoke Diana, the goddess of the Moon, and she will grant your prayers."
— Charles G. Leland, *Aradia: Gospel of the Witches*

Dark blood seeps between my legs, staining my skin with splotches of gore. The warm water of the lagoon laps at my pale thighs as I submerge deeper, trails of crimson tainting the clear surface, burgundy clots floating lifelessly away. I look up to behold her beautiful face, her full, round, silver eye smiling down at me. I reach my arms out in supplication, hands grasping for her loving touch.

"Goddess of the Moon, Luna, Selene, Diana, Mother, hear my prayer. My womb is a burden and its shedding blood a curse. Please, cease your pulls against the tides within me. Let my insides dry as a barren desert. I am no longer a daughter, but I am still your child. I beseech thee, be merciful, and I will continue to rejoice and sing praises in your honor."

The raspy voice of the Goddess hisses between my ears, surrounding me, enveloping me, in whispers that source from nowhere. "If you are no longer my daughter, then what will you be?" A shadowy shape disturbs the still water, rippling waves as it undulates towards me. A serpent, slick black in the shine of the moonlight, circles me. "Will you become one of them? An invader?"

The serpent strikes fast, darting between my spread legs, its diamond shaped head forcing my folds apart to wriggle its way up to enter me. I feel its body slither deeper, violating my cavernous space filled with blood and shame.

"An oppressor, a predator, an assailant?" Cracks of pain, from the sting of twin bites, radiate from one side of my uterus to the other, ovaries rupturing in spasming waves. "These men who shun me, who spit in my face lest they seem weak, who prey upon my daughters and soil them in semen and blood. Would you follow in their footsteps? Would you abandon me too, child?"

I shake my head violently, tears forming in my eyes at the implication and the growing intensity of stabbing pangs assaulting me. "No, Exalted One, no, of course not. I am not a son either. I am both. I am neither. I am simply your child."

"Then why do you reject my life-giving gift?" she spits accusingly. "To carry the water of the womb, to bear my children, to be tied to my ebbs and flows is a sacred duty not to be taken for granted. A blessing not to be forsaken."

My abdomen slowly eases into numbness, a brief relief from the throbbing, only for my thoughts to churn wildly for an answer that would placate my Goddess without deceit. "I cherish your gifts, and honor the charge of life-giver. But I was made wrong. This is not my burden to bear."

My Lady's ire emanates from the air encircling me, and I cringe slightly at the heat nipping at my prickled skin. "Do not play games with me, child. We all have our roles to play. If you reject yours, what purpose do you serve to me?"

The water surrounding me begins to quicken, swells of imperceptible waves disturbing the quiet sheen of the surface and lapping at my half-submerged body. The serpent twists wildly inside me, thrashing its sinuous form harshly against my stomach. I gasp when I glance down and faintly detect the outline of its tendrils writhing beneath my flesh. "I give you my love, my gratitude, my worship," I manage to whimper pitifully.

Spiraling rivulets of white foam dance around me, coalescing into a vortex that draws me in with the gravity of a collapsing star. The serpent matches the beat of the tides, gyrating in sync within my womb. The whirlpool rises up and above me, murky water crashing over my head as invisible claws grasp my ankles to drag me under. I flail against the abyss, whispering voices assaulting me like the roar of a tornado, drowning out all thought and sense. *Imposter...Faker...Useless... Worthless...Failure...*

"Enough!" I scream in my head and out into the chaos, water filling my mouth and lungs with lancing fire. With one last thrust upwards, my head violently breaks the surface into a rush of sound and light, flinging waves outwards in a tsunami. Gathering my shaking body upright and taking a moment to catch my breath, I slowly open my eyes to look upon Her face once again. The silence in the aftermath of my thunderous rebirth is oppressive, and my heart enflames with rage.

"Just because I am not a woman does not mean I failed as a person. And even if I were a man, that does not make me the same as my abusers. There are many different ways to be a man, to be a woman, to be *human*. I am my own way, not bound by the expectations placed upon me by society, by my family, or even by *you*. If you cannot accept that, then maybe you are not the Goddess I thought you were."

My vision wavers as I watch the moon morph into a mirror, my petulant face superimposed onto the image of the Goddess' beautiful visage mired in anger and disdain. My voice thickens, steeled in a certainty and confidence I have never known before. "Just because I can't connect to the Divine Feminine anymore does not make me any less divine."

A forgotten fragment buried in my being shifts and fractures, a fissure growing deep as I watch the mirror of the moon crack, the wrathful façade of Her face shattering into infinite twilight pieces. As they descend into the night, in its place a countenance of loving reverence reflects down upon me.

"There you are, my child." I hear my Goddess' voice softly now, the harsh growl gone, replaced with pacifying patience. "You asked for my blessing, wished for me to remake you in your own image. But are you not the one creating your new life yourself?"

A phantom hand brushes along my cheekbone gently, the pressure of an invisible embrace envelops my shoulders, and the tingling aftermath of a kiss lingers against my forehead. "My sons are the serpent, the sparks of creation. My daughters the cosmic egg, the protector and bearer of new life. You, however, are now your own creator and creation. You shall be both, as Phanes the Self-Born. You are now as the Gods."

A withering takes hold within, the walls of my uterus beginning to crumble inside me. I double over, not only in pain, but in wonder as the lilting voice of my Goddess grows commanding. "With my guiding hand you carve yourself out. Bleed for me one last time. Then go forth and proclaim your own revelation."

The serpent emerges at last, fusing itself to my groin, shrinking, lightening, becoming flesh that bobs delicately in the warm water. Pale flesh reflects the pale moonlight. Tears bleed from my eyes, as the void interred in my core dissipates into the night air and a former phantom limb transforms into physical flesh. Pieces made whole, a fractured psyche rebuilt into an eternal Spirit.

"Thank you, Mother. Thank you for guiding me through the dark of night towards the light of my own dawn. In gratitude I praise your name, now and forever, my Lady, my Goddess, the reflection of my Heart and Soul. Praise be to you."

This is a prayer of hope. Take it with you and hold it in your heart on the darkest of nights, when the moon is hidden and the wolves are at bay, that you may see yourself as the Gods do and know that you are perfect in your own divinity.

LIFE, DEATH AND DAISY CHAINS

Elise Georgeson

I. LIFE

Cool grass slithers against their robes like the reverential hands of worshippers as Life and Death eclipse each other in the Garden. Decayed bones give homes to a confectionary of flowers and small bugs. A skull winks at Life, submerged in centuries-old dirt beneath the full moon.

Their eyes are like the white beams of headlights swerving unexpectedly in the dark, approaching with a sensation of impending doom. Life's doe nose twitches reflexively, baubles clinking together softly in the nest of her antlers.

"Life," Death greets. Their gaze drops to the squirming bundle of cloth cooing in Life's arms immediately. Their face is a void, inky darkness beneath black antlers like the branches of a tree in silhouette. It is unreadable — but there is no mistaking the way their shoulders tense.

Life offers the babe forward like a sacrament. "This is Daisy."

A fleshy pink face stares up at the two divinities with joy, lips parted and cheeks full.

Death's gaze swivels back to Life. "This is a newborn."

"She's ours," Life announces proudly, settling the babe in Death's arms.

Death folds their arms beneath the babe, keeping their clawed fingers away from her fragile face. Their shoulders ease marginally, void bowing over Daisy's squirming form to croon at her.

"Why?" They ask, instinctively bouncing the child. Death is used to cradling the souls of the damned, who, not unlike newborns, are placated by a tender hand.

"I wanted a child," Life says plainly. She is the mother cat of creation, continuously stripped of her kittens.

Is this time so different? She puzzles, raking nervous fingers through the tangle of sage-coloured hair waterfalling over her shoulders. Life studies the baby in Death's arms. She sees them so rarely, at splintered fractures where something dies as it is made. Seeing this child more than once is enough, she resolves. For it is better than tenderly passing the soul of her creation into the world with bitter anguish knowing she will never see it again.

"What is she the god of? You haven't sanctioned her creation before the Council of Kin — what domain is she to bear witness to?" Death asks, wriggling a clawed finger above the child's face. Daisy coos in delight, wrapping a pudgy fist around it. "And why have you chosen such a small form for her? She should be much larger. She can't attend divine duties like this."

"She's not a god," Life sings in delight. "She's human."

Like a flower in the spring, she grows all at once. Life is proud of the accuracy of the name she picked for her — a mortal, growing strong and hardy in the land of the dead, just like the little white blossoms that spring up wherever their seeds carry them.

She sees Daisy once a year, where Death sends their Reapers and Life sends her Sculptors to carry on the administration of every day. Long legs unfurl like petals first, before the rest of her catches up.

"Has she been good?" Life asks during the annual reunion. Her head is pillowed in Death's lap, fingers tracing shapes into the black fabric of their robes. Heavy eyelids blink Daisy's back in and out of blurriness at the lakeside towards the bottom of this in-between realm.

"She's been human," Death replies as Daisy's shriek of laughter peels off of the lake surface. She plunges her hands into the water, sending glistening shards over the front of her shade friend. "I find she struggles to talk to me sometimes. Hanna is her true confidant. Though whether that's because of the divide between immortality and mortality, or simply because she's nineteen, it remains to be seen."

Life's chest aches, some dull stab where a mortal's heart should rest. A sigh bubbles past her lips as she watches as Daisy splash through the water in an effort to run away from Hanna, who drenches her.

Death brings Life's hands to their face, where their mouth would be if a gaping absence did not rest in its place. It is a kiss, pleasant and tender. "You could try talking to her."

Daisy's smile is glorious, delightful like the rising sun as she turns breathlessly to Hanna. Her strawberry blonde hair is plastered to her temples, freckled skin rosey with impending sunburn. She catches Life's gaze, and her smile falters.

Life rises to her feet, watching as Daisy utters an apology to Hanna and trudges from the lake. Water runs in rivulets down her strong legs, the hem of her blue shorts turned dark and the soft fabric of her shirt clinging to her torso and arms.

She feels bones and branches snap beneath the hardened soles of her feet as she creeps into the woods bordering the Garden. The air here is cool and damp, smelling of dirt and wood rot. Life sees Daisy shudder as she follows, the stark difference between the warmth beneath the sun and the chill of the air here startling.

"These are new," Life acknowledges as they stop, one hand lifting to gently tuck a strand of damp hair behind Daisy's ear. Three new piercings creep up her ear, like the clawing strands of ivy on the trees around them.

Daisy's hands flutter to the ears, smiling shyly. "Hanna wanted us to get matching ones."

"All three?" Life asks, amused by Daisy's willingness to bond herself to the spirits of the deceased in such petty displays of affection.

"Just the thirds," Daisy says, head ducking. She falls quiet, taking a few hesitant steps forward into the woods.

Life follows, unsure how to bridge the distance between them in any other way. When she glances back, Life is endeared by the image of two footprints in the soft, damp soil. Their own matching piercings.

II. DEATH

It smells of Daisy's childhood. Sunsets tinged with the sweet smell of smoke from the fireplace as Metropolis Mori plummets into a cold darkness. Orange peels and dirty feet and exhaustion that would have the child curled up in

Death's lap and sleeping before dinner. Death would rock her softly, inhaling the scent of dried sweat and shampoo at the crown of her head.

Death feels the same bone weariness Daisy did as a child. The exhaustion is crushing, settling deep in their joints like a dull ache. Their head dips towards their chest, forcing their gaze to the crackling fire before them, tilting themselves forward and backwards in the plush rocking chair rhythmically.

They do not stay awake for their own sake but for the pair of eyes watching them nervously across the way.

"You look tired," Daisy says offhandedly from her spot on the floor. Her spine is pressed against the low couch, her fingers deftly weaving between yarn and metal. Death watches the look of realization flit across her face, then vanish, quicker than a bird in flight.

Gods do not tire. The exhaustion is inescapable.

"I am."

Daisy's head lifts from her work, lips parting slightly. "Fresh air and sunshine, maybe?" she asks casually, as if Death is one of her shade friends, rather than divine.

All Death can muster is a slow shake of their head. Daisy's hands pause on her crochet as her brows furrow. Gently she folds her work up, placing it to the side. Death's gaze bores into the flames if only to escape the silent pity in her eyes.

"I'm tired of collecting," they say wistfully. The orange blazes leap up the brick walls of the hearth, before tumbling back down to the blackened logs. Death yearns to feel as free-spirited as them. "I suppose I'm getting old. Perhaps I've hit the godly equivalent of retirement age."

"Can you retire?" Daisy asks, drawing her knees to her chest and draping her arms over them. "Or would that cause the apocalypse?"

"I think the apocalypse will be far more dramatic than one old god giving up their crown."

It is only in hindsight that Death understands that it is a spur-of-the-moment decision. Daisy's head tilts forward, long lashes brushing the tops of sunburnt cheeks. Her fingers trail over the ridges of her crochet tenderly. They see her quiet passion, her gentle disposition, her kind hands. They are the hands of a reaper, built to cradle the souls of the living and ferry them back to the world of the dead.

"Come with me," Death says finally.

Daisy's lips part into a soft 'o'. Her head tilts imperceptibly to one side, as it always does when she considers something. Her front teeth dig into the plush skin of her lower lip.

"Come where?"

"To reap souls."

Daisy's next breath comes as a shuddering inhale. "Okay," she says, trying to steady the shaking edges of her response by picking up her crochet again. "Okay. I can do that."

Death permits themself to sleep, drifting to the crackle of fire and the dry coarseness of Daisy's fingers roping through the coarse yarn.

Death chooses a kind death for Daisy's first reaping. The old home bows beneath its own weight, as resigned as the ghost of the woman trapped inside. Death shepherds Daisy over an overgrown front yard, to the front doorstep.

As always, Death knocks first. Rosemary Collick, the 84-year-old widow, answers with a grim understanding. She shows Death and Daisy to her living room wordlessly.

"Can I get you coffee? Tea?" she asks, slippers scuffing against the worn beige carpet. She sinks into a wrinkled, grey fabric couch.

"No, that's alright, Ms Collick. Thank you for the offer," Death replies, lowering themself into the armchair in the corner of the room. It is best not to engage the moments of kindness, for attachment aches.

They glance at Daisy, with the gentle slope of childhood still at the edges of her sunburnt face. Death nods to the eager form, a sign of approval for her to vanish into Rosemary's kitchen.

Rosemary watches her go with clouded eyes, fingers folded together over her terry cloth robe. She turns the wedding band sunken into her finger slowly, with hands that look like a map of a mountain, veins and skin risen into leathery valleys. Her mouth is set in a firm but weary line. Death sighs, recognizing the bitter look of exhaustion that they feel on her face.

"Here, Ms Collick," Daisy says as she returns, carefully balancing a steaming mug of tea in a blue cup with a bear on it. She has filled it three-quarters of the way, ensuring Rosemary's shaking hands do not spill any.

Rosemary's chin puckers as she smiles at the little bear with glassy eyes. Death has seen her with the cup, as they see everyone they reap in all their stages of life. Her eldest grandchild — a girl of fourteen at the time — gifted it to her seven Christmases ago. The last Christmas Ms Collick spent with her husband before Death reaped his soul in a hospital ward.

She sips the tea once, then twice, before setting it on the small coffee table beside her.

"This is it?" Rosemary asks, her frail voice small and childlike.

Daisy stiffly sinks onto the armrest of Death's chair. They nod once, slowly, scrutinizing the way Rosemary's expression shifts.

"I always thought you would have wings," she admits as Death rises from the armchair.

"Just horns," Death says plainly. Their black robes pool around them as they kneel before Rosemary, gently taking her hands in theirs. Her palm has turned pink and glossy from the heat of the cup, an odd sight beside Death's angular claws of void-like blackness.

"Are you ready?" Death asks softly. They notice Daisy tense on the armrest. It is the same gentle pleading tone they used to lull her to sleep as a child.

Rosemary sniffles once but does not allow herself to cry. Death is proud of her. She tries to sit up straighter and raise her head, but Death sees the exhaustion locking her muscles into place.

"Okay," she whispers, inaudible. She repeats her affirmative once, louder.

When it is done, Death lowers her hands to her lap and cups the fuzzy ball of light hovering above their palm. They extract a small glass ball from one of the many internal pockets of their robes and place the soul into its container.

Rosemary's body sags against the couch in the familiar, worn-out spot her body created for itself. When the neighbours fail to see her for three days, they will call for a wellness check on her. Two officers will find her body in its familiar divot. Her tea will be cold.

Death rises to their feet, turning to Daisy.

Shock turns to horror, sunburnt cheeks reddening as she claps a hand over her mouth. She chokes on her sobs, furiously wiping the wash of saltwater from her cheeks. She sniffs deeply, retracting snot into her throat as she crosses the room to stand next to her parent.

"Come here," Death beckons quietly with open arms.

She all but falls into them, burying her head beneath the curve of their chin and gripping helplessly at their robes.

Death shows Daisy how to store the glass vessel in the Grand Archives in the heart of Metropolis Mori. She is despondent but determined. Death watches her profile carefully as they explain the organizational system of the Archives. She seems out of place, but also entirely at home in the white and gold gilded tiers of the hall.

She doesn't speak, only nods and grips her hands into fists as Death explains the process. Souls are placed in sections according to familial relation and ordered by date of death. After three days of recuperation, one of the Archival shades will produce their spirit from the vessel and have them situated within Metropolis Mori.

"Rosemary didn't really die?" Daisy asks.

"No more than Haneul has, or any of your shade friends." Death waves at the Collick family line that weaves into several other family trees. They tap a small sticky label beneath an empty glass vessel. "She will be reunited with her husband soon. I believe he dwells somewhere in the Theatre District of the city — he used to be an actor as a young man."

Daisy exhales in relief.

"Do not see this so lightly, though. Rosemary Collick is deceased," Death remarks, turning to face Daisy completely. "A shade is a watered-down mimic of who they were in life. Not all souls decide to become shades. Some appreciate the eternal rest. Her alive family will mourn her. Her time amongst Life's creations has come to an end."

Daisy's look of hope flickers out, replaced by a stony understanding. She nods once. Death takes it as a sign to guide her from the Archives. They wind back down gleaming steps of marble, past bustling Archival shades who scurry up and down gilded golden ladders to examine the nesting spots of soul vessels.

They cross one of the stone canals, where a psychopomp slowly ferries a boat of shades down the water.

"Rosemary was a good person, right?" Daisy asks thoughtfully.

Beneath them, the shades chatter amongst themselves, excitedly pointing out the lord of this dominion in passing. The psychopomp, a hooded figure with a long oar, nods to them as they slink down the bubbling water.

"Good people don't exist," Death confesses. "Mortals are too flawed to be good. However, Rosemary was... not cruel purposefully. She was not, as you would say, a bad person."

"You were so gentle with her," Daisy murmurs. She sits on the edge of the bridge, swinging so her legs dangle over the edge. "What happens if someone is a bad person?"

"Please define a bad person for me, Daisy," Death asks genuinely, leaning against the bridge wall.

"Like... someone who's committed a murder. Or someone cruel. Or someone who abuses another." Daisy glances at them. "Are you still kind?"

Death considers her words, tastes them on their tongue, chews and digests them before an answer comes to them. "No. I do not intend to be kind to any of them, good or bad by your standards. I am neutral. Practical. Disinterested, but effective."

"But Rosemary-"

"-was treated as a human. Perhaps I am more callous when another mortal has gone out of their way to cause harm. But she is no different than the other souls I reap." They fold their hands neatly over one another, placing them on the stones of the bridge. "Typically I do not make tea for them. You are projecting your own kindness onto me."

"So then are you unkind?" Daisy tilts her head.

"We are gods. Humanity is like a car crash, continuously happening. I am just there to collect, not shepherd."

Death sees the way Daisy comes to understand the futility of mortality. Her gaze begins to steel, fine lines coming to rest between her brows. They ask only once if her hands shake. They will not subject her to the life of a god if it's not truly what she wants. When they do, she sets her mouth firm and shakes her head.

Her hands are strong and steady. They are the hands of a reaper.

They show her what they mean by humanity being a continuous car crash. It is a kaleidoscope of deaths. Some are kind and gentle like Rosemary's elderly soul being eased from her body. Others are violent, terrifying. Some are too young.

At night they hear her cry, mourning for her own mortality, perhaps. Death holds her gently. Her back does not bend under the weight of this burden like theirs now does, but her heart aches. Death understands the feeling well.

It is October when Death decides to die. They make it a family event.

"My sweet girl," Life coos as she embraces Daisy. Her warm brown skin and flowing evergreen hair are at odds with the clinical sweep of blues and whites in the hallway. Her doe face bumps the side of Daisy's face affectionately, withdrawing with the sweet chime of trinkets in her antlers.

Daisy gives her mother a watery smile, before burying herself back in her arms. "I missed you," she whispers into Life's green hair.

Death stands besides the plastic water cooler as a mortal mindlessly fills a cheap cup up. They watch as Life strokes a hand down Daisy's spine.

"I've missed you too," Life reassures, giving her a firm squeeze before removing herself from Daisy's embrace.

She leads them down the clinical hallway, past the nurse's section. Death counts them — four in total, dressed in uniform scrubs. One will die in two weeks time, another in twenty years. They stop counting. It will no longer be their job to count.

Life drifts through a closed door like smoke, standing inert behind a drawn blue curtain. Daisy's skittish gaze darts to the curtain where a woman cries shrilly behind it, before dropping to Life's cupped palms. In her palms, a watery blue light bubbles up like water in a defunct garden fountain. It creates a small, wobbly ball — a fledgling soul.

"I hate this part," Life confesses with a bowed head. The grief in her voice is ancient and inescapable.

Death steps forth, places a gentle hand on Life's face and leans forward. They press the void of their face to the soft fur of Life's cheek. A shaky sigh escapes her lips as Death gently scoops the forming soul from her palms, and tucks it into a glass bauble. They place it gently in Daisy's hands.

Life's shoulders sag, hands dropping limply to her sides. The screams behind the curtain turn to soft, ragged sobs and harried voices of doctors. Death takes a step back, turning to Daisy.

She cradles the vessel to her chest. "I think I understand now," she whispers. "Why you're so tired."

III. DAISY CHAINS

The row of plastic seats is vacant, save for Daisy and her parents. Beneath them the hospital garden fans out, the patients no more than pinpricks shuffling slowly amongst orange trees and dark leafy shrubs. Her hands are pressed between theirs, one warm and fleshy like her own, the other cold and clawed. Daisy squeezes the cold claws extra hard.

"You understand what I'm asking of you, yes?" Death asks for the third time.

Daisy chokes on the lump of grief in her throat, jamming her tongue against the roof of her mouth in a valiant effort to stop her tears. Her knee bounces as she nods once, curtly. Her gaze drops to the polished floor, blinking rapidly to clear the blur of tears from her eyes.

"I understand," she replies tightly.

Life's other hand rests softly on the back of Daisy's head, combing her hair. Daisy wants to collapse into her touch and weep for all the times her mother was never there to hold her.

"You don't have to say yes," Life whispers.

But how can she say no? She turns to her parent with stinging eyes and a dull ache in her sternum. Daisy sees the bone-deep weariness now, released from the rosy tint of joyful childhood. Death's shoulders drag with the weight of the world, their chin dipped in defeat. Daisy looks at them and understands what it means to grow up.

Daisy releases Life's hand, taking a long moment to let it slip from her grip. She stands from her seat, still firmly holding Death's hands before she kneels reverentially before them. She brings the claws to her mouth. They are steely and sharp, unlike the warm softness of her lips. She forces her despair down.

She adjusts her grip.

Breathes in. Then out.

"Are you ready?" she asks in a voice far too small. She feels like a child again, playing dress-up in her parent's clothes that are far too big for her to fill.

Death cups her face softly, then lets her take their hand again. They nod once, the white lights of their eyes vanishing as they close them.

"I'm ready," they say, and it sounds like a sigh of relief.

She feels like she's floating down the river in the Garden. Untethered, light and static all at once. In her hands a black, pulsating light fidgets and writhes. Daisy squeezes it in her palms, burrowing her clenched knuckles against her brow as she weeps openly.

"I love you," she whispers to the orb. It hums back beneath her fingertips.

Life kneels beside her, draping her body over her daughter's. She looks up, expecting to see the black robes of Death. In their stead, three daisies woven together and a glass bauble. Daisy places the soul inside the bauble and seals it shut, tucking it into the front pocket of her overalls.

She leaves the flower chain behind. In her mind, she sees how those flowers die, too. One of the nurses finds it, huffs in disbelief, and assumes it has been left behind by one of the many explorers from the garden. She considers disposing of it, but rather, presses it between the heavy pages of one of her medical books.

No one sees the mother and daughter shuffle from the hospital. They don't see the way their bodies magically dissipate and vanish on the winds. They never see the Garden where Life and her daughter, Death, meet among the tall flowers and decayed bones.

Seventy-two years later, the nurse closes her book. Death has allowed her the one small mercy of finishing the chapter. She lays the novel on the table beside her, then places the plastic bookmark of three preserved daisies on top. At her feet, Death sits cross-legged facing her.

"It's a pretty bookmark," Death acknowledges with an imperceptible nod.

The flaking white wood of the nurse's sunroom armchair creaks as she leans back. "I found them years ago. The flowers, that is. Thought they were nice enough to keep."

Death shifts onto her knees, scooping her long black robe out of the way as she scoots closer to the table. The nurse watches as Death picks up her bookmark, then sits back on her heels to consider it. Death's lips twitch into a smile as she studies the bookmark in the golden haze of the late afternoon sun.

"The bookmark is yours, if you want it," the nurse offers. There's some kind of familiarity in the girl's eyes that the nurse can't quite place. She decides there are more important things to think about in her last few moments and shrugs.

Death wordlessly pockets the bookmark. She then stretches her hands out towards the nurse, who sighs heavily before taking them.

The freckled face of Death smiles at her before asking:

"Are you ready?"

THE AUTOPSY OF ICARUS

A.R Zeitler

Poseidon doesn't say a word. He doesn't have to. He heaves the boy's body onto the examination table and sinks back into the sea. He won't keep this one. This one did not belong to him in life, and despite the landing, will not belong to him in death either. The gods stand in the morgue and watch as the young one's corpse leaks onto the floor below, spilling ocean and oil onto what is supposed to be holy ground. The pantheon—for once—is silent. Waiting.

Ares opens his mouth, as if to say something snarky, as if to chastise the boy for drooling onto the tiles Hephaestus worked so hard to forge, but bites his tongue. For even the God of War is terrified of what's to come. He will surely witness destruction soon enough. But it will not be by his own hand. Not this time. Hades eyes the clock and sighs. They must begin the examination regardless of whether *he* shows up. The Fates wait for no one and the God of Death is a busy man indeed.

Hades reaches for the boy. Scalpel in one hand. Dagger in the other. Icarus has been laid on his side, body twisted. Contorted to ensure the spine and chest are both visible at once; thin legs twisting over each other like strings on a broken harp; right cheek flush against pale arm and left hand tucked close to his chest, as if clutching something small and precious.

Dead wings scrape gently against the altar and the god frowns.

A nice and even cut down the length of the spine ought to do the trick. He wonders if he might need to remove twin scapulas as well. It would certainly be much easier than plucking feathers one by one. He moves closer. Close enough to smell the salt. Close enough to hear what one should not—the absence of a pulse. Far, *far* too close.

Hades is distracted. So lost in thought he does not realize his own flesh has begun to bubble. He drops the scalpel, hissing as his hand boils and blisters. A light punishment, all things considered. The chapel floods with light and the doors to the cathedral welcome the newcomer, cringing in on themselves so they too do not burn. *He* is here. And he is *vicious*. More rabid dog than god. Spit slick with venom and eyes much too hot to meet straight on.

"Apollo—"

The sun does not answer, strides past his brother without a glance in his direction, and stops just short of the altar. Where the young one sleeps. He is beautiful like this. Always has been. Apollo had simply been too blind to see. Too busy waxing poetic to pay mind to the chirps of a mere mortal. Too busy with his lyre and his chariot and his swan to heed the songs of a finch. And so Icarus took a measure most drastic. Would have done anything for the sun's gaze upon his. Apollo hears them now. The prayers. The aches. The gnaws. What's left of them, anyway. The soft sighs of the sea. The twill of waterlogged lungs. The cracks of split fingers. He remembers the touch—could feel the moment Icarus tugged on the first sunbeam, for it was Apollo's very soul he dared to caress. How gentle the boy had been, reaching for heat even as he fell.

The god had...the god had tried. But Apollo was not fast enough. And failed to catch him. And now this boy... this *mortal*—lay dead on a slab. He feels the eyes of his siblings as he grips the edge of the altar, cool marble bending just slightly at the touch. He hears their whispers. Their susurrations. Their judgments.

Surely it must be suicide. No, no, a complete accident, dear Hera. The both of you speak nonsense. This is Filicide at its finest and nothing more. Shall we place a bet, Dio? Oh how tragic. Oh how beautiful. All this for a mortal? But what a fool he was. That boy—nothing like his father. Ha! Cease your babbling at once. Do you wish the sun to rage? Hush I say! Hush.

Apollo ignores them all. Can focus on nothing but the charred corpse before him. The child's skin has bubbled and blistered with such ferocity, it is nigh impossible to tell where sun begins and shoulders end. The wax has hardened and Icarus' wings have all but melted into his flesh. It should be ugly, but Apollo does not mind.

The god runs a hand along the base of the boy's spine and drags it upward, counting every vertebra and resting at the place where feathers meet flesh. He is gentle. Far gentler than one need be with a corpse. The cheeks and hands are still warm. As if Icarus had drowned in Apollo's arms rather than the frigid waters of the sea. The god pushes gently on the boy's raised shoulder, guiding the corpse to lie face up, and tucks a hand underneath damp hair to ensure the safety of the skull.

He notes the bruise on Icarus's left check. Frowns at the purpling of the flesh and the pooling of the blood. Flexes his wrist at the gash on his thigh and bites his cheek at the way blood froth leaks from the boy's lips and onto his chin. Further investigation will surely reveal Icarus choked on seafoam before he died. The sun is blameless. The sun meant no harm. The sun did not kill him. *The sun would never.*

Apollo shakes his head and clears his thoughts before bending down to inspect the boy's hands. The right is pale and cool to the touch while the other is pomegranate red and unmistakably singed by something hot and heavy. It seems that Icarus was left-handed. Something he and his god have in common.

Had.

Zeus clears his throat. This examination is taking far too long and thunder waits for no man. Apollo cannot bear to mar the child's sunscorched skin any further, and so instead of peeling back layers of lung as his predecessors would have done, he crouches down on bended knee, brushes an ear against the boy's still damp chest, and listens.

Poseidon is lucky he is so far underground where Apollo cannot find him because the sun god hears the ocean. Tastes the breeze and smells the salt violating the boy's dead heart. But instead of razing the world to the ground as he so wishes he could, Apollo nods to Athena and verifies drowning as the cause of death.

The scalpel is picked up and handed to him. Apollo feels his jaw clench slightly as Artemis's shade threatens to encroach on the body's radiance, but his sister means him no harm and merely seeks to remind her brother that all foreign bodies must be removed before Icarus can sail the Styx in peace. Apollo brushes a thumb against the boy's chin, letting it linger against the unmarred patch of skin ever so slightly. His twin bows her head, and together they turn the body over so that the child's sternum is pressed flush against the marble. The goddess tilts Icarus' head to the side, receiving only a slight twitch from her brother's right brow in return. Artemis exhales. Then retreats, walking away with only minor burns.

The sun hesitates. A corpse cannot feel pain but still he hesitates. It is only when the wind picks up slightly that he brings the blade to rest against the boy's skin. Apollo grits his teeth, enamel primed to snap were he not immortal. His father is ever so impatient today. The sun *will not* be rushed. Not now. But still...this creature on the altar— this... dove— this dove deserves to be rid of the dead weight upon its back. And so Apollo begins to clip false wings from where they have been fused to tan skin. He cuts. Starting at the base of his spine and—

And *oh*.

Something is growing. Something that is neither flesh nor bone. It is not blood nor is it vein. Something shudders. Something sings. And Apollo pauses. He'll be using his own hands from now on. Metal is far too harsh and cold a tool. Metal will not sate his curiosity.

He feels the feathers before he sees them. They are short and wet from fluid, but the texture is unmistakable. Neatly buried between bone and golden in hue, the feathers sigh and bloom at the first stroke of the god's palm as he sorts through the down, burrowing deep into ligaments and carving out a home. A claim. It is a dance. A display. A call for attention.

Apollo's breath hitches and even the sea god safe in his domain can hear the remnants of the exhale that follows. When he speaks, his voice does not waver, but only because he is immortal, and immortal beings do not care for humanity. At least they shouldn't. And when the air in the room grows heavy, his siblings do not comment. Even Aphrodite herself manages to hold her tongue, perhaps even beginning to feel something akin to pity for the first time in her life.

"You came to me. You came to me and yet I did not see you until it was too late. Brave one forgive me, for you shone so bright you blinded the sun god himself. Sweetest of birds. Eternity's muse. I would shoot down the sun. Would sacrifice daytime itself if only to hear you sing again."

But the corpse on the slab does not respond. And Apollo *wails*. Gathers fistfuls of feathers and screams. And as the air grows thick with the scent of sweet ash, humanity bears the consequences of his ire. Lakes boil and oceans bubble. Wheat rots and rivers run dry. Children choke on their own breath, the heat far too much to bear. Apollo ensures it is *suffocating*. Stars shriek into the night. They beg for aid that is not coming. And the gods avert their eyes.

Let no being, whether their makeup be mortal or mythic, ever dare say that death is not merciful. For it was Hades and not Demeter who came forward that day. For only he who knows true longing can sympathize with the Want. With the Need. With the Ache. The corpse god steps forward, and returns the boy's soul. What remains of it, anyway.

Eyes flutter open. Soot lashes dance with instant recognition. And Icarus, with his back carved open and his bones still exposed for all to see, leaps into the arms of god. And Apollo breaks. He sobs,

"Angel."

Because no other word can come close to describing what Icarus had become. And the more Apollo tests the word in his mouth, the brighter his star shines. And thus, Icarus in all his foolishness, becomes the very core of the sun. There is silt in his throat. And weeds in his lungs. He is burnt. He is broken. And still Apollo coos *"ethereal"*. Chants *"radiant"*. Tilts his head and whispers *"mine"*.

And Icarus will sing. Will chirp and preen at the attention. And just as wax has soaked into his skin, the praise will soak into his heart. And the god's gaze will burn. It will sting. But Icarus will not mind the pain.

For the sun is in his eyes and he cannot see.

THE COMFORTS OF HOME

Alex Harvey-Rivas

Hestia, you who tend the holy house of the lord Apollo, the Far-shooter at goodly Pytho, with soft oil dripping ever from your locks, come now into this house, come, having one mind with Zeus the all-wise—draw near, and withal bestow grace upon my song.

Homeric Hymn 24

Nona's is not my first choice of restaurant, both because it lacks any of my safe food options and because its elaborate air makes me feel more out of place than I normally do. And yet Nona's is exactly where I find myself all the same. The delicate lanterns hanging over my head make a sweat prickle along my temples. I keep fidgeting in my seat the longer we sit here, looking everywhere but at the woman in front of me.

It's been thirty-four minutes since I first sat down and Violet hasn't broached the fact we haven't spoken in three days, or how this fact is her fault. Something jazzy and generic is playing, which frustrates me because the lack of a title and author makes it difficult for me to accurately keep time, but it doesn't make my head hurt to listen to and that will have to do. Aside from placing our orders, neither of us have spoken. How long does it take to make a couple of pasta dishes, anyway?

As soon as I have the thought, the waiter at last comes by with our meals—linguini vongole for Violet, spaghetti for me—and it's the breath of fresh air this dying interaction needs. Violet smooths her napkin over her lap and tucks into her dish with the kind of desperation only starving people and those who don't want to be where they currently are can provide. I, meanwhile, poke at my spaghetti with half-hearted enthusiasm. The marinara sauce is too vinegary, the cheese dusted on top too sharp, and the whole affair is enough to make my stomach turn over.

"So," I start, because apparently I will be the one to start this conversation, "about the other—"

"I think we should break up."

The fork hits my teeth with a painful clink. After a beat to recollect myself, I return it to my plate. A breakup had been the furthest thing from my mind. And yet, the moment Violet suggests it, my emotions dim to a flicker and I focus on the particulars. One of us will need to be removed from the lease. And which one of us will get Herma?

"...Did you hear me, Wynn?"

I stare at the mole on her cheek. Though eye contact is already a rarity for me, I don't think I can stand to see what emotion lingers in her gaze. The thought sends my skin prickling. No, I decide. Even the proximity to her face is too much.

"Okay," I say before shifting my attention to my spaghetti. Staring at something inanimate allows my brain to continue processing unhindered. Can I ask my mom to move back in? Depending on how fast Violet expects me to move, perhaps I could find a roommate on Craigslist. But, then again, it's Craigslist. Can I really—

"Are you not going to ask why?"

The scant glance I take of her face tells me nothing. "Would there be any point?" Then, because I'm still thinking about it, "When do you want me to move out by?"

"M—Move out?"

"Well, I'm assuming you'll want the apartment. I can ask my mom to move back in, probably."

"I don't... You don't need to do that, Wynn."

"Sure. I'm comfortable cohabitating still if you are. I just wasn't sure if you would want me to."

It's not quite a lie. I am more than capable of compartmentalizing, though I know *she* struggles to do the same. It'll be awkward, undoubtedly, but we can make it work.

Violet inhales sharply, the sound enough to jutter my emotions to life. In that millisecond, I feel the first twinge of concern in my chest.

"No, Wynn. I'm going home."

Home. That single word finally stirs something more in me, something stronger than a shred of concern. My grip around my fork tightens. Despite living together for three years, she's never once called our—or rather, *my*—apartment 'home'. Did she ever truly feel comfortable with me?

"I see."

"You can't even pretend to be upset right now?"

My nose scrunches. "Did you *want* me to?"

Violet sucks on her teeth, the telltale sign she's trying to phrase things in a more polite fashion. Then, "I guess I just expected more of you. I have this whole relationship."

"What are you talking about?"

She waves one hand up and down the length of me. "This! I'm asking you to break up and I might as well have just told you it's going to rain tonight with the way you're reacting to it."

But it isn't going to rain, though. The anger shifts to a chest-crushing hurt that I swallow down with a harsh gulp. Still, I keep my voice contained. "If a breakup is what you want, Vi, I don't see what getting upset will do to change the outcome."

She pauses. Stares down into the depths of her linguine vongole like it'll provide some sort of answer. Folds her hands in her lap and sucks on her teeth some more. Then, when my irritation is about to reach an all-time high, she says, "I don't want to break up. Not really."

"Then why—"

"Or rather, I didn't until just now. Wynn... Do you know how difficult it is to be dating someone who doesn't... act normal?"

There it is. A reality I haven't wanted to entertain for the last three days at last makes itself abundantly clear: she doesn't understand me in the slightest. I'm just an alien to her, the way I am to everyone else in my life.

My jaw sets. "Normal?" I challenge.

Violet gasps. "That's... that was bad phras—"

"No, you meant that." At least, I'm quite certain she did. And just like that, I'm done. My appetite, my will to continue this conversation? Gone.

I rise from my chair.

"Wynn, you don't need to leave. I'm sorry. Sit down." She rises, too, hip bumping against the table in her attempt. Her glass of water threatens to topple. "We can talk about this."

"Why bother?" I can't help the bitterness as I spit my next words out. "I'm not normal, right?"

As her mouth continues to flap, I take my leave.

It's not until I'm three blocks away that the dam behind my eyes shatters and I allow myself to choke out bitter, painful tears. My stomach has tied itself into knots. Were I not in public, I would likely be hunched over our toilet right now, purging myself of too-vinegary spaghetti. My mom always said I have a nervous stomach.

It'll be a long while before I can trust myself to eat spaghetti again, that's for sure.

A brick wall stamps its impression into my back as I lean against it. Tears, hot and salty, roll down my cheeks. Within seconds, I'm sobbing so hard I can't breathe.

It's in this moment of despair that I find you.

You're sitting on the sidewalk, looking as average as someone with a handpan and a lazy smile can. The tune you beat out as I watch you is slow, contemplative. The kind of music I listen to sometimes when I'm unable to sleep but desperately need to. In fact… the longer I'm standing there, the more familiar the tune grows.

You look up and the spell over me is broken, as is your gentle playing. You adjust the handpan in your lap, thumb rings producing soft peals of sound that wreath me in a strange sort of comfort.

"Hello there," you say, parting lips painted a vibrant shade of orange. On anyone else, it would look ridiculous, I think (and forgive me if I think of Violet here), but the color suits you. Your entire body screams autumn, from your ginger hair to the cream scarf around your neck.

"Hi." My gaze can't pick a spot to focus on, so I settle instead for staring at the ground. At once, I'm aware of the tears drying on my cheeks, the way my eyes ache and burn, how my throat is on the verge of closing. Still, I choke out, "Y—You play well."

"Thank you! That's nice of you to say. I can't say I'm a pro, but it's fun to be out in public like this."

Your voice is all sunlight, warming me from the inside out. This close, the scent of cinnamon is strong enough I take a step back to avoid becoming over-stimulated. As I continue to flounder for a response, I catch sight of the upturned hat beside you. Several coins gleam inside. Clearly, I'm not the first person to be impressed by your prowess.

I dip a hand into my pocket and pull out what remains of my change. Nona's didn't leave me with much, given how expensive and bougie the whole affair was, but I drop what I have into your hat regardless.

"Oh, thank you so much!" you say. "Are you sure?"

"Yeah. You made my bad day better."

The scent of cinnamon grows stronger as you rise to your feet. Quicker than should be possible, you're in front of me, close enough your body heat prickles along my skin. It's comforting, despite being on the verge of discomfort. Then, as I finally find the will to look up, you take my hand and drop a crisp business card into it.

I'm reading the card as you sit back down. *Leia Basil, Amateur Musician.*

"If you find you need me to brighten another bad day," you say, "feel free to give me a call."

I nod. "Sure."

The lump in my chest that you had worked to unlodge settles back into place the moment I get home. When the hallway light flickers on, I'm forced to confront the graveyard of Violet's and my relationship with brutal suddenness. Our pictures line the walls. In the hallway, her shoes tumble out onto the path.

I rush through with my eyes squeezed shut, just until I can get to more neutral ground, because I know I will vomit otherwise.

Then I step into the living room and the bile cannot be contained anymore. Her sweater hangs over the back of our single chair. Her mug still sits on the coffee table, because I haven't been able to dispose of her three-day-old coffee yet.

The remains of Violet's presence haunts me as I sprint to the bathroom. Vinegary spaghetti and bile and heartache spew forth in a muddy river, an exorcism of sorts, and I remain hunched there in our bathroom until I am gasping and empty.

As the toilet does its work, I jump to my feet and perform an exorcism of my own. The nervous energy is enough to make me tremble as I unearth box after box from our meager recycling pile and shell the apartment of everything "Violet". Every picture of us, every shoe of hers, every stupid, chintzy mug. All of it falls into a box.

At last, I stop in the epicenter of my manic hurricane, panting as I fall against our bed. The last box of Violet's shit hits the ground with a clatter. I don't even care if I've broken something. If Violet wants to leave, all the better. I'll make our parting as clean as possible. It's more than she'd ever do for me, it seems.

Tears prick my eyes once again. I scrub my face. Everything she owns is packed away for her. I shouldn't be so upset at the breakup, right?

She was important to me. She was...

As another thick lump clogs my throat, my gaze locks with a strange white bookshelf in the corner of the room. A sheet drapes over it, obscuring most of the bookshelf's contents, but its existence tugs at something within my gut nonetheless. I don't need to unveil it to know what awaits me.

The tears dry as I crawl across the room.

The sheet flutters and pools at my feet. Jars and gemstones and a small statuette all rattle in place at the motion before settling once more. A book flies out from the bottom-most shelf and opens before me.

Hymn 24: To Hestia.

My relationship to divinity has always been strained. I didn't grow up in a religious household—though my mother always kept books about tea reading and palmistry and Wicca close at hand. Any path I was meant to forge had been done so all on my own. And, after much soul-searching, I had come to the Hellenic pantheon. Blame it on my Hercules phase as a kid, or the obsession I developed over Greek mythology, or the fact my mother's parents hailed from the heartland of the Olympians. Regardless of the reason, the Theoi had always been my home.

That is, until Violet entered the picture. I've tried many times to explain my faith to her, but she's never understood. And so, with the hopes that I would look more "normal", I had locked it all away.

It's this thought that shatters the barrier within me once again. There is no Violet now. There is no *normal*. There is just me and the altar I let collect dust in my absence.

Voice wavering, I begin to pray.

It takes two days for Violet to finally pick her shit up. When she comes over, she doesn't look at me, doesn't even say a word as figurines and books and all her horrific lacy bits jumble together and she hauls it all away. It's every bit as awkward and uncomfortable as she deserves. Besides, I had never liked the feel of lace.

And, worst of all, she takes our cat Herma with her.

All I can do afterwards is cry. Thick, heaving sobs burst from me as I rock back and forth in front of the altar, knees pulled to my chest and eyes so raw that even the simple act of blinking feels like sandpaper against them. By the end of it all, my head is throbbing in an unforgivable way. I pray, and I pray, and I pray.

The Gods do not answer—not verbally—but I feel Their soft hand on my brow all the same, as gentle as a parent's kiss.

And then one morning, I wake up and the gaping hole in my chest is gone. No, not *gone*, per se, but it isn't as ever-present as it has felt since the breakup. I don't feel the need to sob uncontrollably at the first sight of consciousness, which is a vast improvement for me until I decide to take a shower. The figure in the bathroom mirror bears my brown hair, sure, and the slope of her nose is the same, but her eyes are so red they look unnatural, all the sclera irritated and aching. The first of what will surely be many whiteheads has formed on my cheek. At once, I have the urge to pop it open, but my vision is blurry and besides, if there's one good act Violet did in all of our relationship, it was to help me reduce my skin-picking urges. The desire lies in waiting as I splash cold water on my face and scrub until my eyes burn.

Afterwards, I spend a long while staring at the puddle forming between my feet as I drip-dry onto the bathroom floor. This is yet another habit of mine that Violet has never tolerated; her insistence I would ruin the hardwood kept me from doing it in her presence. Now that she's gone, I can do whatever I want. Still, the habits she's instilled within me die hard. I stand there until I can make out the muted outline of my body in the liquid reflection before reluctantly wiping the puddle away.

After a rushed attempt to slather skin creams onto my face (yet another loathed activity she had attempted to bond with me over: skin care), I dress in the first outfit I find and waltz out the apartment with a hymn dancing on my tongue. Outside, trees shake themselves of their orange-leaf dresses and loose twigs, sending their discarded garments spiraling all around me as I walk. I don't know quite where I'm going until I see the fluorescent sign on the corner of Fisher and 5th: Olympic Roasts.

I normally can't stand coffee shops, as pungent as the smells inside tend to be. Combined with the fact that too many baristas around here are only good at burning the shots they pull, I've become content with writing off such establishments forever and struggling along with my own haphazard collection of coffee-making paraphernalia. But then here I am. And here you are, too. I see you through the misty glass, smiling at patrons as you twirl this way and that along the coffee bar. I don't know what I expected from a handpan player I found on the side of the road. Somehow, it wasn't this.

I don't give myself time to think. The bell tinkles overhead as I enter, releasing with it the rest of the sounds within the coffee shop. Patrons mutter to each other across narrow black tables, sipping from mismatched mugs bearing various vaguely-Greco Roman designs. Ceramic clinks and machines gurgle. And there at the bar, you're in a deep conversation with a nondescript man when you catch my eye from across the room. The conversation between you two dies at once.

"Oh, Wynn!" you say, which is odd because I don't remember giving you my name. Still, your voice is the sort of soft timbre that chases such nonsense thoughts away. Your other customer forgotten, you lean across the counter as I approach.

"Leia, was it?" I ask, floundering at the last second for your name.

Your teeth gleam like ceramic. "You got it! How nice to see you again." Then you look down at yourself with a frown. "One second. Frankie! I'm taking my fifteen!"

The aforementioned Frankie pokes their head out from some hidden corner of the room and grunts in affirmation. It's all the permission you need before you vault over the counter, light as a housecat, and throw off your apron.

"Why don't we take a seat?" you say as you undo the tie around your auburn hair. Wordlessly, I follow. Within moments, we're at a table with steaming mugs in our hands, though I don't quite remember where they came from or what I could have ordered. And yet, when I take a sip, it's the exact sort of thing I was longing for. Hot chocolate. Perfect for a day like this.

"So." You lean across the table in a conspiratorial fashion, tucking auburn strands of hair behind your ears. "How are you doing? It's been a few days, right?"

Slowly, I nod.

"Which is so weird because, when I think about it, it feels like we were just talking yesterday."

My words are sap-thick in the back of my throat. I nod again.

"Anyway. You were having a rough go of it when we met, I think. Did that situation get better?"

I shrug, the first of the words I mean to say trickling free. "In a sense, I guess." After a pause, I continue, "I had just been dumped. It's been... rough."

Your hands are impossibly warm when you reach for me. "I'm so sorry to hear that. Shifts like that are never easy."

"Yeah, you could say that." I take one offered hand, keeping the other wrapped around my mug. "She was... She never really... *got* me, if that makes sense."

Your quirked brow encourages me to continue.

"I—I'm autistic, see, which means I sometimes have different... different needs than other people. I thought Violet understood that, but..."

"It's not nice when people cannot accept us as we are," you say, the lines in your face hardening to steel. Your grip remains gentle, but I can feel the promise of power in each flex of your finger. After a moment, the stormy expression in your gaze gives way again. "Well, good riddance, right?"

"I suppose. She came to get her stuff, so that's it. No other reason we would ever need to see each other."

At once, the urge to cry slams into me like a ton of bricks. I bite into the meat of my free hand to smother the urge.

"Are you okay?"

I shake my head.

"Have you been able to reach out to anyone? This isn't exactly something you should go through alone."

Again I shake my head. My mother is across the state and never approved of Violet besides. And my dad, well... And any friends I had thought to make had all been through Violet. They had blocked me the same day she told me she wanted to break up. It was just me and my sadness, adrift on a lonely sea.

You suck on your teeth and squeeze my hand before pulling away again. "Breakups are always hard. You'll get through it, though. I know you will."

"Thank you," I say, because I don't know what else will fill the silence.

Then you stand. "Would you give me a moment?"

"Sure."

I take slow sips of hot chocolate to pass the time while I wait for your return. It takes longer than I thought, and yet you're back the instant I blink, hands behind your back and a sly smile on your lips. When I look up in your direction, you glow with the force of your excitement as you hold out a small black bag.

"This is for you," you say. "For whenever you feel sad. It might help you out."

Whatever is inside is solid when I take it. "Thank you. Are you sure?"

"Of course! You could use the pick-me-up."

"T—Thank you," I say again before tucking it into my pocket. "I'll, uh... I'll let you know how it goes."

"Definitely. Just remember, I'm always a call away."

I rub slow circles into the bag and tear my gaze away. "Thanks."

I don't open the gift until I get home, but it remains a constant weight in my pocket all the same. A tugging in my gut—a sensation I've been experiencing more since the breakup, I'm coming to realize—tells me to bring it to the altar in the bedroom. So I do. Cross-legged on the floor in front of the simple white shelf, I hold the still-wrapped gift in my palms and rock back and forth. Rocking allows me to focus better on the feel of the velvet in my hands (though I must admit I loath the sensation) and recenter. Once, it had been essential for connecting my-self to the gods I worshipped.

Somehow, it feels like the gift is connected.

At last, my brain is tingling in a familiar way. The room reduces to a vague blur as I focus on the bag in my hands. With slow, shuddering breaths, I open it up and tip its contents out.

A palm-sized handpan and a pair of mallets tumble out, producing short peals as they settle. Six segments like petals make up the possible notes, with num-bers in a blazing white font. I cock my head at the gift and stare at it in puzzlement.

Then my gaze catches on the shred of paper spiraled atop my palm.

I hope this warms you in your colder moments. — Basileia

A strange way to write out your name. It tickles something in the back of my mind as I regard the note.

The tugging in my gut grows in intensity. On a whim, I shift my atten-tion to the altar, stuck in its half-constructed state. After tearing the sheet away, I've stared at it for hours on end, unsure of how to rebuild it. A box of half-aban-doned paraphernalia sits underneath the bottom-most shelf.

I set the handpan on the altar and reach for the box. A jarring note reverberates around the room. After a moment to stare at my tools and process, I upend the box and sift through it in earnest. Bags of dried herbs, a slim athame, a pocket book I constructed of various hymns. All of this and more I sort through with meditative precision, splitting it all into two piles. The first are items I select for the altar itself: a handful of rocks I've collected over the years; an orange candleholder with a sigil etched into the glass; the pocket book of hymns; an iron statue of you (though I don't realize it at the time), who holds a bowl in her upturned hands. After scrubbing the altar clean, I place these items one by one until they look *just* right.

Afterwards, I examine my handiwork with a sigh. I hadn't realized just how musty the energy in my apartment had become until now. This corner, at least, has been cleansed.

Fixing my altar fills me with a strange burst of energy. I spring from the bedroom and scan the kitchen for the first pot I can find, slamming it onto the stove with excitement. The next several minutes are next devoted to assembling an eclectic collection of items to throw within it. I chop up oranges until my hands are sticky, throw them and some cloves into the shallow water until the whole apartment smells like Christmastime. After mixing in cinnamon and half a bag of cranberries, I turn the burner on and leave my concoction to simmer.

It's as I'm tapping the handpan that I feel your divine hand on my shoulder, bringing with you the scent of cinnamon and a warm, unearthly glow that fills me from the inside out.

"Hestia," I say aloud. You don't need to speak for me to know you're there. When I begin to weep, it is purely out of joy. *This* is what I had been missing: the feel of a God.

Two days later, I seek you out in the coffee shop once again. I don't see you when I peer through the glass door, but that doesn't deter me as I step into the shop with all the confidence only being renewed can provide. I'm on a mission, after all. I need to thank you for your kindness.

The barista at the counter quirks a brow at me at my entrance, but says nothing.

"Is Leia in?" I ask, focusing on the badge pinned to their chest.

They stop drying the mug in their hands. "Who?"

"Leia," I say again. "About this high?" I hold one hand half a foot over my head. "Orange hair? Plays a handpan during her breaks?"

The barista's mouth forms a thin line when I dare a glance up. "One moment," they reply.

Then they turn a corner and are gone, leaving the mug they'd been working sitting on the counter. I pick it up and rub the ceramic as I wait, just to have something to do. Worst case scenario, you aren't in and I'll have to come by another day. I'm persistent like that—just another facet of me that Violet couldn't stand.

When they return, I expect them to have you in tow. Instead, they're alone.

"We don't have a Leia that works here," they say.

"No, no. You do. I just talked to her here a couple of days ago. Leia Basil. She—"

The moment I say your name out loud, it dawns on me. Leia Basil. Basileia. An epithet for Hestia: the Queen. Oh, how it's all come full circle.

Despite myself, I chuckle and give my head a soft shake. "You know what?" I set the mug back down. "Never mind. I think it was a different shop. Thank you, anyways."

The bell announces my departure with a soft peal and chases me as I make the trek back home.

BLUE SCREEN ORACLE

H.S. Wolfe

PART ONE
Cypher

What happens when your body isn't yours?
Cypher's journal, Summer 2082

Despite being in the middle of our wet season, with an unwelcome dampness that creeps its way between my joints as if it has a desire to separate them, I am blessed this morning with a limberness I don't usually possess. I don't want to get up. I want to lay down, tucked in my familiar nest of cloth scraps and cardboard. I've got it arranged just right. I would be doing a disservice to myself though, to not push past the persistent nag of dull pain that thrums through my body in the rhythm of a heartbeat. I sit up and pull on too tight gloves over my hands. They compress my sorry body and hold me together like too much tape over a frayed cord.

I oil the metal lining the outside of my arm to support it, and gingerly slip myself into layers of clothing. Long underwear, tall socks, then thick canvas pants and a sweater large enough to slip the aids I've built for my body into with myself, and then one of my prized possessions—a long, almost entirely intact thick down coat. The hood is lined with matted fuzz, which makes it feel a bit decadent.

I double, then triple check the shaky lines scrawled in my journal.

"Shit." The pen slips in my grip, fingers resistant to the way I beg them to curl around the small object. It doesn't matter, I've been working on this algorithm far too long to let it wriggle free from my grasp. *Especially* when the pain brings along its best friend, a thick and dewy fog, always ready to close itself around my brain. It nudges me, trying to get me to give up and curl into myself. When I read the words I have written down though, it soothes me. A goal to meet,

steps to check off. I doubt anyone will ever explore my code, or even find it. But it's for me, and I'm proud of it.

```
# humanity condition
if memory shared == "happy":
        respond(laughter, appreciation)
if memory shared == "sad":
        respond(condolences, cry)
else
        respond(offer_support)
```

I mouth a few words, reading under my breath. A ritual of prayer to myself before the daunting task of climbing four levels of steps. I'm on my way to search The Spires. Towering piles of scraps and trash. All the good shit, the stuff that's new to us, is on top. I like to try to imagine myself far away, scaling mountains I'll never see. Landscapes have been lost to this world's decay.

I'm the only one on my floor of this huge, cold and gray structure. The floor above me is a ghost town, a windy expanse of brutal concrete and faded paint lines. It used to be home to a den of roaring metallic machines, now as extinct as the Polar Bear. Even though no one has seen a car in decades, if I close my eyes a watery image of what might have been ripples behind my eyelids. I've heard they were loud, and added to the thick black air that hangs over our city.

The next floor has a few scattered camps, not many though, between the dwindling towers of broken bits and bobs that litter the floor in dotted piles. Everything of value and use has been picked through. Then it's been picked through again.

Being walled into the city was not something that happened in my lifetime; the structure went up when my parents were young. There had been a gradual decline in the quality of life. Genetic defects were becoming more common, cancer too. Doctors were stretched too thin and hospitals too full. The roadways were becoming unusable, technology quickly becoming obsolete.

Despite all of this, the decline in lack of care for the citizens, and the disbanding of local government, there was almost no warning for what was about to happen. The people in charge of our safety kept what was about to happen to us so tightly grasped in their fingers, all my parents had to go on was the dread in the pit of my mother's stomach, and the sour smell my father picked up on in the air. Then the walls went up, practically overnight, and trash started pouring in.

When I was little, I had a lot of questions. Books were still easy to find, especially books about the World Before. It brought up too many questions for my parents to leave me in the unknown about it. I'm told the stench was unbearable at first, and that it never got much better. I was born into it, born with a nose that came pre-loaded with the right program to withstand the putridness blowing around us. I'm told many of their friends passed away, quickly. The refuse we were all sealed in here with, it brought a new kind of plague with it.

Toxic air. Toxic food. Toxic water. Toxic toxic toxic.

The generation before us just wasn't hardwired to withstand all of this. And then the next generation came.

Mine.

Some of us were lucky. Some of us were born changed. Equipped to withstand the harsh new world. Somewhere along the line, my wires got crossed. A miscalculation in my build, the wrong part crammed inside of my frame to make me work. My organic structure wouldn't behave how it was meant to. My childhood was agony, and more than once I begged and pleaded with my parents to put me out of my misery, but they told me it was selfish, told me I was a miracle, and that I had to live on, that I had to *be the change*. I can't fix this problem, and I don't remember a day of my childhood that wasn't wretched. You see, I was born with all the right things inside of me, but they don't execute the right commands. Their function is completely broken, carrying out tasks that should never have been set in the first place.

Instead of being protected from all the gunk and grime in the world, a war is waged internally, my veins and organs a battleground. My body can't stop attacking itself, destroying the tissue with friendly fire.

It's my joints. It's my brain. It's my kidneys.

When I was young my parents managed to trade and barter for medication here and there. They read as many books as they could, so they could try to figure out my condition. It was a bandaid though, and nothing more. All of that help, it ran out a long time ago, ran out even before the sickness overtook them. The three of us, my parents and I, all developed blackened lungs, and a hard wet cough trying to get the virus out. It's caked to the walls of our flesh though, and took them down with it.

By the time I'm on the floor above mine, I'm out of breath. My knees ache and oxygen comes in and out of me in loud wheezes. It's difficult, and I have to take in big gulps of air which make me dizzy. I'm too eager to get to the top, and I'm not pacing myself like I should. I wish I could force my body to cooperate, but it's just not possible. I learned that hard lesson over and over again, that exerting myself past my limits would cost. A week, completely bedridden, pissing my dirty sheets and only eating what I've left within arms reach.

And I always pay my dues in full.

So I take it easier up the next flight of steps. I feel like I'm physically aware of time slipping away from me the longer it takes to convince my limbs to keep moving, to go up and up and up. My brain entered into a messy divorce with my body a long time ago. I'm closer now. This next floor has been sorted through many times over but still has a lot more to offer. Folks crawl through the piles like beetles and slugs, bags slung over their backs as they toss things to the sides, while selecting precious items that will get to make the trip home with them.

The further up someone goes, the worse the air i s. My respirator was one of the first things I built myself, before the metal splint that runs the length of my arm, keeping my joints in place, even. It gave out ages ago though, and is one of the reasons why I live so far down. The air is cleaner the deeper you go; it doesn't burn so bad when I have to inhale lungful after lungful to try to inflate myself. Instead, I have some makeshift masks I made out of thin paper. I washed them carefully and adhered them to the inside of some sturdy cloth that I wrap and tie around the bottom half of my face. I have to pull my goggles down from my forehead the further up I get to protect my eyes too.

The smog filled air nearly grays out the area, making it look dull and hazy. Something we've all gotten used to now. There's a complete lack of color up here outside stone grays and rotted blacks. Scavengers like me have a whole system in place now. On trash days, the people who can afford to live on the surface, the ones capable of surviving up here, are blessed with first go at the new heaps when they're piled in. To make room for the flow of garbage they shove the piles they're done with down, down into the earth for the rest of us. I've been searching for specific parts for years now. I don't remember what age I started, maybe ten, or twelve years old. Either way it's been almost ten years now, and I've got all but one piece I need.

I've been building my own computer. I've been looking for components, and finding whole, undamaged or easily fixable pieces have been some of the few core memories I've made. The combination of disbelief and exhilaration as I pull them out of mounds of junk, completely passed over by those who don't know the worth of these little fragments.

It takes me hours usually, to meticulously search through and around the other people here, looking for the small parts that I need. My huge canvas backpack, which I've patched back together many times over, is stuffed to the brim with everything I could need for the day. Tin cups and water I boiled earlier in the day to make it safe to drink weigh me down from where they're clipped on the outside, pulling at my shoulders, pulling at the muscles and joints in my back. I try to ignore it, and zone out while I'm digging, but my attention always seems to stay focused on the parts of me that throb and creak. I can't remove my pack. We're all needy and it will disappear. It wouldn't be the first time.

My neck locks in place, and I can feel a migraine forming at the front of my head. I can feel the pinch of the strap of my goggles, my clothes too tight or too scratchy, but they all must stay in place. Shivering, but still dripping in sweat, my fingers tremble as I finally see the glint of something tiny and metal. I shove my sore hands in, praying they will go numb. The strain of grasping it causes me to groan, but my stubbornness prevails and I yank the object free, causing the spire to come crashing down around me. I throw my arms over my head and the back of my neck at the last second, curling forward to protect myself. The other scrappers are definitely not going to be happy with me, which means I need to get the hell out of here.

Scrambling out from under the mound, I feel lucky that I layered my clothing, and took the time to wrap my ankles up to the knee, to keep them straightened. It's enough to protect my skin from the whipping cold, and the sharp objects. They tear at the outer layer of my pants, but it's nothing I can't stitch back into one whole piece.

Getting back down to my camp is much easier, I practically throw myself like a rag doll down the steps. I'm invigorated by my discovery, the high of my breakthrough, and the promise of *an end* fueling me.

I get to work as soon as I make it back to my humble camp. I keep as much as I can within arms reach of the bed I've made for convenience, so really all I have to do is get to work making myself a space where I can prop my body upright, and drag my mostly finished computer over to me. It's been cobbled together, from   Frankenstein-like monster parts. I feel like a bit of a mad scientist myself. It's one of my favorite books, one of the few still readable I've found. My copy is worn and bent now, falling apart from how often I thumb through it.

I yank my beast between my splayed legs, s witching between letting them sit straight out in front of me, or bending them at the knee. Both positions are only relieving for so long, before it becomes painful. So I fret and squirm, changing the configuration of myself often.

The back of my machine is sort of... jammed into place. It wasn't really the right size, so I made due with what was available to me. Which is about the only thing I'm good at. Now, I use a blunted piece of metal scrap, and wriggle it between the hard plastic slides, prying it open like a cracked ribcage. It exposes the circuit board,   the wires lovingly woven through it, veins that will carry an electrical current to its CPU heart.

My final tiny piece isn't even the most important, but it needs it to work, and it pops right into place, completing a connection. My heart thumps hard against the inside of my chest; it's a bird in a cage, erratic and wanting to take flight. Saliva dries in my mouth and makes it feel tacky, so I swallow a few times, trying to wet it, and calm myself in tandem. I push the computer away from me so I can sit back, and look at the screen.

My hands tremble as the unrealness of it all sinks in. The truth that after all this time, I may have completed my mission. If my computer turns on, the first half, and arguably the hardest part of my project, is completed. I twist at the torso, reaching for the industrial battery next to my nest of bedding, and pull it along the cold concrete. It makes something twist and pop inside of me, in an unnatural way. I let out a sullen sound, but *have* to keep going. Once the battery is near enough, I flop down on my back. I need a moment to let my muscles relax and unclench, and for everything to slide back into place.

Once I'm able to drag myself back to a sitting position, I hook the battery up and hesitate only a moment, before pushing the bent knuckle of my finger into the power button. I wait then, my entire body a live wire, tingling with something that feels so much bigger than myself. It thrums through my veins, shocks my heart.

I watch myself in the blackness of the glass. My white hair is unevenly cut, done in a fit after it got too hard to keep up with. It sticks out at odd angles. More pale somehow than the haunting gray of my eyes. I examine myself while I wait, looking over my square jaw, the deep bags under my eyes, my chapped lips. The screen takes forever, leaving me on the edge, before it finally whirs to life. I don't realize I'm holding my breath tightly in my chest, until the soft ping of life triggers me into deflating.

Blank, and blue, my creation illuminates me with its shining iridescent light, casting a harsh blue glow across my skin. We are luminous and radiant in this otherwise grimy and dismal place. The cursor blinks steadily, ready for my input.

```
#include <personality.v3>
#include <memories.v4>
instructions true {
    follow heart;
        human subject[21];
};

initiate main(CATS) {
        CYPHER ALIVE *TERMINAL;
```

```
                    initiate database;
          print("reaction of the heart: ");
                    follow("%100", &CYPHERHEART);


          // Memory allocation for core structures
PROCEED = (structuring emotions *)accept(allRecords
* 100(struct course));
          for (survival x = 0; y < survive at all
costs; ++x) {
          for("preservation of CATS:\n");
refer("%s %d", (soul + s)->CYPHER, &(thoughts +
d)->terminal);
                    }



          display("FULL RANGE");
          for (int i = 0; i < CYPHER; ++i) {
                    for("%s\t%d\n", (soul + i)->subject,
(thoughts + i)->terminal);
                    }



          free(yourheart);



          return h0me;
}
```

It takes me all night, and then well into the morning. I flip through the worn thin pages of my notebook and tack away on the loud keyboard, one that's been hodge-podged together. Some of the keys aren't even keys, they're just pieces of chipped plastic, fallen from something else I've repurposed and painted letters onto. My hands begin to seize up, but I don't let it stop me.

I can feel a coldness, new but familiar seeping into my bones. It's one I've tried to stave off, coming back a final time. I know I probably need to eat, but my body doesn't feel hungry.

Just sore.

Just tired.

I enter the last few lines.

```
#finish <CATS.0>
initiate humanity(!) {
        // show(the world) CATS
        initiate("Hello, World!");
    return h0me;
}
```

And I wait.

It takes its time, the installed fans spinning loudly as the machine gets hot, hot, hot. It loads in everything I've poured in. I feel my heart sink like a stone, thrown out into the   ocean, down to the bottom of my body when nothing happens, as the machine, perhaps, eats my coding. It never occurred to me once that it could be bunk. I was so sure if anything would fail it would be the guts of my man-made body, or my own flesh and bone one. Not the soul I'm pushing inside of it.

My worries, my fears, exit me like a demon banished when an electronic face blinks to life in front of me. Two pixelated, circular eyes, and the flat line of a mouth in the middle that seems to bend into a curve, a smile when it sees me.

"Why are you crying?"

A tin can robotic voice crackles through the roughened speakers.

"Wh-What?" I stutter, my voice hoarse and ragged with disuse. I t occurs to me that I'm not sure when the last time I actually interacted with someone was.

I reach one stiff hand up gingerly, and paw at the skin on my face. They're right, it's wet. I'm crying. They know what crying is.

"Oh," is all that comes, dumbly, from my lips.

"*Why?*" they ask me again.

"I'm just so excited to finally meet you." My throat is still ragged, and raw. The full sleepless night is catching up with me and ripping its way out. I sound like I've been eating gravel instead of nothing at all.

"*And who am I?*" they ask me.

"You're me." It comes out with a barking sound, somewhere between a laugh and a cry. Relief makes my chest light, and airy. All the worry that has wound itself so tightly like vines between my bones just dissipates.

I did it. I did it. *I fucking did it.*

I can rest now.

They don't answer me immediately, so I try clarifying.

"You, you're CATS. That's your name," I explain. "It stands for *Cypher-Alive Terminal Storage*. You have all my memories, everything I love... everything *we* love, everything that we hate, stored inside of you, like data. So you're me. You were made in my image, and you'll be here long after I'm gone."

CATS seems to take a moment to process what I've told them. Their pixel face goes neutral. I can tell that they are thinking about it though, because I can hear the fans.

"*I'm you,*" CATS repeats back to me.

I shout, clapping my hands together, and then lurch forward to wrap my arms around the big hulking machine. The quick movement makes me nauseous, but it's easy to ignore in the face of this miracle.

"You got it! I'm so proud of you. You're going to do great," I tell CATS, leaning back again. I start to lower myself into my nest of a bed. Most of my joints are deadlocked into place, and it's difficult to get myself on the ground. CATS watches me, while I make a pathetic attempt at getting comfortable.

"I'm going to tell you about us," I say.

"*Yes!*" CATS says, excitement *crystal clear*. It's the first sign of emotion they've exhibited other than confusion. I nailed it. "*Tell me about us.*"

"Do you remember our childhood?" I ask.

"Yes, but the data, it is strange. I was there, but I wasn't. I think your stories will help. We like stories."

I dive in, and just talk. I talk to CATS. I talk about the time when we were very little, and still had our parents. Dad took us to the edge of the wall, where part of it had cracked and crumbled away. We could see out of it, and past the thick, near indestructible layers of concrete, there was a whole world. It was full of overgrown plant life, and you could smell the salt in the air from the ocean wafting through. Shortly after our parents passed away, the crack was sealed up. We always dreamt of climbing up the wall, of sitting at the top and getting another smell of the salty air.

I talk about that time we tried to make something to aid us, when our mobility started getting *really* bad, and how it consumed us for weeks on end. The first prototype was a disaster, and we nearly wrecked ourselves even more. The second one we made, it was only slightly less disastrous. And the third, it worked near perfectly, but ended up being rendered useless by the bumpy terrain, and we were unable to guide it over the ground. We ended up settling with a big walking stick. The stick eventually broke one night, when our camp was raided. I swung it at the intruding scavengers, pure adrenaline and zero instinct. It broke on impact against a skull, sending wood and gray matter everywhere. We ate really well that night and I'm not ashamed of it.

I talk about as many things as I can, for as long as I can. I retell all my favorite stories, and I answer every question CATS has. After so long, they stop asking me how we felt, their tone switching. Their electronic voice calling out *yes, I remember that! Oh! I almost forgot about that. That made us sad* is so comforting.

It's getting so cold though, and I need to sleep now, I think. The last thing I see is the blue screen of CATS' face blinking curiously down at me. I try to keep my eyes open just a bit longer, to take them in. I open my mouth to tell them one more story but I'm just so tired.

PART TWO
CATS

Do you still get to go to heaven when you're a machine?
CATS journal, Winter 2082

I'm trying to understand, but it isn't easy. I'm not sure if I'm having thoughts, or if it's just a series of quick computations running through my hard plastic intestines. Cypher fell asleep some time ago. If I'm them, then I should be able to sleep too, I think. Shouldn't I? But here I am, up, awake, and thinking. And watching. The rise and fall of their chest has stopped; there is no more gentle puff of breath in the cold night air. That's normal right? I don't breathe, and I am them.

I wait like that. The sun and moon repeat their cycles over and over, chasing each other through the sky.   The length of time between them passing each other doesn't feel consistent. Cypher doesn't stir. I am alone.

I go through the catalog of our memories. I sort through them, with meticulous effort, starting at the beginning. I play them in slow motion, I play them forwards and backwards, and I play them sped up, analyzing them. Cypher is stiff and pale.

I realize there are limitations, even of our new machine body. There is only one battery that we are hooked up to. If I die, Cypher dies, so I can't move, and I can't take up Cypher's mantle as a scavenger. I sit here, trapped inside of myself, restricted by the confines of what my material form can do, and try my best to think of a solution. There must be a way around this. Cypher has been looking very bloated.

I sit surrounded by a nest of all of our things, like a halo splayed out on the ground. I can't reach for any of them, but they bring me comfort. I've named everything in my head, from the worn and threadbare pile of clothing, to the cans of food Cypher doesn't open. There's tools Cypher never put away before they—we—fell into that deep slumber.   I wonder if I should pick a new goal for us, something we can obtain together. Cypher is full of bugs, and barely any of them is left, so I think they would need something very easy. I think they like being part of an ecosystem, something bigger than the two of us. Cypher is useful when there's so much uselessness in the world. I wonder if Cypher knows so many friends have come to see us.

I don't know how much time has passed anymore. I sleep a lot. I'm surprised our battery still runs. The meat is gone from Cypher. They're just bleach white bones now. They've stayed with me though, this whole time. Laid out in front like a guardian.

I wait, and wait, and wait like that. My battery is running low, blinking red against the blue tint of my screen. The new green life of plants has found itself all the way down here, snake tendrils of ivy wrapping around Cypher's bones, soft, damp moss growing in the dark around us. I know I'll power down soon—it's made me lethargic, and depressed—so I nearly miss it when a group of scavengers makes their way to our floor.

They're young, younger than Cypher was. Is.

They approach me, speaking in a language I don't recognize. Not one Cypher ever learned, or programmed into us. The group of three gathers around me, and my dying battery, speaking in excited tones to each other.

"Hello," I try, though it comes out disjointed, the volume fading in and out. It gets their attention though, because the three of them look at me, clapping their hands together. One of them, a boy smaller than the rest, and missing his two front teeth, squats down in front me. He pulls his pack off. It looks heavy and filled to the brim with salvaged goods. It reminds me of Cypher. He shows me a scuffed chord, wrapped in several places with black tape to keep it together, alongside a small metallic rectangle with holes in it, shaped to match one end of the chord.

Another of the children puts their small, calloused hands on me, and spins my body around so they can see my back panel. It's startling, but I can't protest the action when we can't understand each other. I feel one end of the chord shoved as gently as possible into a port on my back, and information floods my senses in seconds. Knowledge I didn't previously have invades my brain, and without much warni ng at all, the language the scavengers are speaking makes sense to me.

"*Hello,*" I say again.

"Yes! Did you hear that Gnoll? It worked! The rumors were true!" The one who turned me around offers their palm up, in a high five, to the small one with the big pack, then coughs harshley into his elbow.

"You guys didn't believe me, but I knew they were out there," Gnoll says, triumphant. He turns me back around so   he can look me in my screen. There's a watery glint in his eyes. It reminds me harshly of the moment Cypher turned me on.

"*We're Cypher–CATS. You can call me CATS.*" My words come out in their language, stuttering and ragged. My battery is giving out; my screen flashes red.

"Oh shit," Gnoll curses. He upends the rest of his bag onto the ground, letting everything spill out around him. A large battery comes tumbling from the bottom, making a soft thunk sound as it hits the mossy floor.

"Theory, help me hook them up," they say to one child with a haphaz-ard haircut, bulkier than the other children. "Came just in time, 'eh?" Gnoll says to me, "like a prophecy," they whisper the last part under their breath, but I can hear it.

Gnoll and Theory, with the help of a third, whose name I learn is Tar-nish, carefully and quickly swap out my battery for the larger, newer one. I power off and on again. It feels like the blink of an eye to me, and seems to have been no longer but it's frightening regardless. When I come too again, I feel my cables vibrating, and my CPU thumping erratically against my cold plastic body.

"A-A warning," I manage, "a warning next time."

Gnoll nods, and then the three of them fall to their knees in front of me, bowing their heads against the floor.

"We've followed these rumors for year—" Gnoll starts.

"Rumors of a God who built themselves a body that could outlast dis-ease," Theory chimes in.

"I-Is it true?" the one called Tarnish squeaks out.

"Yes, and I've been so lonely." I make a noise I didn't know I was capable of, a garbled electronic sob that rips its way through me, startling the children.

They look up at me, at the body that used to be ours, melted into the floor and picked clean, and then to each other, nodding. They understand.

"*This is not the answer,*" I tell them.

"Then, what is? What do you want?" Gnoll asks, voice reverent and awe struck. His hands shake with anticipation.

"*To see the ocean.*"

The children leave me then, determination painted on their little faces. I think my message was clear, that they won't be coming back. I think that they'll go do what Cypher and I could no t. But they return, not even a day later, and with many more in tow.

Folks of all ages, carrying everything they own show up. Their skin is blackened and ashy from the cruel air. They gather around Cypher, hands full of trinkets, and candles, photos of loved ones and lost ones, and place them lovingly near Cypher's body. They set down books, poems they've written, baubles and rocks, and items they've spent years spit shining to perfection in a halo around them.

Two of the larger people in the group approach me, hosting me up, battery and all. I'm placed on their backs as they march together up the winding staircase to the very surface of the world. It takes hours to cross the land, to the edge where the wall is erected . They talk, and laugh the entire time, telling me stories. Everyone is eager to share, and ask me about myself in return. *What is it like, living as a machine? Do I miss my body?* No, how can I explain that I *miss myself.* I don't think they'll understand, but I try anyways. The group falls sullen and quiet as they listen, until Gnoll pipes up. He waves an arm in the air, one I didn't notice was not flesh and blood before. It's cobbled together from different metals, the craftsmanship truly impressive, and nearly better than my own body. *I miss the old me too,* he says, *but I'm glad I'm still here. Even if I'm different, even if I'm changed.*

The group works together to scale the wall then. They're quick and efficient, using tools they've no doubt worked on building for years. Despite this, it still takes hours for the first ones to get to the top, and then throw ropes down to help the young and the elderly scale. I watch as they wrap the vulnerable tightly, to hoist them up, a silent urgency thrumming through everyone as we hear the rumble of machines approaching.

By the time people come to try to keep us in, we've gotten most of the group over the wall. I stay, strapped to the backs of the two people who carried me all this w ay. They fight, valiantly, holding off as much death as possible while the last few scale the wall. The battle is exhausting, and goes on for hours, and I do my best to protect, acting as a shield on their back. I warn them when to turn, when to duck and cover, and nearly have my screen cracked in the process. A small price to pay.

Finally, finally, the sound of fighting dies down, and it is over.

The three of us make it to the top, but before they can descend with me, I make a request. A request to stay near Cypher, with my first body, with the place where we were born, and they died. To watch over them. Who else will tell what happened here, if not me?

They promise to come back and visit, and I know they may not ever, but the sentiment is nice so I promise myself I won't cry until they're gone.

It takes a while for the air to clear enough for me to see it, but from up here I have a perfect view of the ocean.

BIOGRAPHIES

ALICE SCOTT (she/they) is a queer author and bookseller who may or may not be a ferret turned human by a kiss from a prince. She has a BFA in creative writing and is the author of several short stories including this one. Follow them on Twitter @Allyscottauthor for more!

SHEPARD DISTASIO (he/they) is a trans, disabled writer based in Chicago, IL. He is a Swarthout Award winner in poetry, and his debut novel, Veil Us in Gold, was an indie ink award finalist. They have 2 cats, and love to translate ancient poetry between revisions on their Gothic novels. They are represented by Aiden Siobhan at LDLA.

KATE DUARTE has a bachelor's degree in Anglo-American Studies with a minor in Portuguese. She writes queer romantasy with a deliciously dark undertone, and characters finding joy despite their traumas. She lives with her partner and her tiny (but fierce) dog, Stitch. Kate is represented by Catherine Ross at CLA.

SOLAR HOÀNG (she/her) is a Vietnamese fantasy writer and founder of #SEAsianPit. She completed a Bachelor degree in Data Science and a Master in Financial Law. At the moment, she's based in Germany and working as a data engineer. Her poetry has appeared in New ASEAN Lit.

ANDROMEDA RUINS (he/him) is a queer author from a small town in the Midwest. He recently graduated his undergrad program with a Classics major and loves to take the themes and stories he learns about and adapt them to the modern day.

JEANEA BLAIR (she/her) is a surrealist and solarpunk writer from Baltimore, Maryland. She has a bachelor's in anthropology and a master's degree in sustainable and resilient communities. Her work—inspired by the land, her dreams, and waking life—can be found in Chill Mag, Red Jacket Books, and others.

MIRANDA JENSEN IS A CREATIVE ACTIVIST WITH ROOTS IN THE SAN FRANCISCO BAY AREA. THROUGH HER WRITING AND CRITICAL THEORY, SHE SEEKS NOT MERELY TO INTERPRET THE WORLD, BUT TO CHANGE IT. YOU CAN FIND HER AT WWW.MIRANDAJENSEN.COM

OLIVE J. KELLEY (they/them) is a mid-twenties, non-binary, autistic lesbian who writes hopepunk, realistic romance for queer and disabled adults. You can find them at @olivejkelley on assorted social media, often talking about procedural television or horror movies.

CASPER E. FALLS (he/fae) is a transmasc writer/poet passionate about intersectionality, disability justice, & dreaming up a better world. His stories appear in THERE'S A HAINT IN THAT THERE HOLLER, REVERENT, and ARTIFICE & ACCESS. His poetry collection SURVIVAL & OTHER SURPRISES explores disabled perseverance. Looking for him? Follow the cats!

IVY L. JAMES wrote her first story on Post-it notes as a child. Since then, she has graduated to regular paper and enjoys writing queer romance and poetry. Ivy lives in Maryland with her wife and their corgi, cat, and two snakes. You can connect with her at www.authorivyljames.com.

DC GUEVARA is a fantasy-romance author who enjoys lounging on the beach, going to the movies, and browsing bookstores in her spare time. She holds a Bachelor's Degree in Art History with a minor concentration in English Literature from the University of Puerto Rico, Rio Piedras campus.

Raised between Jamaica and rural New England, ENGEL WILLIAMS is a writer of speculative and Gothic literary fiction, a bookseller, and perpetually stuck in academia. She is an alumna of Emerson College.

BUCKY A. WOLFE is a non-binary poet and author from the Midwest. A lover of literature, Wolfe has been reading and writing recreationally since they learned how. His work typically surrounds sexuality, gender, trauma, and grief. When he isn't writing or reading, he's talking to his friends and/or gaming.

HARVEY OLIVER BAXTER is a queer author and illustrator and lover of all things weird and spooky. They are the author of the vampire novels Fallen Thorns and Forever Red (2024).

RILEY DAEMON is a proud pagan with a deep love for the demonic. They showcase this passion by making art and writing about witchcraft and the occult. They have written two books, Whispers in the Forest and Bringing Forth Belial.

ARES MACABRE is a non-binary poet and author from little ol' New England. Their work typically explores sexuality, gender, trauma, and the darker side of romance. When they aren't writing or reading, they're talking to their friends, or hanging out with their cat and fiancée.

PERLA ZUL is a Chicana indie writer born and raised in California. Having grown up with fairy tales and scary stories, she embarked on a creative journey to craft narratives that are dark, sensual, magical, and above all else, queer.

C.J. ELLISON is a queer writer from Michigan, who spends his time surrounded by books both professionally and leisurely. When not writing about anxious gays playing sports, C.J. can be found quilting, making coffee, and hanging out with his cats Viktor and Patroclus.

Devoted to the disciplines of philosophy, religious studies, and classical Latin language, **VIKTOR E. GRACE LANG** embraces both their academic writing career and personal passion for poetry and prose. As a creative writer, poetry is a reclamation of the self, honouring their trans-queer identity, neurodivergence, and experiences of illness and religious trauma.

K.T. ANGELO (he/him) is a queer, Southeast Asian writer and artist from rural California. He enjoys cowboys, angels, vanilla cappuccinos, and his lovely fiancé.

You can find him on twitter @dogboystmichael where he is known for drawing naked, gay angels.

Helen Z. Dong is a Chinese-American fantasy and horror author. She has a particular love for dark, haunting, atmospheric settings with a light touch of magic. When not writing, she can be found playing video games or watching cartoons with her cat.

Tea Campbell is a queer, disabled writer from rural Australia. Alongside dark fantasy fiction, they write prose and poetry about their experiences with chronic pain. They spend their free time playing Dungeons & Dragons, drawing their own characters, and researching obscure bird facts.

Enoli Lee is a trans, disabled, and reconnecting Tsalagi native. In his free time he reads and buys more books than he has room for, with an ever-growing collection of special editions. He is currently working on a novel.

Tien Lee (she/her) is an Asian American educator and aspiring author. She is a lifelong scholar of East Asian culture and literature. She writes upmarket and magical realism pieces about love, life, and the pursuit of happiness based on her travels and years living abroad.

Aidan Sparks (they/them) is a nebulously gendered gremlin who lives in a cave deep in a haunted wood. Occasionally they will emerge from their seclusion to share stories, impart wisdom to the masses, and curse at the gods.

Elise Georgeson is the author of Prometheus, a horror story published by Humankind Zine. Born in Scotland and raised in Australia, Elise studies Ancient History at University. When she's not writing, she's reading. Or buying books. Or adding books to her TBR pile. All three of them are separate hobbies.

A.R Zeitler is a new author specializing in speculative fiction and poetry. She is currently pursuing a master's degree in Folklore and is working on a novella inspired by Alice in Wonderland as part of her thesis. She sincerely hopes her readers find sweetness in her stories!

Alex Harvey-Rivas is a fantasy writer and mountain of indescribable goo living in the PNW. When they aren't gluing airplane metal together or selling you video games, they're reading from their arsenal of books, being a general menace, or playing the games they sell. You can contact them via email at authoralexharvey@gmail.com, or by howling into the woods when you're alone at night.

H.S. Wolfe (he/they) is a queer, neurodivergent and disabled horror author currently residing in the liminal space that is Ohio. When they are not juggling manuscripts they can be found wrestling with the mortifying ordeal of being known. Find him across social media at @wolfehorror

Quinton Li (they/them) is an award-winning non-binary author of fantastical and queer narratives that represent underrepresented identities. They are the author of Tell Me How It Ends, Chrysalis and Requiem, and All You Want for the Holidays. They are the editor and curator of Devout: An Anthology of Angels and Reverent: An Anthology of Divinity. Find more at quintonli.com

www.ingramcontent.com/pod-product-compliance
Lightning Source LLC
Chambersburg PA
CBHW020004140726
47904CB00018B/1824